ALL
THAT
TIME

ALL THAT TIME

STEVE LIDDICK

All That Time
Copyright © 2015 by Steve Liddick
Published by Top Cat Publications
Editorial Production: Diane O'Connell, Write to Sell Your Book, LLC
Cover: Joleene Naylor
Interior design: Karen Hudson
Cover image courtesy of leungchopan & CanStock Photo

Following is a work of fiction. Any similarity to persons living or dead, places, characters, and/or incidents, is coincidental and unintentional

Printed in the United States of American for Worldwide Distribution
ISBN # 978-0-9714193-4-6
E-book: 978-0-9714193-2-2 (e-Pub); 978-0-9714193-6-0 (Mobi)

TO SHERRY

Thanks

So many people have said to me that they should write a book. Few realize what a hard job it is or the difficulty of the process that is involved. Sometimes I think writing the book is the easiest part.

No book that gets all the way into the hands of readers is ever the work of a single individual. It is a collaborative effort involving the advice and support of researchers, experts of all kinds: family, friends, editors, agents, publicists, and more.

I am grateful to those who have helped me to get this book to you.

Special thanks to the California Writers Club, Sacramento branch for exposing me to knowledgeable people with expertise in the various aspects of steering a novel from idea to bookshelf. Thanks also to my original writing mentor Nora Profit who started me on the right writing track.

Much of the credit for helping to make this story the best it could be goes to the editing team of Diane O'Connell, Brianna Flaherty, Janet Spencer King and Jolene Paternoster.

No small measure of credit goes to my critique partners Jo Chandler, Sandra Sullivan, and Madelon Phillips, all accomplished writers themselves. Without their encouragement and valuable input I might have given up.

My wife Sherry has encouraged me through the entire process and I would have given up long ago without her total backing.

We're a team. With that kind of support, I've become confident I could do it again. Maybe even again and again and again.

—Steve Liddick

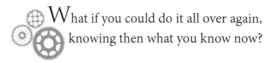 What if you could do it all over again,
knowing then what you know now?

Chapter 1

Early spring, 2005

Ted McBride watched from the window of his apartment as the last of the winter ice flowed slowly down the Susquehanna River. A new day was easing into Pennsylvania's capital city. Ted was not sure whether to embrace it . . . or go back to bed.

A loner by preference rather than phobia, Ted's teaching job at the Penn State University Harrisburg campus did require some mingling, but that was manageable.

Now there was a new challenge to his semi-hermit status.

Arnie Hoffmeier's words of the previous day kept coming back to him: "You're always saying how your life would be different today if when you were a kid you knew everything you know now. Well, I'm offering you a chance to prove your theory."

His friend and fellow university professor had invited him to take part in a radical experiment. Ted could think of little else since then.

Frightening to consider, yet Ted thought maybe it would chase away some of the demons he had carried with him for most of his fifty-five years.

Ted spent many mornings sitting on this same spot sipping coffee and running a lifetime of regrets through his mind like an old movie.

Now he had Arnie's project to add to the whirlpool. That in addition to the news he got the previous evening.

Meanwhile, the antique schoolhouse clock on the living room wall tick-tocked toward another day to be dealt with in the wider world. Ted got the clock in the divorce settlement. His wife got the house.

His coffee had cooled. On the way back to the kitchen to reheat it he noticed a spider had become stranded in the sink and was trying desperately to climb the slippery porcelain sides.

"I know the feeling, little fella," Ted said. "You take one step forward and slide back two. The story of my life." He put a hand down so the tiny creature could climb onto the offered lift to safety.

"Just so you know," he said, as the spider scampered up the wall, "you're going outside when it gets warmer."

Reheated coffee in hand, Ted went back to his spot at the window to continue considering Arnie's offer . . . and to review all the things he should—and should not—have said and done over the five decades of his life.

If I only knew then what I know now, he thought.

Ted McBride took his coffee with cream, sugar and torment.

CHAPTER 2

THE PREVIOUS DAY

SINCE THEY BOTH BEGAN TEACHING THIRTY YEARS AGO Ted McBride and Arnie Hoffmeier had gotten together in the university's food court most mornings for coffee and conversation.

The usual early arrivals were scattered around the big room. Voices and kitchen clatter echoed off hard surfaces. Students and faculty members were taking in sugar-coated, goo-filled carbs and cholesterol and getting a caffeine fix before facing the daily routine . . . caffeine being the only mood-altering non-prescription drug permitted on campus.

"A grand and glorious springtime morning, Teddy," his friend called out when he spotted Ted.

Ted looked to the ceiling and rolled his eyes. "Have you no regard for the rotten disposition it has taken me a whole day to acquire, Professor Hoffmeier?"

"Be of good cheer, Professor McBride," Hoffmeier said, spreading his arms theatrically. "'Tis great to be alive."

"You're not gonna burst into song, are you, Arnie?"

Arnie was a supportive friend and the only person other than Ted's mother who still called him 'Teddy'. A few years older than Ted, Arnie had the finest mind in the Penn State computer science program. He was the archetypal professor: bearded, rumpled and smelling vaguely of aromatic pipe tobacco and Old Spice, with an air of good-natured goofiness about him.

Ted drew a cup of coffee from the tall chrome urn and reached for the last jelly donut on the carousel.

At the same time, another man pushed Ted's hand aside and snatched up the donut he had been aiming for.

"Oh," Ted said. "Sorry." He stepped back. The man scowled at him and walked away. Ted chose a plain donut instead.

"Teddy," Arnie said. "Why did you let that guy take your donut?"

Ted shrugged. "It wasn't that important to me."

"But it was your donut. You got here first."

"It's just a donut, Arn."

"It's not about the donut, Teddy. It's about getting what is rightfully yours. Don't you ever get angry?"

Ted ran his fingers through his thinning hair. "I kinda got out of the habit when I was a kid," he said. "The only one allowed a temper at our house was my father."

"Well, you really should be more forceful. It's a wonder you don't have ulcers."

"You sound like my ex-wife." That thought sank Ted into an even gloomier mood.

"I'm saying if you don't change your ways, Teddy, people will always walk all over you and you will always end up losing what is rightfully yours."

Ted plopped down in a chair at their table. He really wanted to change the subject and said, "Are you ever going to finish your big secret project . . . the one you won't even tell *me* about?"

"You know why I've not been able to say anything, Teddy. Federal money. Hush-hush stuff. But we've completed our research and I was planning to talk with you about it."

"So. . . talk."

"Not here my grumpy friend. Meet me in my office after lunch. Right now you can tell me what's making you more of a grouch than usual."

Ted looked down into his cup as though the words he was looking for might be hiding there. When he found them he said, "Maggie is getting married, Arn."

Arnie's mouth formed an O. "When did you find out?"

"My son let it slip when I called him last night."

Arnie smiled broadly. "The good news is you won't have to keep paying alimony."

"Well, there's that."

"Not jealous, are you?"

"Oh, God no. There was nothing left of our marriage when we ended it. Looking back, it was pretty obvious we were both coasting. But it's another reminder of one of life's big failures."

"I hope you're not taking on the whole load, Teddy. It takes two to fail in a marriage."

"I guess it's the way the breakup happened that sticks with me. Maggie came to me one day and said 'Ted, I want a divorce'. Just like that. As casually as if she were asking me to stop off on the way home for a quart of milk."

"As I recall, you were having some problems before that."

Ted thought back to one particular incident where Maggie suggested they go out for dinner.

"Where would you like to go?"

"Up to you," Ted said. "Anyplace is okay."

"But, don't you have a preference?"

"Yes, they absolutely have to serve food."

"You know, Ted, that's one of your problems."

"How is my wanting to go anywhere that pleases you a problem?"

Maggie gave him a sour look. "It's not just about which restaurant. It's about which car we should buy, which shirts I should pick out for you."

"A car is a car, a shirt is a shirt. A car is a way to get from one place to another. I don't really care who built it. Society requires I wear a shirt, so I wear a shirt. If it keeps me legal, anything you choose is fine with me."

"But why do I have to be the one to decide every little thing?"

"You think I'm indecisive?"

"You lack assertiveness, Ted."

"Maggie. . . most women would be glad their husbands agree with them and want to accommodate them."

"It's just that it shows a lack of . . . strength."

Ted thought for a moment. "All right then," he said. "Let's go to that new riverfront place."

Maggie cocked her head, her hands on her hips.

"We don't know anything about it."

"We don't know anything about any restaurant until we go there for the first time."

"Well, what if the food isn't that great?"

"Okay," Ted said. "Then you decide."

"See?" she said, throwing up her hands. "There you go again."

Ted shook his head at the memory.

"She tried to make me into the person she thought I should be. I realize some compromises have to be made in a relationship, but she wanted a whole different person."

Arnie nodded. "That period of your life is over, Teddy. You are a free man now.

It's time to stop torturing yourself with things you can't change. Time to move on."

Ted knew it was true, but did not know how to be anything except what he had always been. He took a bite out of his donut. "Maybe she'll have a better time of it with Mr. Perfect."

"There's no one better than you, my friend. Maggie just doesn't know it yet."

"You're a lucky man, Arnie. Your life is going just the way you want it. My life, on the other hand. . . how shall I say it. . . ah. . . sucks."

"Maybe what I want to talk to you about will give you some perspective."

The only thing Ted knew about Arnie's project was that it had something to do with quantum physics. Ted's own mathematical skills were remarkable, but Arnie Hoffmeier's were into the stratosphere.

Arnie was the most complete person Ted knew. The man was organized in his thinking, yet flexible in ferreting out the abstract. His right brain and left brain were in regular contact, the lobes working in concert rather than conflict. Arnie had close friends among both Democrats *and* Republicans. He understood . . . and actually *liked* . . . children. He was endlessly energized by the same things that wore down most humans.

On top of all that, Arnie was married to a woman who worshipped the water he walked on.

"You ought to find something to keep you occupied and mentally stimulated," Arnie said.

"All I have is my job, my martial arts classes and my music."

Ted played the trombone and had recently joined a group of fellow professors.

"Our Dixieland group is playing at the American Legion this Saturday night."

"That's good, but even that can become routine. What you need is a passion."

"I was passionate about computers when they first came out. That was many, many haircuts ago."

"How can you *not* find something to engage your mind? There's an exciting world out there waiting for your attention if you'd stop dwelling on the past and look to the future."

Ted shrugged. "I guess I'm stuck in the present. The past wasn't that great either."

"There you have it. You've hit the very heart of the matter, my friend. Your *memories* of the past. As you bring an image to mind it changes from the last time you thought of it. After many years of recalling the event, it bears little resemblance to the original."

"Well, things sure would be different today if I had known everything I know now when I was a kid." Ted tucked a bite of donut into his cheek like a chipmunk.

"I'm bored to death with my job and my life in general. I bored my ex-wife and my ex-son, who hates me. I even bore myself."

Arnie sighed. "You're right, Teddy. You're boring. Shut up and eat your donut."

Ted wrinkled his brow, which was getting wider as the hairline receded.

"My childhood was no picnic," Ted said. "Being smart was not a plus in a town full of tough, brain dead children of railroaders."

Even though many years had passed, the hurt from his treatment by his peers still burned in Ted's psyche.

"Kids can be cruel," Arnie said. "Especially to people who are different or whom they don't understand. They don't know anything at that age, Teddy. People are a lot like computers. From the moment they're born . . . and for the rest of their lives . . . they continue to add mental data."

"Yeah, then their hard drive crashes and they die."

Arnie threw his hands in the air and shook his head. He held up his cup of coffee. "Half full," he said.

Ted held up his cup and said, "Half empty."

Arnie sighed.

Ted noticed the new sociology professor taking a seat across from them. She was wearing a clingy red dress that was more likely to keep her male students focused on anatomy than on social dynamics. It certainly was having a warming effect on Ted. He guessed she was in her mid to late forties. Spectacularly put together for a female of any age.

Arnie smiled as Ted's eyes tracked the woman. Ted noticed Arnie noticing. Embarrassed, Ted said, "I sure could use an 'edit-undo' command on my life. I'd make everything right that went wrong if I had known then what I know now. I'd sure know how to handle the bullies that made going to and from school a battlefield."

"Are you sure?" Arnie said. "You let people walk all over you now. How would knowing what you know now have improved your life then?"

"I think I've learned a few things along the way."

"Knowing what you know now, you didn't defend your donut this morning."

Ted knew Arnie was right. Thinking how he might have handled that incident and so many more like it, he could not come up with an answer. What would he do, fight with the guy in the Great Pastry Smackdown? Would he have gotten into a shouting match? Would he have risked the scorn of those who witnessed it?

Ted took another bite. "Arn, I've been thinking. What if none of this matters . . . life. . . our existence. . . consciousness? Maybe this is all just a gazillion mega-pixel illusion generated by an immense cosmic computer with some kid at the controls, playing us like a video game. Great graphics, by the way," he said, taking another look at the hot sociology professor.

"Boy, you really do have the blues. What would it take to make you happy, Teddy?"

"If I knew that, I'd do it. A king-sized bed would be a good start. And someone to warm the other half."

He'd had a few dates since the breakup of his marriage, but none led to anything he would want to continue.

"You're a kind and generous man, Teddy. Not exactly a snappy dresser," Arnie said, noting Ted's casual attire. "You're not bad looking. No competition for George Clooney, but you'd give Dan Aykroyd some anxious moments. You probably clean up pretty good. Get out there, man."

"It's too cold out there."

"Be bold my timid friend. Carpe diem. Seize the day. Take some chances. Put on your dancing shoes. Mingle. Find a woman." Arnie lowered his voice and leaned over conspiratorially. "You probably don't remember what those are, do you?"

"I'm pretty sure that's one right over there," Ted said, gesturing to the woman seated across from them.

Ted recalled when the opposite sex was the number one topic of male-to-male conversation in those teen years when his comrades-in-horniness had only rudimentary knowledge of the sub-species.

As an adolescent Ted considered Marlene Sutton to be the standard by which all 'women' should be judged. From the time his body started manufacturing testosterone in troublesome quantities until his family moved away from Carbonville, the girl had him in perpetual heat.

His mind wandered to that time when she was the star of his youthful fantasies.

Marlene Sutton's shiny, black hair made her eyebrows and eyelashes look as though she wore eye makeup, although she did not. She probably had some Italian blood that was more prevalent in the capital city and regions farther to the north. German and Polish genes dominated Ted's hometown, where pudgy plainness was the norm.

Ted and his friend Charlie Freeman passed by Marlene and her group at the usual spot in the school hallway.

"Hi, Marlene," Ted said nervously.

Ted had the impression she was looking through him, as though he was not there. But her face came alive when she saw Charlie. She practically swooned over the boy. She didn't know him like Ted did.

In spite of the knowledge that he would never be noticed by Marlene beyond a reluctant nod, young Ted had been a member of the drooling crowd just the same.

Someone told Ted years later that Marlene had come to a bad end; drugs, prostitution and all that went with that life.

"Hello," Arnie said from across the food court table. "Anyone in there?"

"Oh. Sorry. I was just thinking about my success record with women."

"And . . .?"

"And I don't *have* a success record with women . . . my marriage aside. And look how that turned out."

"Friends have recommended eligible women and you always turned them down."

"I tried that. I don't go out with women suggested by friends anymore. It's kind of like when you call an electrician and he's too busy to do a rewiring job for you. So, you ask for a referral. It is more likely the electrician will recommend someone because he is a friend than because the friend is a skilled electrician. You end up with a half-assed job. It's the same way with someone who recommends a single woman they say is a 'good match'. I have enough regrets in my life. I don't need to add to them."

"You understand, don't you," Arnie said, "that there is a difference between regretting and wallowing?"

"Well, I apparently rank pretty low on the eligible bachelor scale. I doubt there are many suitable women out there who are compatible with a fifty-five-year-old divorced, balding, slightly overweight computer nerd."

"And one who has a whipped puppy look about him," Arnie added. "Surely there's someone out there who would be willing to lower her standards and do some charity work."

"This is why I so enjoy our morning confidence-building sessions, Arnie."

Ted resented when friends tried to fix him up with an airhead or a man-damaged divorcee who could vent on him. He had been assured by well-meaning friends that they were the 'perfect match' when the only thing they really had in common was their singleness. As for the man-damaged ones, Ted could not understand why he should be the focus of their hostilities. Whatever they were angry about wasn't his doing.

Just another conflict to be avoided by a man who dodged conflict.

Ted often wondered what kind of woman would actually be right for him . . . and him for her. Certainly not the high octane type at the next table that he was trying not to stare at.

As though reading Ted's mind, Arnie said, "You probably wouldn't want one of the 'Zowie' type anyway."

"Why not?"

"Because that sort of woman often believes she is already everything a person has to be and the world should dedicate itself to fulfilling her every whim. Having a lot of choices, she is quick to move on to the next male down the line when things don't go exactly as she assumes she is entitled to."

"There is a slight chance you could be right for once," Ted said. "But I'm not going to let that keep me from having Zowie thoughts."

"I guess you'll just have to be content being stuck with women of character whose neuroses match you own."

"If such a person exists. Blind dates are not the answer. That would mean someone else has chosen for me, like some countries where mates are assigned by the family. In America we get to screw up our own lives."

Ted had long ago concluded that any woman on the street was as much a prospect for a future relationship as one recommended by a friend.

"I'd have more success if I went to a mall, walked up to the first female who looked interesting and asked her whether she was single and available. If she hadn't called a cop, I could invite her to lunch so we could check each other out before deciding whether we'd like to go so far as to have an actual date . . . and children."

"Seriously, Teddy, you should ask that nicely decorated professor out."

Ted frowned.

"I happen to know," Arnie said, "that she is divorced and within your socially acceptable age range. If you can't fit her into your 'happily-ever-after' scenario, at least think of her as *practice*."

Ted shook his head. "I'll bet her first word as a baby wasn't 'Mama' or 'Papa'. It was probably 'No'. I don't handle rejection well."

"She won't go out with you if you don't ask her my timid friend, and she might if you do."

"She'll just have to be the one who got away."

"No, Teddy. She'll be just one more you didn't go fishing for. You're living your life passively and getting a poor result. You've got to download new data. To put it bluntly, you should check the compatibility of her software with your hardware."

Ted screwed up his face at Arnie's suggestion. "Until that unlikely eventuality I'm off to my classroom to continue the appearance of molding young minds. I'll see you in your office this afternoon."

Arnie shrugged and looked at his watch. "Upward and onward then," he said, whipping out a ballpoint pen and thrusting it skyward.

Down the hallowed halls they went to carpe their separate diems.

CHAPTER 3

TED'S CLASS ON THIS DAY WAS NO DIFFERENT from any previous session. No better, no worse.

Despite his increasing lack of enthusiasm for life in general, Ted still felt a responsibility to his students. They ranged from basically competent to stunningly brilliant. He had to stay constantly alert to keep the super intelligent ones from overwhelming those less intense.

The Einstein wannabes waved their hands to answer every question, demanding to demonstrate their superior intellect.

"Wait until I call on you," he said. "Don't just blurt it out."

Showoffs.

Ted knew they knew the answers. He tried to concentrate on the less gifted students to be sure they understood the material.

Ted had vowed early in his teaching career not to be like some of the worst examples of teachers he had suffered in his own educational experience. But there were the good ones, too. His high school English and science teachers, Grace Simpson and John Wilson, were both capable, caring people. Their nurturing ways resonated with him these many years later . . . and impacted his own attitudes and teaching style. Wilson had been a role model, both as a teacher and as a man to pattern himself after. Thinking back Ted realized that in many ways Wilson had been more of a father to him than his own father.

"What do you want to do with your life, Ted?" John Wilson said.

"Something involving computers, that's for sure."

"If that's your dream, follow it."

"My dad thinks it's worthless."

"Meaning no disrespect to your father, Ted, but it's your future we're talking about, not his."

"I wouldn't be able to afford college on my own."

"Well, let's look into scholarships."

Wilson helped Ted get scholarships and other financial aid for the education he wanted in the field of his choice . . . despite his father's continuing objections and refusal to contribute anything toward what he considered a frivolous fad.

As burned out as Ted sometimes felt, he still gave his students his full attention, in and out of class. A year earlier a young female student appeared to be acting out in ways that suggested sex-related problems.

Angela Freitag never seemed quite fully attentive to the material . . . as though in a fog. She was barely passing the course. She was, however, a flirt to the extreme and hyper-attentive to every male in the place. Ted had the impression she had even come on to him.

One day he took her aside after the class.

"Angela," he said. "Is something troubling you?"

"No," she said too quickly. "Why would you think that?"

"Certain observations I've made suggest that you might be having some personal problems."

"No," she insisted and practically flew out the door.

Her speedy retreat convinced Ted something was going on. He arranged for her to see the university psychologist.

Six months later Angela came to Ted to thank him and let him know that he had guessed correctly about her having some personal issues. Ted would never have asked for details, but she told him anyway.

Her grandfather had started molesting her when she was ten years old. Although that had stopped when she got older, guilt and fear swirled around in her head ever since then. It resulted in her hitting on every male within flirting distance. It was apparently the way one who felt worthless and damaged tested her value to the opposite sex.

Angela had identified her feelings and the blame was properly assigned. From then on she behaved no differently than any other girl her age and became an outstanding student.

If anyone would know how deeply someone could be affected by childhood trauma, it would be Ted McBride.

Chapter 4

When Ted arrived at Arnie's office he was again amused at the cluttered workspace and décor. The place had a unique smell to it: books, dust and pipe smoke . . . ignoring the university's ban on smoking in campus facilities.

Arnie was seated behind a scarred wooden teacher's desk of the kind rarely seen since the days of one-room schoolhouses. The office was jammed with books, scientific journals and an interesting assortment of gadgets. A vintage Felix the Cat wall clock wagged its tail. A gumball machine sat on a shelf next to a small TV. A large, moth-eaten stuffed moose head was mounted high on a wall. A plastic flower lei hung from one antler. A bent cigarette dangled from its long dead lips.

Ted closed the door behind him and settled into a chair. "What did you want to talk to me about, Arn?"

"Teddy, what would you say was the most critical part of your early life?"

Ted had a ready answer for that. "Easy. My teens. I never felt more out of control. Why?"

"You've often said you wish you had done a lot of things differently in your life."

"Sure. Everyone wishes that sometimes."

"Of course they do. But, what if the adult Ted could go back and see how things really were in those days?"

It was hard to take Arnie seriously with a dead moose looking down at them.

"What are you getting at, Arn?"

"What I am about to tell you is top secret stuff, Teddy. I cannot emphasize too strongly how important it is that you say nothing about this."

"I'll take it to my grave, Arn. Will that do?"

"I know this will sound crazy, Teddy, but . . . I think I can make it happen."

"You're right, Arn. That does sound crazy."

Arnie continued. "A few years ago I wrote a paper for a scientific journal. Some government types read it and the next thing I knew, I was up to my ascot in feds.

They were sitting right where you are, pushing money at me to take on a secret research project on the subject of my article."

Arnie took a deep breath, let it out slowly and went on. "There had been quantum physics experiments in which an electronic pulse . . . provably . . . was received a nano-blink before it had been sent. Time could now be seen as a variable rather than the sequential flow we have always known."

Ted shifted in his chair. "Well, Albert Einstein theorized that time could have a certain degree of flexibility. Something to do with the effects of gravity on light."

"Right," Arnie said. "We've developed what we believe is an expansion of that miniscule time reversal right here in the lab."

That got Ted's attention.

"You're talking about time travel, aren't you?"

"I wouldn't call it time *'travel'*, Teddy. We believe it may be a way to get an accurate look at the past."

"I've been looking at the past my whole life and not liking what I've seen."

Arnie shook his head. "You're looking at your *memories* of the past, Teddy. That's not necessarily the same thing. Now, suppose we knew exactly where a person was located in the universe at a given moment, say, forty years ago. I believe we can connect someone from the present with that moment. In other words, we could put a fifty-five-year-old university professor inside his fifteen-year-old mind, looking out at what he actually saw as a youth."

"Me? I guess my first question is: does your time machine . . . or whatever it is . . . work?"

"We think so."

"*Think* . . . so?"

"It hasn't been proven, Teddy. That's why we call it an *experiment*. It's the reason I thought of you. You'd be perfect for it. You're always saying how your life would be different today if when you were a kid you knew everything you know now. Well, I'm offering you a chance to prove your theory by looking in on that period in your life and seeing what you might have done differently."

"I hope you don't mean you would send me out there into the cold ether on a hunch."

"No, no. We're not sending anyone anywhere."

Ted had an intellect described by some as being way up there in the upper brainy brackets, but Arnie was making his head hurt.

"Come with me," Arnie said, getting up from his chair. He led Ted into a small room that was partitioned from the rest of the lab. A double bed was surrounded by electronic monitoring equipment of the type used in hospitals to keep track of a patient's vital signs. A window to the adjoining room was covered by curtains with a drawstring.

"Here's the way it would work, Teddy. The subject would be on the bed, in a kind of sleep state, hooked up to equipment to provide nutrition, hydration and exercise. Brain activity, heart and respiratory functions . . . all of it . . . would be constantly monitored throughout the experiment."

"For how long?"

"For as long as it takes to find out whether our theory is correct. We're prepared to keep the experiment going for up to a couple of months."

"A couple of—I have one word for you, Arnie: bed sores."

"That's two words and we've got it covered." Arnie pressed down on the bed and it continued to move for a moment.

"A water bed?"

"Not water," Arnie said. "A thin mixture of mud. It was developed for burn patients. As the subject breathes, the bed undulates and pressure is relieved on the body. In other words, the bed does the subject's tossing and turning for him."

"Well, mud or no mud, if you're talking about making me the 'subject' I can't be lazing around for that long. What about my classes?"

"Teddy, if you were to get sick, the university would have to find a substitute. If you took a sabbatical they'd make other arrangements. Since this project would be part of a university research project you would remain on the payroll. It's not like it's gonna kill you."

"Why me?"

"Because you're always moaning about your dull life. I thought you'd jump at the chance."

"Sounds risky."

"Not at all. I admit we don't know every detail for sure. We do know that if it doesn't work you would be perfectly safe. If it does work we'll have made history."

Neither said anything for what seemed like a very long time as Ted considered the possibilities.

Finally Ted said, "You would need proof that it succeeded. The human lab rat might be having these virtual experiences. But from your point of view it would just be an unconscious guy on a mud bed."

"Now *that* we do know something about for sure," Arnie said as they walked back to his office. He turned on the television, reached behind his desk and pressed the 'Play' button on a video player.

Dream-like images came slowly into focus, taking shape, then becoming clearer on the TV screen.

"What you're seeing, Teddy, is pictures made through the eyes of Harold, my assistant."

Ted's jaw dropped at what he was seeing and hearing.

"You've converted thoughts to pictures?"

"Not thoughts . . . sights through the eyes and sounds through the ears. It's part of the same project we've been working on."

"You could monitor what the subject is experiencing?"

Arnie nodded.

Ted said, "We're talking about a major disruption in my life."

"What life is that, my boring friend?"

"Well," Ted said, "it may be boring, but at least it's manageable. Sort of."

"Remember Einstein's other theory? 'Insanity is doing the same thing over and over again and expecting different results.' If you want things to change, Teddy, you have to do something different."

"Some things are bigger than me."

"Bigger than *I*, professor," Arnie corrected, ". . . and this is not one of them."

"There's nothing I can do about who I am or how I got this way."

Arnie rolled his eyes. "A convenient cop-out if ever I heard one," he said. "If I understand correctly, you're telling me that if your car is headed for a cliff, you're not going to turn the steering wheel to avoid plunging to your death?"

"I think this is a little different, Arnie."

"Teddy, nothing will change unless you change it. If you wait around hoping things will improve, they won't. Things will happen *to* you, not *for* you. Unless you take control of your life, your life will take control of you."

Ted leaned back and didn't say anything for awhile. He surely knew that Arnie was right about what a meaningless life he had been living.

"When would this adventure begin?"

"Shortly after you give the go-ahead."

Ted got to his feet and headed for the door. "I'll have to think about it."

"I need to know soon, Teddy," Arnie called out to his friend.

CHAPTER 5

TRAVELING THROUGH TIME. A bizarre concept when Ted McBride opened his emotional gate a crack and considered what he would be going back to . . . if he decided to take part in the experiment. It would be nice to see his old English and science teachers, Mrs. Simpson and Mr. Wilson again. The idea had him at once excited and apprehensive . . . feelings he had not experienced in many years. Unsettling because Ted had gotten into the habit of not allowing himself to feel much of anything. He rejected life's 'ups' so the 'downs' would not come as a disappointment.

In his youth Ted had been smaller in stature than his contemporaries. He enjoyed a growth spurt in his late teens and grew to six feet tall by the time he was twenty. But in his own mind he was still the small boy who was a natural target of bullies in the mean little railroad town where he spent his formative years.

Even though he could claim many professional successes as an adult, those had not made him the confident person he deserved to be, especially in one-on-one relationships. Being bullied as a kid and treated coldly by his father still poked at his psyche.

"Get those ridiculous ideas about computers out of your head," his father had said.

"Computers are the future, Dad."

"If the future includes having machines doing our thinking for us," Ed McBride said, "I won't spend a dime on such nonsense."

Ted's prediction had come true, of course. His father did not live long enough to see the impact the technology had on the world.

His failed marriage did nothing to boost his self-esteem. A sense of failure was never very far from Ted McBride's consciousness.

Ted had skipped one grade in elementary school. Administrators were so impressed with his intelligence they wanted to skip him yet another. His mother would not permit it. Ted was already a year younger than others at his grade level. She reasoned that he would suffer socially if placed among students who were so much older. As it was, Ted had no real connection with his grade-level classmates or with those a grade back. So there was Ted on his own lonely island.

He had little in common with the rough children of rough railroad men living alongside the industry that kept the town going . . . and kept it from going further. The town served as an incubator where each new generation of railroad workers was hatched. The town's male children would eventually replace their fathers and grandfathers in those jobs and continue their blue collar dynasty.

Ted's family's economic status was equal to just about everyone else's in town, so wealth, or lack of it, was not the great social divider. Still, differences could be found or invented by those with a need to feel superior.

He remembered one particular incident long ago that was typical of the cruelty he suffered while growing up.

A scruffy-looking boy lay in wait among the cornflowers, Queen Anne's lace, thistle and wild mustard growing alongside a path worn through sharp brown shale of the kind that supported only the hardiest of plant life. It was a regular after-school ritual.

Without warning, Jimmy Deavers sprang from his hiding place to block Ted's path.

"Hey homo."

"Let me alone, Jimmy." Ted tried to get past the bully. "I've never done anything to you."

Since fighting was not in Ted's nature, the only other choice seemed to be to endure. It was all the more humiliating because Jimmy was a year younger and a few inches shorter than Ted. However, what Deavers lacked in size, he made up for in meanness and had no limits on the damage he was willing to inflict on his prey.

Jimmy walked behind Ted, stepping on his heels as they continued down the hill.

Suddenly Jimmy pushed Ted to the ground. The knee was ripped out of the pants his mother had so carefully pressed that morning. Ted's glasses flew into the weeds so that all he could see were fuzzy images of his trombone case and books bouncing down the dirt path. Papers fluttered onto the street and into neighboring yards.

"See you tomorrow homo," Deavers called out. His laugh echoed off buildings as he ran toward his house, just four doors away from the McBrides.

Gasping for breath and fighting back the urge to throw up, Ted got unsteadily to his feet and brushed dirt from his torn, dirty clothes. He located the glasses he could barely see without his glasses. He rounded up as many of his scattered items as he could find and walked painfully the rest of the way home.

Even at fifty-five years old, the psychological wounds were as painful today as the physical wounds had been all those years ago. Ted regularly flashed back to incidents that profoundly affected him.

Post Traumatic Stress Disorder did not only apply to war veterans.

Ted had an appointment that evening with his kickboxing instructor at the YMCA. He had never considered himself athletic, so he was surprised that he had become fairly proficient at the martial art, which required a high degree of agility. It also required a level of aggression that was not in Ted's nature.

"Ready to grunt and sweat, Ted?" Abe Kirby said.

"I guess we'll soon see."

Ted had gotten involved in kickboxing, ostensibly to keep his aging body in some kind of physical shape. Digging deeper into his psyche, he knew that punching and kicking sparring partners was also good emotional therapy . . . a socially acceptable kind of violence against demons that had pursued him into adulthood.

The two men bowed and went at it.

In seconds, Ted found himself on the floor, looking up at the instructor.

Abe offered Ted a hand to get him back on his feet. "I know you have the ability, Ted, but you need to go after your opponent with blood in your eye."

"I know, Abe. It's hard for me to play rough."

Ted often wondered whether he would ever become truly proficient in the self-defense discipline.

"Your skill level is far beyond that of the average mugger, Ted. This is not for the meek. You could probably defeat any of my other students if you aggressively used everything you know. But, if you hesitate because you think it's not the polite thing to do, you're gonna get knocked on your ass a lot."

Ted thought about what Abe had said and how he might have applied his self-defense skills against the bullies of his youth.

"If you want things to change," Arnie had said, "you have to do something different."

If Ted had any self-esteem at all, he credited his mother. Alma McBride had always been on his side. He believed that if his mother saw him standing over a dead body holding a knife and was covered with the victim's blood, she would insist that, "my Teddy would never do anything like that."

His father was another story entirely. Ted could never count on any backing from Ed McBride. Like when Ted expressed his interest in computers.

"Not one cent for it," Ed McBride had said when young Ted approached him about taking an introductory computer science course. "I've told you before, I'm not going to waste hard-earned money on something that isn't worth a hill of beans."

Frustrated, Ted said, "Dad, computers will change the world."

"Gadgets. A fad."

"Tools," Ted said, as insistent as he had ever been with his father.

"Learn something productive."

"Maybe my idea of what is productive is different from yours," he said. "I'm interested in computers. What's wrong with that?"

"You're good at math," Ed said. "Do something with that and you'll never have to work on the railroad like the rest of us."

"That's just what I'm telling you, Dad. Computers are pure math—"

"A waste of time . . . like that damned trombone."

"Music is math, too."

"This discussion is over."

Ted felt his frustration rising.

Ed McBride said, "And don't give me that look, young fella."

As he always did, Ted pushed his feelings deep down inside himself. He tried logic instead.

"The day will come when unbelievable amounts of information will be stored on computers," Ted said. "Data will be sorted and organized at the speed of light."

"If machines did our thinking for us," Ed said, "we'd stop thinking for ourselves."

"If you believe that, Dad, then you believe that putting seatbelts in our cars will make us drive less carefully."

Ed glared at his son and Ted realized it was very possible his father actually did believe that.

"If computers are the future," Ed said, "Lord help us. I don't want to hear another word on the subject."

Ed McBride was not a man to be challenged when his mind was made up.

The prospect of seeing his father again was troubling. Ted could not say he hated Ed McBride. Neither could he say there was any love.

Ted's great-grandfathers and grandfathers on both sides of his family had been railroaders. His maternal grandfather had retired to a farm a few miles farther north. Following another railroad tradition, his mother's father died a few years after his last day on the job.

The prospective husband pool offered few choices, so Alma Patterson also married a railroad man.

If history was any indicator, Alma's son would also work on the railroad. Ted vowed at an early age that was not going to happen. So had his mother.

Alma had grown up with people hardened by a sad lack of prospects. They became the parents of the children who now bullied her son. If anyone could have understood what Ted was going through, it was Alma McBride. On the other hand, Ted's late father never had a clue, nor did he make an effort to know his son that well.

Ted recalled one occasion when he again tried to connect with his father.

Ted went down the stairs to his father's basement workshop. In a corner sat the tools of Ed McBride's job as a railroad brakeman: A suitcase contained signaling flares and other paraphernalia related to the trade.

"What is it, Ted?" Ed said impatiently. He looked up from his work on a lathe as his son descended into the cool cellar. Ted's father's hideout smelled of dampness mingled with cigarette smoke and new wood heated by the friction of a steel chisel against whirling oak.

In his own way, Ed had become an abusive man, although he would never have accepted the description. Ted was a living reminder of Ed McBride's responsibilities.

"I just wanted to see if I could help," Ted said, noticing his father's frustration that a woodworking project had not been going quite right.

"It's a one-man job," Ed snapped. He turned his back and shut his son out. It effectively delivered the message that the boy was not welcome in this private space.

Ted went back up the stairs and never again tried to become part of his father's world.

Ed McBride died before their differences could be resolved, but the hurt lived on. Ted did not want to be like his father in dealing with his own son. Still, he and young Tim had a strained relationship. He remembered one of the last times he talked to his son. It was all Ted could do to keep the boy on the phone, let alone spend time with him.

"Hi, Tim," he said. "It's your dad."

"Uh. . . oh, hi."

"Maybe we could get together this weekend, do something."

"Uh. . . this weekend? I think. . . my scout troop has a thing."

"A thing?"

"Yeah, uh, merit badge stuff. . . and, uh. . ."

"Since we don't see each other that much . . ."

"Uh huh. But I'm working toward Eagle Scout , and , uh, if it wasn't for that . . ."

"Okay, Tim. Another time then."

"Sure."

Ted concluded that his efforts to stay in touch with his son may have been more a matter of obligation than affection. They had done things together when Tim was younger, but they seemed to have gone off in different directions as the boy got older. Maybe it was because of Ted's refusal to accept his son's obsession with flying. Maybe Maggie sent silent . . . and maybe not so silent . . . anti-Ted messages to their son. Maybe it was simply because he didn't understand teenagers. It was quite clear that Tim had little interest in a relationship with his father.

Another regret to add to Ted's life list.

CHAPTER 6

TED COULD THINK OF LITTLE ELSE BEYOND Arnie's proposal since their talk. The plan seemed insane, even frightening. Yet the possibilities were exhilarating. Who would not want to peek at their earlier life the way it actually happened? That would certainly be more interesting than the life he was living right now. It was all Ted could do to drag himself out of bed every morning and drive the few miles downriver to teach the complexities of computers.

Arnie had said Ted needed to do something different. Well, everything he had done so far had turned out badly. Traveling back forty years in time would certainly qualify as 'different'.

Ted arrived at the university earlier than usual and stopped by Arnie's office. Arnie's bifocals slid down his nose as he looked at Ted and waited for his friend to speak.

Ted's heart was threatening to come through his chest wall when he forced himself to say, "Okay Arn. I'm in."

"Good man!" Arnie shouted, practically flying out of his squeaky old swivel chair to shake Ted's hand. "We can be ready in a week."

"A week?" Ted's heart rate went to warp speed. "I hadn't expected it to be that soon. I have some things to do first."

"As do I," Arnie said. "Both of us had better get started then. And remember, it's hush-hush."

"I hope I know what I'm doing, Arnie," Ted said. "More important, I hope you know what *you're* doing."

"One more thing Teddy. We need to know where you were at the age of fifteen at a particular day and time. It has to be at a precise time when you were awake and you positively know your physical location to within a few feet."

Ted was astonished. Arnie wanted a guy who often forgot where he put his car keys to know within mere inches where he was positioned in the vastness of the universe four decades earlier.

"That's some homework assignment, Arn."

"Just to show what a sport I am," Arnie said, "I'll buy the coffee this morning."

CHAPTER 7

IT DIDN'T TAKE TED VERY LONG TO SET THINGS UP for his absence. Arnie alerted the university administration about Ted's participation in the project. A substitute was lined up to handle his classes.

There were very few appointments or obligations on Ted's personal schedule.

Pathetic, he thought, *when it only takes a couple of phone calls to cancel a person's agenda for three whole months.*

Arnie also arranged for Ted to have a complete physical exam, which he passed easily.

As the big day approached, Ted waffled dozens of times. He paced and agonized, coming close to calling the whole thing off. But he never got beyond picking up the phone and putting it down again.

Except for playing in the Dixieland band, he had no active social calendar and no girlfriend. Arnie was probably the only person who would notice his absence.

McBride, you are pitiful.

Ted paid the rent on his apartment three months in advance, in the event the experiment worked and it took longer than expected. He told the landlord he would be traveling. No need to mention that he would be traveling through time.

He had called his mother to let her know he would be away on a research project. Another call to his son.

"Hi, Tim. It's your dad."

"Uh. . . oh. . . hi."

Ted could feel his son fidgeting at the other end of the line.

"Just wanted you to know I'll be out of the area for maybe a couple of months."

"Okay."

In the first ten seconds of the conversation Ted realized he was not going to be missed. It was obvious Tim could not wait to end the call.

"Just checking in. See you when I get back."

"Okay, bye," the boy said and hung up.

Ted sat with the phone still to his ear long after the dial tone changed to an irritating squawk. What had he done, he wondered, to alienate the boy to such an extent? When did a call from a father to his son become a chore for the boy? Ted realized that if he had not made the call Tim probably would not have noticed he was gone.

Their biggest disagreement was about Tim's wanting to pursue a career in aviation. Ted saw flying as dangerous and pushed for something in computers. He had complained to Maggie about what he saw as their son's frivolous use of his PC.

"Here's a tool that could solve the mysteries of the universe," Ted said. "The only thing the boy wants to do is shoot down space invaders."

He had often expressed his objections to his son.

"Tim," Ted said, "I don't see how destroying computer-generated Martians figures into an aviation career."

"It's great for developing eye-hand coordination, Dad. That's real important in flying."

"Why flying?"

"Just look up in the sky, Dad."

An airliner and a small plane were passing over.

"Somebody's gotta fly 'em," Tim said.

"Why you? There are much less dangerous things to do for a living."

"Far more people die in car crashes than in airplanes for every million miles traveled."

"Well, you have a few years before you have to get serious about a lifelong occupation."

"I won't change my mind," Tim said.

Ted decided to wait until they got together over the weekend to tell his bandmates of his upcoming absence. He canceled a dental appointment and did not reschedule because. . . well. . . you never know.

The possibility of actually revisiting parts of his youth made him consider more carefully how he might have handled certain situations if he had been as mature, disciplined and knowledgeable as he was today.

His younger sister had been troublesome when they were growing up. He wondered what he might have done differently there, as well.

Emily, was five years younger than her brother. There was the usual sibling chafing and squabbling, although it seemed to Ted to be more intense than in most families. She was demanding and quarrelsome. While young Ted was able to push his anger at adults down inside himself, he had no such restraints where his frustrating sister was concerned. However, the adult Ted was now considering that there might have been a lot going on inside that little head that was not so obvious. He recalled those times when his mother asked him to take Emily with him to the movies in the city.

"Aw, Mom," Ted said. "Do I have to? She never behaves."

That was in the days before there was a fiend on every street corner. Ted suspected his mother wanted to get the girl out of her hair for awhile, so he got stuck with her.

"I'll pay for both of you," his mother had said.

He liked the part where his mother paid for the movie tickets and the popcorn. He hated the part where Emily had to go with him. She would talk through the film and never listened to him when they were on the streets of the city.

When they got there Emily constantly ran toward the curb.

On one occasion he said, "Damn you, Emily."

"I'm gonna tell Mom you swore."

Frustrated, Ted said, "Yeah, then you can tell her how I bashed your head against that building."

"Eek! You better not."

He didn't mean it, but the threat had its effect.

"Then behave yourself. I'm never bringing you with me again."

"Mom will make you."

"If I have to take you along, I'd rather stay at home."

The bus ride home was uneventful. When they were within site of the house Emily ran the rest of the way, faking crying as she went inside.

"Teddy hit me and said he'd bang my head against a wall," she wailed. "And he swore, Mom . . . Teddy said a bad word."

It wasn't just the movies. It seemed to Ted that every aspect of his dealings with Emily as they were growing up had been a battle. They fought over everything, from who got the first toast that popped up out of the toaster, to which TV shows they would watch.

Emily managed to impose herself on Ted in many ways. She got into his personal belongings and constantly complained about things that Ted got and she did not, such as a room of his own while Emily slept on a daybed in an alcove off the living room.

The last time Ted visited his mother on the family farm, Alma McBride was fixing lunch. Emily was her usual sulking self, sitting at the kitchen table reading a magazine. Her hair was uncombed, as though she cared little about her appearance.

"Hi Mom," he said. "Hi Emily."

Without looking up from her reading, Emily said, "Yeah. . . whatever."

"Nice to see you too Emily."

"What do you want me to do, sing the hallelujah chorus?"

"A civil greeting would be nice."

Alma McBride said, "Teddy. . . Emily. . . let's not have this contention. It's time you two got over your childhood differences."

"Well he started it," Emily said.

"All I said was 'Hi, Emily'. My deepest apologies."

The weekend engagement with the band was unexciting. When the last song had been played and the members were packing up their instruments and equipment, bandleader Al Manning took Ted aside.

"What's going on, Ted?"

"What do you mean?"

"Your playing didn't have the usual spark tonight," Manning said.

"Sorry, Al. I've got a lot on my mind these days."

Ted had already told his bandmates he would be gone for as long as a couple of months.

"Maybe the time off from the routine will do you good," Al said.

Ted was feeling more nervous as the countdown continued to the day of the great voyage. Or the big flop, depending on whether it worked. He actually found himself taking comfort in a daily routine that had previously become tedious.

CHAPTER 8

IF THE TIME AND SPACE ADVENTURE HAD BEEN A NORMAL, everyday, non-science fiction event, Ted thought the day would have seemed like forever in coming. Instead, it arrived almost before his living room clock could say "tock". It felt like the first day in a new school . . . multiplied by thousands.

Ted was nervous as he turned his car toward the university campus. A bead of sweat ran down the middle of his back. He had showered before leaving and thought he might have to do it again at the rate he was perspiring.

He drove five-miles-an-hour under the speed limit. He didn't want to see a flashing red light in his rearview mirror and have some cop yelling at him. Besides, he thought, what's the rush?

Even with Arnie's assurances of the experiment's safety, Ted would have defied anyone to honestly say they would not be apprehensive.

If Arnie had not been a trusted friend, and if the man had not gone to all the trouble of preparation, Ted thought he might have turned around and gone back home.

He pulled into the computer science building's faculty lot and parked his car beside a monster satellite dish. Arnie had agreed to drive Ted's car home once a week to keep the battery charged up.

He walked without haste to . . . to what?

Arnie had charted the location of that place in time he had asked Ted to recall. When he was fifteen years old Ted was a volunteer at the fire company's fundraising carnival that spring. It was the first weekend in April. He had worked the penny-pitch concession that Sunday evening. Ted knew that for sure because his mother's birthday was the next day and he won a stuffed bear for her at the wheel of fortune.

The penny-pitch board was contained within a twelve-foot-square fenced enclosure. Ted would have been the only person inside the one-hundred-forty-four-square-foot area that night.

The information satisfied Arnie. Presumably, he had tweaked his magic machine and fed in the data.

Just outside the computer lab a group of people was seated. Ted wondered why they were there.

The curtains in the room with the mud bed were open and Ted could now see the equipment next door.

"Not exactly what I expected, Arnie."

"Did you think the lab would be something out of Star Trek?"

Actually, that was exactly what Ted did expect—a sleek control room, blinking lights, Mr. Sulu at the controls, Captain Kirk barking orders. He imagined a life-sized screen on which to watch the galaxy whiz by. Instead, the technical side of the window resembled a computer geek's storage space. A desktop PC and keyboard sat at an unimpressive-looking workstation. A second keyboard was positioned on a table to the side, much like a piano player who could swivel to his left and continue playing on an organ. A microphone was mounted on a flexible arm affixed to the desk. A color monitor on a wall shelf at eye level was connected to yet another computer. A bank of black electronic devices with blinking lights was panel-mounted against a wall. Wires and cables ran through a conduit from the bed to the technical array in the adjoining room.

"Who are those people in the waiting area?" Ted said.

"They're the medical team who will be taking care of you during the experiment. Their duties will be limited to your physical needs. They won't know anything about the nature of the project. You're in capable hands. Relax buddy."

"Relax? Holy frijoles, Arn. How would you feel if you were about to go where no man has gone before . . . to a galaxy far, far away . . . ?"

"Oh for heaven's sake."

"And then some," Ted said, trying unsuccessfully to keep the tremor out of his voice. "I don't normally have medics and a nerd squad hovering over me. This isn't normal, Arnie. Of course I'm nervous. How many times have you gone back in time? How many times has anyone gone back in time?"

"None that we know of, although I've heard some of the administrators referred to as 'dinosaurs.'"

"All right then."

"Okay, Teddy. You can be nervous. Now take off all of your clothes."

"Why Arnie, you randy devil."

"Your shoes and socks too, sweetie," he said. "And put on this gown." He tossed Ted one of those thin hospital gowns with tie strings in the back. He pointed to an adjoining bathroom.

"You don't leave a man with a shred of dignity, do you?" Ted said.

Ted took his time dressing. In part because he was not anxious to get started and partly because he was having trouble tying the blasted strings at the back of the blasted gown.

When the inevitable could no longer be delayed Ted left the relative safety of the bathroom. He held the troublesome rear opening in the gown closed as best he could.

"My, my you look lovely in that outfit," Arnie said with a snicker.

Ted frowned, mumbled something vague, possibly profane, and climbed onto the bed, pulling the sheet over himself.

Responding to a signal from Arnie, the medical people moved into the room. They surrounded Ted and went into action.

One of the nurses inserted a needle with an intravenous tube into a vein on the back of Ted's left hand.

"Ouch."

"Hold still," Arnie said. "Stop being such a baby. We're hooking you to a line to keep you hydrated and nourished."

Gel-coated suction cups were connected to wires running from various points on Ted's body to the electronic equipment in the adjacent room.

Arnie put a set of earphones on Ted's head and went into the control room where he spoke through the sound system.

"Only you can hear me now, Teddy. Those are hearing protectors as well as earphones. They will shut out any sounds in the room and let me communicate with you. I'll spot check what's going on and I'll call you each evening at seven o'clock sharp. I won't be able to hear your thoughts. You will have to speak up. If you're not in a place where you can talk, just don't say anything. Or you can give me a one-word answer like 'later', or 'uh huh'. Got it?"

"Uh-huh."

Arnie's assistant, Harold, was carrying what looked like a black Lone Ranger's mask, but without eyeholes.

"You don't mind if I call you Igor, do you?" Ted said, lifting the earphones.

"Not at all, Doctor Frankenstein," Harold said.

He put the mask on Ted's head, but had not yet brought it down over the eyes.

Then he slipped on a stainless steel helmet that resembled something out of a 1930s Buck Rogers movie, with hundreds of sensors on the inside that were connected to wires on the outside.

"Arnie, I imagine this is quite fashionable among those who wear a colander on their head."

Through the small window to the tech side, Arnie had positioned a TV monitor that only he and Ted could see. On the screen was another screen within a screen within a screen within a screen . . . into infinity. It took a moment for Ted to realize that what he was seeing on the monitor was what he was seeing with his own eyes, picked up by the sensors and converted to visual images.

The wizardry was working so far.

Then Harold pulled the mask down over Ted's eyes and it was lights out. The only sound he could hear was his own breathing.

A syringe had been poised at a junction on the IV tube. Those stationed at equipment related to their realm of medical and electronic expertise looked to Arnie for the order to start the process.

"Okay, Teddy. A sedative will relax you. That will make it easier to get into the flow. At some point you should fade from this reality to another at the point we discussed. That could be unsettling, but knowing it in advance should help you to adapt more quickly to the transition. Have a nice trip. If all goes well I'll see you in a couple of months. If it doesn't, I'll see you in a few hours, after the drug wears off."

Ted's pulse pounded in his ears and he could feel the drug taking effect. He was growing numb. His mouth was suddenly dry and he had the impression he was moving, as though the bed were on a giant turntable at a thousand RPM. A faint beeping sound beat a cadence that increased until it became a continuous tone.

Then Ted's world turned very strange.

CHAPTER 9

PEOPLE WERE TALKING. . . some nearby, some farther away . . . out there in the darkness. There was a clacking sound off to Ted's right. A thumping noise and the clang of a bell to his left.

The smell of freshly popped popcorn. And hot dogs. He could feel a slight chill.

There were snatches of conversations, the words increasing in volume, then fading as though they were passing by: . . . "then she said I don't think I" . . . "hey Fred, over here" . . . "won a stuffed duck" . . . "some cotton candy" . . . "looks good in a T-shirt . . ."

"Hey, kid," Ted heard a man's voice say. "Hey!"

He was yelling into Ted's left ear.

Where the hell am I?

"Wake up boy."

Images were beginning to come into focus. Kind of foggy. Odd shapes. Moving. It was like coming out of a deep sleep. He was standing in something like a small corral, holding onto one of the railings. People were leaning on the top rail, throwing things. Coins. They were tossing pennies; occasional cheers.

"Hey," said a clearly irritated man. "How about my change?"

What the . . . .?

Then Ted realized he was wearing an apron with pockets containing a lot of coins. There were lights above and all around him. Above those was a black, star-filled sky such as he had not seen in many years.

Arnie actually did it. It's 1965 again.

He recognized the Carbonville Fire Company carnival and knew he was looking at something that had occurred decades before.

"Kid," the man shouted again. "I gave you a quarter. Gimme my pennies."

Ted stood there, open-mouthed and immobile until he fully realized what had happened.

"Uh. . . Sorry." Ted said. The voice coming out of his mouth startled him because it wasn't actually his voice. Not exactly. It was more nasal; higher pitched.

He dug the coins out of the apron and handed them to the player.

A familiar-looking man approached the railing.

Jesus. It's Skip Doutrich.

Ted heard Doutrich had died in the 1970s. The man was . . . is . . . chairman of the fire company carnival committee. The old man had a pencil-thin moustache like actors wore in 1930s movies; . . . the ones who never got the girl.

This is so weird.

"Are you all right Teddy?" Doutrich said.

Ted's first thought was to get to a place where he could adjust to this new reality.

"Mr. Doutrich," Ted said. "I'm not feeling well."

That's sure no lie.

"Let me find someone to take over for you," he said, looking around the lot for a likely replacement.

Although he felt like he was swimming in a thick liquid, Ted continued to make change and pay off winners until Doutrich returned with another young boy in tow. The boy looked familiar.

I know that kid. He was in my high school algebra class before I moved away. What in blazes is his name?

"Walter will finish the evening," Doutrich said.

Walter . . . Walter Minnich. Right. I haven't even thought about him since I left Carbonville.

"Will you be okay, Ted?"

"Huh? Oh, yeah . . . thanks Mr. Doutrich," he managed to say. Ted took off the change-filled apron and handed it to Walter.

The fogginess was clearing up, but he wanted to get away from the place as soon as he could.

As Ted ducked under the railing he could hear Doutrich instructing the boy on how to determine a penny-pitch winner.

The thumping and clanging sound he heard earlier turned out to be the local macho men using a sledgehammer to ring a bell for prizes. The clacking noise was the wheel of fortune. Ted remembered that his Uncle Ken used to run that concession.

Sure enough, there was his mother's older brother, looking much younger. And alive. He was spinning the wheel and handing out prizes to those who had placed their coins on the number the wheel stopped at.

"Hey Teddy," Ken said to the man disguised as a boy. "You gonna play?"

Ted's Uncle Ken was in his mid-seventies when he died in Ted's future world. This man was not yet forty.

Ted felt for a coin in his pocket, not at all certain one would be there. He found a quarter.

"Sure," he said, bringing out the coin and placing it on the number seven.

"A quarter?" his uncle said. "We certainly are a big spender tonight."

A quarter was . . . is . . . big money in this time period. Even bigger if minted before the mid sixties when coins actually had a much higher amount of real silver in them.

All bets were down. Kenny the Younger reached back, grabbed the edge of the wheel with a meaty hand made tough from years of shoveling coal into steam engine fireboxes and gave it a spin. "Round and round she goes. . ." he called out in a monotone, ". . . and where she stops. . . nobody knows."

The wheel spun about a half-dozen times before coming to rest on the number seven.

Ted knew his number would come up because it had happened before.

"We have a big-time winner," Ken said. "A winning quarter player gets choice of prizes. Is it for Alma's birthday?"

"Right. Mom's birthday," Ted said. "I'll take that big stuffed bear."

"A teddy for a Teddy," Ken said with a chuckle, handing over the huge stuffed animal.

"Thanks . . . uh . . . Uncle Ken."

Ted was halfway down the street before it occurred to him there were major differences between what had happened in the past few minutes and what had happened the first time around.

The sounds of the carnival crowd faded as Ted, still dazed, walked down the dimly-lit street toward where his home had been four decades earlier.

Then he heard a voice.

"*Teddy.*"

"Yeah? Who—"

"*Ted. Can you hear me? It's Arnie.*"

"Arnie." he shouted. Then he looked around to see if anyone had heard him. He realized someone might think he was talking to himself . . . which, in some bizarre sense, he was. Ted scanned the neighborhood to be certain no one was nearby before he answered. "Arnie, you did it. You crazy man, you did it."

"Harold and I went nuts when we saw images coming through. How are you feeling?"

"I feel great," Ted said. "No aches. I think I could run ten miles without getting out of breath. And nothing hurts, Arnie. Funny how you don't think about a bum knee until the ache isn't there anymore."

"It's a strange sensation to be talking to you Teddy. Right now I'm looking across the lab where you're asleep, even though your brain is wide awake. Your teenage voice is not exactly the one I'm familiar with."

There was a lot to tell Arnie . . . and ask him.

"You think it's strange for you? How do you think I feel?"

"Pretty cosmic, I'm sure."

"It's going to be awkward talking with you if there are people around, Arnie."

"I understand. I'll check on you each evening at seven o'clock. If you're not alone I'll wait until you are. Remember, you have to speak out loud, since I can't pick up thoughts."

"Testing, one, two . . . over."

"Ten-four . . . loud and clear good buddy. How do you feel physically?"

"I can't remember when I've felt this good. I have spring in my step I'm not accustomed to."

"In other words, you are experiencing your teenage world . . . again."

"Yeah. Now what do I do?"

"You need to keep your eyes open to see if your memories were accurate."

"You know, Arnie. Something odd; I'm seeing differences between what I remembered and what I've just seen."

"That's bound to happen if my theory of remembered memories is correct. Rather than recalling people and events as they occurred, I believe they actually remember their immediate previous recollection of a person or occurrence. As time goes by, the memory recurs with miniscule changes. Recalled frequently, the image evolves into something entirely different from the original."

Ted thought that would explain why his Aunt Millie got so upset with his Uncle Kenny for recalling the same event differently from her own version of what happened.

"More than that, Arnie," Ted said. "I'm not sure what to make of it, but if I'm just watching a video of my original life, why are some things so different?"

"Well, I told you memories were likely to vary from the real thing."

"No, Arn . . . I mean really different."

Silence.

"Arnie."

When Arnie spoke again, it was very quietly.

"Different how?"

"Well, I did win a teddy bear at the wheel of fortune and I did work at the penny-pitch that night, but I didn't leave early. I absolutely know I worked until closing time. And, if I'm watching a replay, why are all my senses working? Not to mention talking to you, which I didn't do the first time?

There was an even longer pause.

"Arnie . . . you there?"

"I'm here. Just trying to figure out what's going on."

Ted stopped walking. "You're starting to freak me out, Arn."

"I assume you're on your way home."

"Yeah, it's the next left turn."

"Instead of turning left, turn right."

"There would be no reason to—oh—"

When he got to the corner, Ted expected to turn left, just as his 1960s self would have done.

That's not what happened.

"Uh-oh."

"What do you mean, 'uh-oh'? Arnie, do not ever say 'uh-oh' to me when I am stuck forty years in the past. Now what do you mean?"

"Well. . we had this other theory, but didn't give it much thought at the time . . ."

"You mean this is not a rerun of my early life."

"Teddy . . . I think you are actually re-living that part of your life."

"How is that possible?" Ted said, having a moment of panic.

"I haven't figured that out yet. One theory has it that other dimensions exist. You may be living in one. I think we can prove it."

"How?"

"Is there someplace . . . some object . . . structure . . . that is the same today . . . my today . . . as it was then?"

"Sure. The Baptist Church right over there," Ted said, making certain he was looking at it so Arnie could see it in the dimness of a street light. "It will still exist forty years from now."

"Okay, here's what I want you to do. Find a remote spot on the building and scratch your initials into it."

"Huh?"

"I'll drive up there and see if I can find your mark. If it's there it will mean that you

are not just viewing your past as it was. . . you are actually living it."

"And you knew this was a possibility?" Ted said.

"The thought occurred to us, but it seemed too far-fetched."

"Far-fetched? Arnie, this whole experiment is pretty far-fetched. I wish I had known earlier about that theory."

"Would you have done anything differently?"

Ted considered that for just a moment. "Now that you mention it, probably not."

Ted hurried to the back of the church and found a spot that could not be seen from the street. He located a bent nail on the ground that had probably been dropped by workmen and scratched 'TWM', for Theodore Winston McBride, into a brick.

"Can you see where I am?" he said, looking at the mark.

"Yes. I'll call you as soon as I get back."

Ted knew the wait was going to be excruciating. To pass the time he walked up and down the familiar streets.

Even in this place that held so many bad memories of being bullied by the local thuglings, where he never quite fitted in, where he feared his dreams would never come true, he was overwhelmed with nostalgia.

An occasional car passed by, including the Ford roadster "Cappy" Johnson had bought brand new in 1930. Many wondered which would give out first, the old man or the Model A.

The butcher shop on the corner would be replaced by an appliance store as supermarkets and strip malls edged out his hometown's Mom and Pop shops. On a vacant lot where a house would one day be built there were trees and shrubs, behind which Ted had kissed a girl for the first time. He was nine and Patty Gibney was eight. Ted heard that Patty got kissed a lot after that. Not by him.

Carbonville was the only town Ted knew of that did not have a Main Street. But then why should it? None of the town's streets were different from any other, so none could rightfully be considered the main one. Each house was the same as the next, built from a single set of plans, as though no individuality were permitted by the railroad company that built them to rent out to its employees.

Two hours of walking and thinking later, the anticipation had Ted in a sweat.

"Teddy."

Ted jumped, startled at Arnie's voice in the otherwise quiet neighborhood. "Yes Arnie . . . it sure took you a long time."

"I drove like a maniac."

"You always drive like a maniac. What's the word?"

"The word is, your mark is there and—"

"—anything I do here will affect the future."

"Absolutely. You may be in a parallel universe, which some believe are as infinite as the universe, itself."

"Translation please."

"One theory is that the Here-and-Now we are experiencing is just one layer of time, that there are other layers, like those of an onion. Activity in each layer, or universe, is based upon all the events that are occurring differently in each layer adjacent to the one we are living in."

"If that's true, then how did what I scratched in the brick in this layer of the 'onion' turn up in yours?"

There was a long pause at Arnie's end of the conversation.

"You're trying to ruin my day, aren't you, Teddy? I'll have to give that a lot of thought."

"If I murdered my eleventh grade history teacher," Ted said, "the world would be completely changed because of all the things the demented bastard was too dead to do after that."

"As they say, Teddy, if a butterfly flapped its wings in South America, the action would create a tornado somewhere in the world."

"The Chaos Theory."

"Be very careful, m'boy. This could have enormous consequences. Maybe we should bring you back."

"No . . . no . . . don't do that. Now that I'm here, let's see where it goes."

"Okay, but if I sense any problems, I'll pull the plug."

"All right, but please check with me before you do that," he said, and started for home. "I'd hate to be halfway up a ladder when you called off the project. That really would change the future."

"Deal. I'll spot-check your activities every day and talk to you again tomorrow night. Signing off."

"Roger. Over and out."

Ted wondered why, if science could locate his younger self at a pinpoint in the infinite universe, he had not been able to find a satisfying place for himself on one lousy planet.

CHAPTER 10

THE FRONT DOOR TO 220 RILEY STREET WAS UNLOCKED, as it always had been. It was unlikely that anyone in the family even knew where to find the key to secure the house where Ted spent his early years. He was never able to convince his mother that times had changed for the worse. She still would not lock the doors at the farm where they moved . . . would move . . . when school let out for the summer.

A small nightlight provided only slight illumination in the entryway. The smells and the feel of his old home enveloped him, bringing forth emotions he had no idea were still there. The place seemed smaller than he remembered it.

A low squeal came from the darkness. Ted recognized the sound.

"Daisy," he whispered, as the stubby little terrier skittered toward him. A lump appeared in Ted's throat and a tear trickled down a cheek.

"I never thought I'd see you again," he whispered, hugging the little dog.

She wagged her tail more briskly than one might expect of a dog that died in 1968.

He placed the stuffed bear on the telephone stand and scribbled "Happy Birthday Mom" on the pad by the phone.

Now, if I can just get to my room without making any noise.

He thought he would need more time to adjust to all of this before he got into a conversation with anyone. His father worked the night shift on the railroad, so Ted would not have to face the man right away. It was almost ten o'clock. His mother and sister should be asleep.

He had forgotten that the third step on the wooden stairs creaked. It always had. It creaked again.

Oh please God, don't let Mom hear me.

"Teddy?"

Aw, man . . . God never listens to me.

He stiffened, knowing that he risked her sensing that something was different. "Yes, Mom."

The door to his parents' bedroom opened as he got to the top of the stairs. His mother was wearing a powder blue terrycloth bathrobe and green plastic hair curlers. She had on a pair of pink fake fur slippers.

Blue, green and pink. My mother is a walking, talking rainbow.

Alma McBride had dark brown hair instead of the gray she had when he last saw her. And she was thirty-five-years-old again. Or she would be tomorrow.

Alma would have no reason to believe her son was anything but the boy she had known for all of his fifteen years. Standing before him was June Cleaver, Margaret Anderson, Martha Stewart and Betty Crocker, all rolled into one person. Seeing her this way made Ted a little sad to think of the life that lay before her. She had a crease between her eyebrows that would deepen over the years as worries piled up.

"Did you get anything to eat at the carnival, honey? Let me fix you something."

The question startled him. He didn't know whether he had eaten anything. His confusion must have shown on his face.

"Um . . . I'm not hungry, Mom."

His mother cocked her head slightly and raised an eyebrow. Ted often wondered how it was possible to raise just one eyebrow. He read somewhere that it was hereditary. He didn't think he inherited the gene. Maybe it skipped a generation. Maybe his son had it.

He was certain that some mothers and all female elementary school teachers have built-in antennae. Ted's mother was one of those. She tuned in on him, picking up anything that didn't quite fit. She was doing it again.

"What's going on, kiddo?"

If you get me out of this God I promise I'll . . . oh . . . never mind God, I'll handle it.

"Nothing, Mom," he said. "Different day, same old stuff."

She never let me get away with anything.

After being busted a couple of thousand times, it was likely you would try to stay out of range of a mother with ESP, X-ray vision, radar, sonar, eyes in the back of her head and a generous supply of pixie dust. Maybe even some voodoo business going on that let a rare parent hold a kid's soul up to the light.

How could I possibly explain that I am older than my mother?

"You'd tell me if there was something wrong, wouldn't you?"

"Of course I would."

It wasn't exactly a lie. Nothing was wrong in the normal sense, although he was having a little trouble defining "normal" at the moment.

"I'm just tired."

He would have to act like a teenager if he hoped to pull this off. Ted continued to work his way toward his bedroom, wanting to get the ordeal over with.

"I shouldn't have let you stay up so late on a school night."

"I'm fine. Really."

"All right. Good night then," she said, and went back into her bedroom and closed the door.

Ted resolved to work on his kid skills. Simple answers; lots of "I don't knows" and oafish grunts. He couldn't have Professor Theodore McBride leaking through from the 21st century. Maybe he could pick up some pointers from other kids at school tomorrow.

School tomorrow. Now there's a scary thought.

Ted's bedroom was the same as he remembered it. Hanging from the ceiling was a tissue paper-covered yellow Piper Cub J-3 model airplane with a black lightning bolt along its side. Also, a P-51 Mustang fighter plane and a Korean War era Sabre jet fighter. Ted hung them there when he was nine years old and never took them down after he lost interest in airplanes. Technically, he built them forty-six years ago and suspended them on fishing line held in place by thumbtacks.

Same faded wallpaper, same cracked linoleum on the floor, same single bed pushed against a wall.

I can't believe I ever slept in a bed that small.

There was his roll-top desk . . . and the dresser with at least a half-dozen coats of paint. Physically, the room was just as he last saw it.

But something was different.

Ohmygod! My ears aren't ringing.

He'd had tinnitus for years. It was a constant sound that had been there since he was in his thirties. He had to buy a clock with a more robust alarm because the tones in his ears were louder . . . and at roughly the same frequency . . . as his old clock's puny wakeup call. All he could hear now was the clacking of the eight-day Big Ben windup clock in his parents' bedroom down the hall and the muffled rumble of distant freight trains.

Ted was enjoying the lack of aches and pains of aging that had been creeping up on him.

I could get used to being fifteen again. Well, the physical part, anyway.

He felt as though he could leap tall buildings in a single bound.

He was also thinking impure thoughts of women he'd known.

Omygod! Hormones!

CHAPTER 11

A RAY OF MORNING SUNLIGHT HAD MOVED ACROSS THE BEDROOM and found its way to Ted's face. He sat up with a start and looked around.

Where—?

Then he remembered that he was fifteen years old again and this was the first full day of the rest of his past life.

"Teddy," his mother called up the stairs. "It's time to get ready for school."

"As soon as I shower and shave, Mom."

Silence.

Oops.

"Kidding Mom," he said quickly. He had forgotten they had a tub, not a shower. Nor did the teen Ted have to shave yet, although the fuzz on his face was thickening to the point where he would soon need a razor. He thought how nice it would be to never have to shave. If he had not been in such a rush to do the grownup thing when he was a teenager he might never have had to shave at all. Wishful thinking.

Ted was almost finished with his morning bathroom routine when he heard the front door close. His father . . . his not-yet-dead father . . . just getting home from work.

Ed McBride plodded up the stairs to wash off the railroad grime when he spotted Ted.

"I'm gonna have to get in there," his father said.

He who wins the bread gets first dibs on the bathroom.

"Sure," Ted said. He went back to his room, resentment mingled with longing for the relationship with his father that should have been. Ted often wondered, as his friend Arnie had suggested, why he didn't have ulcers, considering all the emotions he suppressed.

Ed McBride's attitudes had created a rift between them that never healed. Yet here Ted was, feeling . . . something. When Ted lived in this moment the first time he would have raced to the kitchen, wolfed down his breakfast and beat it out of the house before his father came downstairs.

By the time Ted was in his teens, Edward McBride had become a shadowy figure in his son's life. Father and son lived in the same house, but rarely spoke or had much direct interaction.

Ed rode railroad freight cars six nights a week and slept evenings before returning to his job. Ted would only catch small glimpses of his father before he went back to work. The schedule made it easier for Ted to avoid the man.

After his father finished getting cleaned up he would have breakfast. Maybe take a nap. Typically, Ted would already have left for school.

But Ted decided this day would be different.

The smells of breakfast wafted up the stairs from the kitchen. Ted headed that way.

"Happy birthday, Mom," he said.

"Thanks for the stuffed bear, Teddy."

On the table were bacon and ham and sausages. There were eggs fried in the fats from all the others. A heap of browned, crispy fried potatoes sat steaming in the middle of the table. Toasted homemade bread was slathered with farm fresh butter from the cow his grandmother milked twice a day on the farm.

A cardiologist's nightmare, but what the heck. I know I've lived at least four more decades on a diet like this.

In the 21st century, just to be on the safe side, Ted's breakfast usually included two eggs fried in olive oil. He figured the alleged good cholesterol in the olive oil should cancel out the alleged bad cholesterol in the eggs.

Ed joined them for the morning meal.

"Good morning, Dad," Ted said.

Ed seemed surprised that his son was still in the house and had actually spoken to him.

"Uh . . . good morning."

Alma McBride also seemed a little surprised at the exchange . . . and that Ted was joining them at the table.

"How are things, Dad?"

Ed looked at his son for a moment before speaking.

"Things are the way things have always been," Ed said looking down at his plate.

Ted was still chewing his breakfast when he got up from the table. It was clear that any in-depth conversation with his father would have to wait.

Alma said, "Don't forget to pick up Benny's mail, Teddy."

Ted stopped chewing, trying to place the name.

Benny? Oh, yeah, I remember.

"Okay," Ted said.

Benny Hubbard was the town bookie. He had contracted polio as a boy. By the time he was an adult, he was wheelchair-bound full-time. He lived farther up Riley Street and ran his horserace betting operation out of a spare bedroom. The town cop never bothered him because, although gambling was illegal, the lawman cut Benny a break. The betting was pretty much penny ante stuff anyway. Never any big money involved. Nobody got hurt. Bettors paid him in quarters, dimes and nickels more often than in dollars.

"Don't forget your trombone," his mother said as Ted finished his breakfast and started for the door.

He had forgotten about that, too. He had probably forgotten a lot of things.

This is going to be a strange day.

"Teddy," his mother said. "Are you awake?"

"Any minute now, Mom."

As he walked to the top of the knob behind his house Ted noted springiness in his legs he hadn't felt in years. He started to run. When he reached the crest, he soared over it. It was almost like flying. If his older model self had tried that, he thought he would probably need a chiropractor. He vowed to make jogging a regular part of his daily routine when . . . if . . . he got back to his own time.

It occurred to Ted as he walked to school that by the next millennium nothing would exist as it was on this day. The maple trees lining the town's streets were barely full enough to cast a shadow. In his future they would have reached full maturity and be gone, victims of disease and old age.

Arriving at the old two-story red brick high school, Ted experienced a mixture of déjà vu and dread.

The building will still be here in forty years, but it won't be a school anymore.

Ted thought back . . . or was it thought *ahead*? . . . to the school as it would be four decades in the future. As the population grew, districts would consolidate. The several hundred students from the town of Carbonville would be bused to a larger campus that would accommodate many more hundreds of young people transported from other towns.

High school buildings that had been used for generations would continue to serve for a few years as elementary or middle schools. Eventually they would no longer be big enough for the growing student body and not worth the cost of upkeep. They would be sold off to generate revenue toward the cost of new facilities. The Carbonville High School building would become a dozen or so apartments. Ted's old homeroom would be turned into living space for people not yet born. The gymnasium would be several two-story townhouse-style units with picture window views of the Appalachian Mountain ridge in the distance.

Ted never got a close look at the inside of the structure after his family moved away, although he had driven by a few times when he got his drivers license.

Finally he got up the nerve to go inside.

This is going to be a really weird day.

A nostalgic blast of air struck him when he entered. A school gave off a particular blend of aromas. The same combination probably permeated schools around the world; a mix of cleaning chemicals, floor wax, sweat from the same clothes some kids had worn previous days, and oranges, bananas, and bologna sandwiches in bag lunches. The cafeteria sent out its own special essences.

As he roamed the hallways he could see the remembered parade of heroes and villains, strutting boys and posing girls. They looked smaller and younger than he recalled.

These people are . . . children.

From all outward appearances, Ted was also a child.

"No running," shouted one of the male teachers as a young boy tore down the hallway.

Trying to calm the herd had little effect. The teachers were dealing with kids with one foot in childhood and the other on a slow course to adulthood. The sound and motion in the halls was intense.

What did I ever have in common with any of these people?

When he actually was that young, Ted McBride had no clearly identifiable peer group. He knew that most teens felt alone to some degree, convinced they were the only ones in the entire world with their particular set of woes. Given the shallow intellectual reservoir in his hometown, Ted really was pretty much alone. Even an intelligent teenager with a well-formed ethical sense longs for wider validation of his worth. The need at that age tends to allow for acceptance of differences in people not exactly like him. As they got older, they became more discriminating and distanced themselves from those with mismatched tastes and values. Meanwhile . . .

"Yo, Teddy."

Oh, Lord . . . it's Charlie Freeman.

Charlie was walking toward Ted, belching loudly with each step.

"Where the f—" Charlie caught himself mid-obscenity. "Where ya been?"

Charlie was rough in look and manner. He projected an aura of defensiveness. If one were judged by the company one kept, Ted McBride might have lost a few points because of his association with a boy like Charlie.

"You're late, Teddy," the swaggering, gum-chewing boy said.

"How observant you are, Charlie," Ted said.

Knowing someone from the time they were toddlers and going through most of the same stages of growing up was a good way for each to understand the other and be more likely to forgive what was lacking. Ted and Charlie had known each other practically since they were sperms. As they got older, Ted became more aware that there were some missing ingredients in Charlie's makeup, especially in the areas of logic and ethics.

Ted McBride and Charlie Freeman had been friends by default.

"It's a shame we gotta go to school," Charlie said, bouncing on his toes, cracking his knuckles and checking out girls passing by. "We could be off somewhere, humping our brains out with some of these women."

Women? These girls are babies.

"Some of them are pretty ugly," Charlie said. "Maybe we ought to burn them like they burned those witches in Maine."

"They didn't burn them, Charlie, they hanged them. And it was Massachusetts, not Maine."

"Teddy," Charlie said, looking at Ted as though he were being patient with a small child, "everybody knows about them burning witches."

"Funny thing about what 'everybody' knows, Charlie. Sometimes they get it wrong. This is one of those things."

"Look it up. You'll see."

From long past experience, Ted knew that Charlie was certain of just about everything and could not be convinced otherwise.

Ted spotted the girl who had been his youthful fantasy princess. Marlene Sutton was at her usual place at a hallway intersection, standing with her regular group. At that spot the maximum foot traffic would assure that she could be seen and admired by the greatest number of people.

Marlene's short, tight skirt and low-cut blouse were just barely within the school administration's range of acceptable dress. The combination, Ted noted, sent the wrong message to the wrong kind of boys.

"Before too long I'm gonna have a piece of that," Charlie said.

Ted was appalled at the thought of someone like Charlie taking advantage of a young girl.

"Is sex all you ever think of, Charlie?"

Charlie looked at Ted as though some alien being had just landed. In a way, he was right.

"What the hell else is there to think about in this lousy town?"

The girls were looking around at passers-by and giggling. Ted wondered whether they were laughing because they thought something was actually funny or to keep others unsettled, wondering if they were being laughed at. Ted interpreted their silliness as a display of immaturity rather than the superiority they seemed to be trying to project.

Marlene looks much younger than I remembered.

Ted had often thought about people with a serious "look-at-me" need. People like Marlene seemed to be focused on themselves in the extreme.

Once again Arnie's theory of evolved memories was proving itself. Marlene was pretty, but not the sex bomb image he had carried with him into adulthood. His mental picture had evolved to movie star beauty and had added at least ten years to her age.

As they got closer to the cluster of girls, he looked more closely and saw a Marlene he was completely unfamiliar with.

Something other than her looks is very different.

The girl of memory had always appeared to Ted as supremely self-assured. This Marlene was unlike the girl he remembered, vacillating from arrogance to angst, like a switch rapidly being turned off and on. One moment she projected self-confidence. The next, with strobe-like speed, she was searching faces for approval. Ted had never noticed that before.

In the years since he last walked these halls, Ted had observed thousands of people in a great many situations.

Marlene, you poor child. You're a fraud.

Seeing the boys approaching, she purred, "Hi Charlie."

Charlie mumbled something unintelligible. He gave her a brief nod and shoved another stick of gum into his mouth.

Then Marlene did something she had never done in Ted's previous life. She spoke to him.

"Hi Teddy," Marlene said, throwing in a little head tilt, hair flip, and some minor eye work.

Ted had been studying Marlene rather than admiring her. That was apparently equal to being ignored and had activated the girl's seduction system—a radar-like mechanism where she sent out a ping to see what bounced back.

"Mmm," Ted said without embellishment, eager to move on.

He could see she was probing for clues, but his usual puppy dog demeanor was not there. It was a condition that would have been quite unfamiliar to Marlene. Ted's absolute lack of romantic interest must have been evident.

It was hard for Ted to believe this girl had been the star of his teenage imaginings.

"What's the matter, Teddy?" she said. "Aren't I good enough for you to talk to?"

Before he could stop himself, Ted said, "too young, Marlene."

Ouch. I can't believe I said that.

He regretted the comment the instant he made it, but realized that anything he said now would only make it worse.

The other girls started to laugh. Her smile vanished and Marlene did not seem to know whether to be hurt, embarrassed or angry. Ted suspected she would eventually get around to all three.

"Gotta get to class, Charlie," Ted said as they walked away from the group. Marlene's carefully-crafted tableau now lay in ruins. She had fired off practically her entire wily repertoire. She apparently expected Ted to react as all the other boys did. Except Charlie, of course, although she could not have known that ignoring her was contrived. It was part of Charlie's tactic to make himself more attractive to her.

"Treat a queen like a tramp and a tramp like a queen," Charlie had once said. "They'll be ripping your clothes off."

Ted had inadvertently done that very thing. He now realized that the reason Marlene had ignored the old Ted was because she already had him—and any other male who openly fawned over her—where she wanted them. She knew he was hers if she chose and there was no need to waste any more energy on him. On to other challenges. When Ted displayed no interest, he landed right in the middle of her playing field.

That is, until he insulted her.

"What was that all about, Teddy?" Charlie said.

"What do you mean?" Ted said, knowing exactly what Charlie meant.

"Usually your mouth doesn't work when you're around Marlene. Today you acted like she wasn't even there."

"She's a kid, for crissake."

Oops!

"She's the same age as us."

"Nice looking," Ted said. "I'll give her that."

"She's a beauty queen, Teddy."

"I used to think so."

"Yeah, 'used to' yesterday."

In the years since high school, Ted had learned that females responded to confidence in males even more than to good looks. Sadly, there was also a certain type of woman who was attracted to men who mistreated or ignored them. Those were skills he had never mastered, nor would he care to. Charlie, to the detriment of females and to his own advantage, had the ability to fake both confidence and disinterest.

It was a rare thing, but for once Charlie was right about something.

Marlene had been dismissed by Ted in full view of her friends. She, who had always been the dismiss-er and never the dismiss-ee.

Ted was mentally kicking himself, but her response convinced him there was more going on with Marlene than he had been aware of.

Ted put his observations together with an incident when he followed Marlene home those many years ago. He had seen a man watching her from the doorway as she approached the house. He assumed at the time it was her father.

The man stood in an aggressive pose; thumbs hooked in his belt, feet far apart, watching as Marlene approached the house. To complete the picture, he wore a sleeveless T-shirt, an apparent attempt to project masculinity he may have been in doubt of. There was a cigarette at one side of his mouth, a sneer at the other. It was clear from Marlene's hesitation and body language that she did not want to enter the house. She shrugged her shoulders. Even from a distance Ted could see that she let out a long sigh before going inside.

Thinking back over the incident, the cynicism Ted acquired through the years told him that no normal parent would look at his daughter in that way. Now he was convinced that something sinister was taking place in that house.

I think I may have been looking at the boogie man.

He decided to check it out.

It was becoming easier for Ted to see why adolescents appeared overconfident one moment and completely lost the next. As an observer Ted realized that a teen's world was one of constantly swirling emotions—wrestling with physical changes and the frustration of no longer being children. But neither were they adults. While their parents were doing the heavy lifting, kids lived in a bubble.

They would not fully realize how insular their lives had been until it was their turn to carry the load. It had certainly come as a shock to Ted.

Unlike the kids in his 21st-century world, these 1960s young people's activities included hanging out with friends in actual one-on-one interaction. Granted, talk was seldom deep, though he overheard occasional flashes of wisdom and maturity. It was human contact of the kind he knew would be all but lost in his own time as electronic communications infringed on genuine conversation.

Charlie was prattling on about an alien spaceship that had landed in Nevada in 1947. He assured Ted the U.S. government was covering it up.

"It's a well-known true fact," Charlie said, snapping his gum as he swaggered down the hall to his first class.

How did I ever become friends with this crude young man?

In his past life, Ted had always been willing to concede a point rather than argue. He avoided trouble so completely that his own ideas and opinions were smothered. But an unfamiliar feeling was boiling up within him. This kid was really irritating him.

Ted knew it was useless to tell Charlie the 'alien spaceship' found on the New Mexico CIA test site that became known as Area 51 was actually a downed experimental stealth spy plane. That would not be known publicly for many years. But government officials did little to discourage the UFO myth to keep the public attention off the top secret purpose of the site.

CHAPTER 12

GRACE SIMPSON TAUGHT ENGLISH. Ted especially admired his favorite teacher because she was a straightforward person whose only goal in her professional life was to add to her students' bank of knowledge, taking nothing from the experience for herself except the satisfaction of having done so.

Mrs. Simpson's classroom was at the end of a hallway directly ahead. Ted could see the teacher sitting at her desk as he approached.

Wow. Why hadn't I noticed she was a babe when I was a kid?

On this day, Ted was a fifty-five-year-old man in the body of a fifteen-year-old boy. He was thinking adult thoughts about this kindly woman who appeared to be at least two decades older than the boy ogling her from the hallway. To complicate matters, the teen Ted was experiencing a massive hormone infusion, the prime motivator of adolescent males on the cusp of manhood.

If Ted thought Mrs. Simpson looked good, a couple of his mother's friends also had him wanting to write poetry.

Even from a distance, Ted could see that Mrs. Simpson was crying.

He remembered back to this very incident. She had been dabbing her eyes with a tissue, just like now.

In the original version, no one else had arrived yet for his first period English class.

Mrs. Simpson's elbows were on the desk and her hands covered her eyes.

She had not noticed him standing there. Rather than impose on what was obviously a personal moment, Ted stepped back into the hallway and waited for the rest of the class to catch up. He held the teacher in high regard and wanted to respect her privacy.

He had heard that Mrs. Simpson's husband was an adulterous rat. The whole town knew it. She had apparently found out, as well. Ted thought it was bad enough her husband had a girlfriend on the side. The man, with a kind, elegant wife and a sweet young daughter, did not even have the decency to be careful about it.

A girl was passing by the classroom. "Hi Nancy," Ted said. It was both a greeting and an alert to Mrs. Simpson.

Ted wished he could do something to help. He waited a moment before going into the room. By the time the other students arrived, no one but Ted was aware that anything was out of the ordinary.

Experiencing the same incident once more, Ted thought it would be criminal if he again failed to comfort this woman he so admired.

Ted took a deep breath and went into the classroom. "You okay, Mrs. Simpson?"

"Wha . . . oh, yes," she said, doing her best to regain her composure.

"Sorry to intrude on a private moment."

Your philandering husband is an idiot who should have his skin peeled from his body.

"I'm fine, Ted. Thank you."

Students were clattering down the hallway, some on their way to her classroom. Ted reached over to the teacher's desk and lifted a tissue from the box. He handed it to her, just as several students came through the door.

"If I can ever help," he said quietly, "please call on me."

Just loud enough for the approaching students to hear, Ted said. "Take care of yourself Mrs. Simpson. Those springtime colds can hang on all summer."

After the class, Charlie Freeman said, "Hey brown-noser."

"Why do you say that?"

"I saw you doing some close work with Mrs. Simpson. I watched you buttering her up for a better grade."

"Right, Charlie. You may have noticed, I'm already a straight-A student."

"I guess it worked then."

Charlie's mind was made up. No use pushing the issue. As irritating as Ted found the boy, he resolved to try to be more understanding of young people.

"You know, Charlie," Ted said. "Some day we'll call these the 'good old days.'"

"What's so damned good about them?"

"Looking at them today it doesn't seem so great. One day we'll forget all the bullshit and compare our lives then with our lives now. The memory will look good by comparison."

Charlie glared at Ted. "I think I have a better memory than that, chief," he said, and walked away to his class.

Alice Simpson was looking at him from down the hallway, trying unsuccessfully not to appear to be waiting for Ted's arrival. Mrs. Simpson's shy, awkward twelve-year-old daughter had a large crush on Ted in those . . . these . . . days. Alice was three years younger.

Alice is so young. And I thought she was young when I actually was this age.

"Hello, Teddy," she said, almost too quietly to be heard. Alice rarely made eye contact with anyone she spoke to. Ted was the exception.

"Hi, Alice."

Ted thought it would be impossible not to be nice to anyone this sweet. Kids could be cruel to those who were shy or different. In a way Alice was bullied as much as he had been. In less physical ways, perhaps. But being ignored or teased could be equally damaging. Alice smiled through a grid of shiny metal braces. She looked directly at Ted with hazel eyes behind thick, horn-rimmed glasses.

Alice had not quite grown into her face and body yet. But underneath the dental and vision hardware Ted could see a beautiful young woman emerging.

"How's life, Alice?"

The girl just shrugged. The domestic pressures troubling her mother had to be affecting her, as well. At least her father was out of the house now. His presence would have been harder on her than his leaving.

"What would you wish for that you don't already have, Alice?"

With only slight hesitation she said, "I'd wish I were pretty."

Ted was so surprised that he stopped quickly, his sneakers squeaking on the waxed floor, startling her. The Simpsons were originally from an area north of the capital, the deep end of the gene pool, where early southern European settlers' descendents continued to produce lovely blossoms.

"Alice," Ted said, "you're already the prettiest girl in town. What more could you ask for?"

Alice took in a giant breath and her eyes desperately searched for signs he might not be sincere.

"Don't say that, Teddy. You know it's not true."

"It is true. Why would you think you're not pretty?

"I wear braces," she said, pointing to her sparkling mouth.

"And one day you'll take them off and have perfect teeth."

"And glasses," she said, pointing to the nerdy rims.

"I wear glasses, too. They keep me from bumping into things," he said, taking off the glasses, squinting and groping along the hallway wall.

"You still there, Alice?"

The girl laughed, quickly putting her hand up to cover up the retainers.

Ted gently pulled her hand away from her mouth.

"Don't hide your smile, Alice."

She was probably also aware that her clothes were not in tune with her contemporaries. Ted knew the answer to that, too. Her mother purposely . . . and wisely . . . dressed her conservatively so her daughter would be judged for herself and not for her looks. Marlene Sutton dressed like a tart and that's the way she was perceived. She would pay a terrible price for accepting that kind of notice.

"I have trouble talking to people," she said.

"You're talking to me."

"You're different, Teddy. I've known you since we were both little. You . . . you've always been nice to me."

"Anyone who is mean to you isn't worth your time. It's their problem, not yours. Stop beating yourself up."

"Marlene Sutton is pretty," she said, looking down at the floor.

Ted knew she was not fishing for a further compliment. He shook his head. "More important than looks is that you're smart and you are a good person. It's what's in here that counts," he said, gently tapping her head. "Marlene is provocative."

"What?"

"Marlene poses and prances. She's showy. That's not what pretty is. That's false advertising."

Alice giggled. She started to cover her mouth, but changed her mind.

"Please don't tell anyone I said that," he said. "I don't want to hurt feelings. Marlene wants a lot of attention. She's probably trying to make up for what she doesn't get at home. No, Alice, you are a pretty girl and you will be a beautiful woman, just like your mother. In the long run, looks aren't as important as you think. They can even get in the way. If the boys your age weren't such jerks they'd be following you around instead of Marlene. They wouldn't recognize character if it bit them in the—nose."

Ted thought the child was going to swoon on the spot.

Oh crud. Now I've really done it.

If she had a crush on him before today, he had only made it worse.

She was starting to get teary.

Nice going McBride.

"I heard you're moving away," she said, barely able to get the words out.

"We're moving to my grandmother's farm. She's getting too old to live alone."

"I wish you weren't leaving, Teddy."

Ted regretted that he had unwittingly endeared himself further to this sweet youngster.

"Some decisions you make for yourself, Alice. Others are made for you."

The girl looked devastated as she walked down the hallway, and there was nothing he could do about it.

Ted spotted Mr. Wilson, another of his favorites on the Carbonville High School faculty. A tall man, Wilson walked with a slouch, like someone suffering from persistent disappointment. He wore a gray suit that was a decade out of fashion. The narrow knit tie and white shirt were of the same era. The elbows of the jacket and the seat of the pants had a shine from wear.

John Wilson was clearly a man making do.

"Good morning, Mr. Wilson," Ted said.

"Are you sure about that, Ted?"

"Better than yesterday, not as good as tomorrow."

Wilson smiled and said, "Nobody likes an optimist first thing in the morning, young man."

"Somebody put vinegar on your Cheerios this morning?"

"A regular part of my diet, thank you."

Ted could see that the man's spirits had been lifted by the brief exchange.

Unlike many of the other teachers, Wilson took extra time with the slower learners and did not berate them for not immediately absorbing what he already knew so well . . . things students like Ted soaked up without effort.

The man and the boy often stayed after school, talking about science and whatever else came up in conversation. Ted loved the subject. But, even more, he enjoyed spending time with an adult who valued his opinions and who had never treated him like a child.

Having spent a lot of time with the man in a more casual setting, Ted had learned some things about John Wilson, though not directly. More by inference and interpretation.

Squeezed between crushing family obligations and a long list of unfulfilled dreams, Wilson had put aside his personal aspirations and settled for the stable world of teaching. But Ted knew there was a serious gap between teaching high school science and the career path Wilson once dreamed of. Ted was aware that the man had math skills at least on a par with his own.

Maybe I can do something for him.

The rest of the day was one weird experience after another; seeing children who would reach adulthood with varying degrees of success . . . or lack of it. There would be news stories about some of them, trumpeting their triumphs and lamenting their tragedies. There were those who would never make it beyond their youth.

A young boy named Clark Erickson walked by Ted in the hallway. Clark was an effeminate young loner who avoided looking directly at people.

Nice kid. Probably gay and everyone treats him like he was diseased.

"Good morning Clark," Ted said.

The boy looked up and seemed surprised that someone was speaking to him.

"Oh. . . uh . . . hello Ted," he said and walked on, looking back over his shoulder, perhaps to be sure he had heard correctly.

Someone had told Ted that Clark committed suicide when he was in his twenties.

Robert Carson taught civics. Ted knew Carson wasn't a bad guy, but the man did not have a lot of patience. His basement classroom had none of the usual refinements of the upper-level rooms. No acoustical tile on the ceiling, just open joists and plumbing. Except for the desks and chalkboard the room could easily be mistaken for a storage area.

Carson looked at one of the students. Sam Scott had his head down in his textbook.

Ted knew what was coming because he had experienced it before.

"Mr. Scott," Carson said, interrupting his lecture, "go to the office."

Ted looked at boy, who had his eyes covered with his hand.

"What for?" Sam said.

"For sleeping in class."

"I wasn't sleeping, I was following along in the book."

"Go to the office."

"That's not fair."

Ted knew exactly what had happened. Despite his usual habit of avoiding conflict, Ted needed to set it straight.

"Wait a minute, Mr. Carson," Ted said. "Sam wasn't sleeping."

All eyes in the room shot to Ted.

"Stay out of it Mr. McBride."

"But you're wrong."

Historically, Mr. Carson was not one to be challenged.

"This is none of your business."

"I think it is the business of everyone in the room, Mr. Carson. This is civics class isn't it?"

"That is correct. It is *my* civics class."

"And civics includes the study of our constitutional government, right?"

"Mr. McBride, you are wearing on my patience."

Ted went on. "The Fourteenth Amendment guarantees the right of due process."

"What's your point?"

"My point is that you accused Sam Scott of a civics class crime and gave him no opportunity to refute the charge."

Carson had to think that one over for a beat or two.

"I heard him snoring. What more do you need?"

"Evidence."

"Snoring is convincing evidence to me."

"So, the United States of America stops at the door to your classroom?"

Carson exhaled to an almost insulting degree.

"All right Mr. McBride, just for the entertainment value, what can you offer to support Mr. Scott's claim that he was not sleeping in my class."

Ted turned to the accused and said, "Sam, read as you were before."

The boy did so, slumping down in his seat, his hand over his brow."

"Notice," Ted said. "The light globe above Sam is broken and the bare bulb shines directly at him."

The teacher looked up.

"That would seem to justify shading his eyes," Carson said. "How about the snoring?"

"See the pipes running through the ceiling?" he said. "Those are water and drain pipes to and from the restrooms directly above."

"And . . . .?"

"And . . . listen."

An intermittent hissing and buzzing could clearly be heard when one actually focused on the room's ambient sounds.

"Now, look at Sam."

The teacher did so and saw a young man who appeared to be asleep at his desk, with a sound above him that could be mistaken for snoring.

Carson hesitated for a moment, apparently stuck somewhere between embarrassment and admiration.

"Mr. McBride," he said, finally. "I believe you have made the case, both for Mr.

Scott and for the Democratic process. I apologize for my lapse. From now on you may be assured Democracy will reign supreme in this room and, hopefully, in the rest of America."

The class applauded. Ted stood up and took an exaggerated bow.

"Do you plan to be a lawyer, Mr. McBride?" Carson asked.

"Are you kidding?" he said. "I hate lawyers."

The teacher smiled and said, "Further evidence of your intelligence and strength of character."

CHAPTER 13

THE SUN HAD TUCKED ITSELF DOWN BEHIND THE APPALACHIAN ridge and it was getting on to time for Ted's evening meeting with Arnie.

Ted had finished practicing his trombone in the basement. It was a good time of day for it because his father was at work and could not object to the 'noise'. The smell of stale cigarette smoke saturated all surfaces, the result of his father's use of the space as his woodworking shop.

"You're sounding really good, Teddy," his mother called down the steps.

"Thanks, Mom."

"It's trash night, you know?"

"Just getting ready to take it out."

Ted wiped the shiny brass instrument clean with a cloth and put it back carefully into its case.

The evening air was cool as Ted carried the family's trash cans to the curb. Neighbors on both sides of tree-lined Riley Street had set theirs out for pickup the next morning.

Suddenly there was a loud crash of metal cans coming from the Deavers home four doors down the street.

"Get your ass out there and do what I told you."

Oh God. I remember this incident.

It was a replay of Blaine Deavers' assault on his son Jimmy that Ted had observed those many years before.

Ted had actually been disappointed that Jimmy had not been waiting for him on the way home from school. It was what Ted had most looked forward to in his return. However, not being at his ambush spot was not unusual, since Jimmy was a regular truant. Ted had not seen the boy and assumed he was holed up somewhere to avoid school.

Brutal slaps to Jimmy's head and body echoed off houses. Ted watched him struggle with the cans. Even from that distance he could see the boy's face was twisted in fear.

Blaine Deavers was a drunk and a tyrant with a "little man" complex. Even though the elder Deavers was smaller than most adults, he still had a physical advantage over his son.

Victoria Deavers would not win "Mother of the Year" honors either. Rumors persisted that Jimmy's mother cheated on her husband. If they were making a movie and were looking for someone to play a tart, they could not have done better than to cast Vikki Deavers in the role. She worked part-time as a waitress at a local diner. Her makeup was outdated and too heavily applied. Attractive in a sluttish way, her hair was done in a style typical of party girls of her era. As new styles came along, the hairdo had not changed. Neither, it seemed, had Vikki Deavers.

Ted had seen the inside of the Deavers home once. He was walking past the house one evening after dark. The curtains were open and the living room lights were on. The wall facing the street had holes in it, as though heavy objects had been thrown against it. One of the doors visible from the street had fist-sized punctures. Given the violent nature of Jimmy Deavers' father, it was easy to imagine how it happened.

Even after the trash was set out, Jimmy continued to sit on the curb.

In the 21st century Teddy knew a man like Blaine Deavers would be locked up as a child abuser.

Ted snapped to attention when he heard the familiar voice inside his head.

"This is the future calling Ted McBride . . . come in Teddy."

Ted walked to the woods to continue the conversation.

"This is the past speaking. Hi, Arn."

"How is the life re-lived young man?"

"Really strange. You were right about memories. I'm seeing things very differently from the way I recalled them over the years."

"I could say 'I told you so', Teddy, but I'm a bigger man than that."

"Uh huh."

"But I did tell you so."

"You never disappoint, my friend. Do you remember Angela Freitag, that girl in my class . . . the one whose grandfather was . . . ah . . . taking liberties?"

"I remember her. One of your students. An overly sexual girl, I believe."

"That's the one. She came on to just about every male in the place. I noticed she seemed stressed and I approached her about it. She got really nervous and denied anything was wrong. She reacted so strongly that I became even more convinced there was a problem.

"You arranged for counseling."

"It came out that her grandfather had been molesting her since she was a kid. She was filled with guilt and feeling worthless. I only found out about it because she came to me later, told me the whole story and thanked me."

"Why are you bringing that up?"

"Because I'm seeing similar behavior in a young girl here."

"Are you sure it's the same situation?"

"No proof whatsoever," Ted said. "But I'm sure she is troubled. I've got to find out more."

"Tread lightly, Teddy. Where there's a molester there's a man who could get violent if threatened with discovery."

It was obvious to Ted that Marlene was a person with a great need to control men . . . or, perhaps, to know where she stood with them. Although he had no hard evidence, Ted would have bet the girl lived in an abusive home, possibly sexually abusive if his previous experience was any gauge.

In his youth, Ted had followed Marlene home from a distance just to watch her. He had made up his mind to follow her again. But his motive this time would be pure.

"What other observations have you made with your new perspective, Teddy?"

"Arnie, I've only been here a short time and I'm convinced 'Lord of the Flies' is a true story. Some of these kids are savages."

"Children run largely on instinct, Teddy. It takes many years to tame those who can be tamed. Those who cannot are in prison or serving in the state legislature."

"There's this one kid who is absolutely sure of every word that comes out of his mouth, but is actually wrong most of the time."

"Kids don't know they don't know everything, so they think that everything they do know . . . is everything."

"Thanks for clearing that up, Arn. I shouldn't be too hard on them, I guess. I had forgotten how tough it was to be a kid. I could probably have handled things differently with my son. Young people are not highly regarded by most adults."

"True, but they get a two-month vacation every summer, so it's a trade-off."

"Then they graduate from high school . . . maybe college . . . and, if they are fortunate enough to find a job at all, they get a lousy week of vacation after they've worked there for a year. I still wouldn't swap being disrespected for a two-month vacation."

"And you, poor boy, are now one of those suffering slings and arrows."

"It doesn't bother me because I know who I am. But I can't tell you how starved I am for adult conversation. I have to speak a whole new language or I'll blow my cover."

"Uh huh. If you spoke in multi-syllable words, people would immediately know you were from the future."

"They would know something wasn't right. Especially my mother, who has honest-to-God ESP."

"Be careful, Ted. We don't want this to get out before the right time."

"When will there ever be the right time to re-adjust the past?"

"Hey, buddy . . . didn't you say you'd like to go back in time with all the knowledge you accumulated over a lifetime?"

"Yeah, but I never thought it would actually happen."

"Well, ready or not, my friend, here we are . . . the past has come to your future."

Ted looked down the street. Jimmy Deavers was still sitting on the curb rather than going back into a house where he was not loved.

CHAPTER 14

THE NEXT DAY SPED BY, BUT SLOWED PAINFULLY as the final class of the day neared.

In the short time since he arrived in Carbonville Ted's adult sensibilities often clashed with young people. While his maturity allowed him to overlook most faults in the young. . . or at least not become too impatient with them. . . the kind of emotions he had not permitted himself in adult life were growing more intense as he witnessed unjust treatment of kids by their elders.

When it was time for the final class, most of the students were antsy and couldn't wait to get out of there. Unfortunately, the last period on this day was World History. Ted had always disliked history. Not the subject; the teacher. He regarded Ralph Taylor as a destroyer of self-esteem.

When local men of draft age were called to serve in World War II there was a critical shortage of teachers. There were sixty-thousand teacher vacancies nationwide. The local school district was among those hard-hit as draft-eligible male teachers went off to fight the Germans and the Japanese. Many never returned.

To fill the teacher void, anyone who could demonstrate anything close to a skill in a particular subject area could take a short course and be awarded a temporary teaching certificate. There were far more female teachers.

And there was Ralph Taylor.

Taylor had glassy eyes common to career drunks. The man was overweight, had high blood pressure, a heart murmur, and one leg shorter than the other. Classified 4-F, he was ineligible for the draft during World War II. He applied for and received his temporary teaching credential. It became permanent around the time the war ended. With tenure there would be no getting rid of him.

The class had barely started and Ted was already feeling irritated. He tried pushing it down the way he always had, but it kept coming back up.

Taylor took particular delight in making his students look foolish. His heavy-handedness had touched each of his students at one time or another.

A lecture took up most of the class period. It featured Taylor strutting and posing.

When he finished, Taylor said, "Your homework assignment was to read chapter sixteen."

The air was thick with disdain.

He was one of those men who looked as though he had lifted weights at one time. When he stopped working out, the muscle turned to flab and he added to the bulk one forkful at a time. He had a red Irish face, a redder nose with broken capillaries and those glazed eyes . . . the hallmarks of a dedicated drinker.

Here it comes.

"Has anyone actually read the chapter?" Taylor asked in his condescending manner.

The smell of breath mints doesn't fool anyone you jackass.

Many of the kids in the class came from homes where there was liquor when there was no milk.

"Someone?" Taylor said. "Can anyone tell me why Hannibal chose to take his Carthaginian army by way of the more dangerous route through the Alps to do battle with the Romans?"

No one ever volunteered in Taylor's class. But Ted knew what was going to happen next because it had happened before. He raised his hand. The teacher ignored him.

Then Taylor whirled around, stomped his foot on the floor, and shouted, "Hammaker!" Tommy Hammaker jumped as though he had been struck by a speeding semi. Taylor laughed out loud.

"Stand up and enlighten us," Taylor said.

Tommy struggled to his feet.

The boy was the son of a domineering father and a mother too afraid of her husband to interfere. He had little self-confidence to begin with. Taylor descended on him like a buzzard on roadkill.

"Ah . . . Hannibal . . . ah . . . well . . . he went up . . . uh . . . "

Ted was aware that Taylor did this on purpose. He knew very well that Tommy fell apart when he had to get up in front of the class.

Ted was feeling an unfamiliar emotion. He was actually getting angry. It was upsetting, but he knew he had every right, considering the injustice that was taking place right before his eyes. He was not going to let this man get away with it.

Tommy kept trying and the teacher was obviously enjoying himself.

"... he had ... these elephants ... and ... uh ... a lot of ... uh ... soldiers ..."
Hammaker looked like he was going to have a stroke.
"... and ..."

"Wait just a minute, Hammaker," Taylor said. "Hold it right there." Taylor hurried out the door and raced around the corner.

In less than a minute the teacher was back. With him was hawk-faced, overly made-up Carla Buckley.

Buckley was second on Ted's most-hated-teachers list. She taught biology in the classroom next to Taylor's and had her own brand of cruelty.

Buckley was as unattractive as Taylor, although the physical opposite. Taylor was at least a hundred-pounds overweight, whereas Buckley was in the flyweight class with a face that looked like skin stretched over a doorknob. She had a small chin. Taylor had many chins. Together they averaged out, chin-wise.

Beauty is said to be only skin deep, but Carla Buckley was ugly all the way to her core.

If these kids only knew what I know about you two.

Ted had not shared that knowledge with anyone, not even Charlie Freeman, about an incident he witnessed when the two of them went to a movie matinee in the city one Saturday.

Ted and Charlie were waiting in the theater ticket line, Ted happened to look past Charlie's shoulder, across the adjacent alley, through the lobby window of the St. Marks Hotel.

Standing at the registration desk was a nervous-looking Ralph Taylor. Off to the side, browsing through a rack of tourist brochures, was Carla Buckley.

Taylor was married. By some miracle... possibly her husband's extreme myopia, desperation or catastrophic bad luck... so was Buckley.

Ted was partially hidden by a pillar. He had a clear view of them. Neither teacher spotted him.

Rather than share with Charlie what he saw, Ted tucked it away. It pleased him to know something about the pair that no one else knew.

A twisted smile in place, Carla Buckley was primed to be amused at Tommy Hammaker's discomfort. She was one of those pretentious people who spoke with grating precision. It's EYE-ther this and RAH-ther that, throwing in an occasional mispronounced French word or phrase in an attempt to demonstrate her sophistication. Instead it amplified her peasanthood.

Kids know imposters and drunks when they see them.

To a college professor who had seen it all before, Buckley was clearly back row trailer trash.

"Continue, Thomas," Taylor said.

"Uh . . . Hannibal . . . ah . . ."

"Oh," Buckley said, "how droll."

Droll, your ass, lady.

All of the years of thinking back to this incident and regretting that he had done nothing about it came bubbling to the surface. This man in boy's clothing had spent a lifetime avoiding trouble. But today he would take his martial arts instructor's advice.

"Self defense is not for the meek, Ted," Abe Kirby had said. ". . . if you hesitate because you think it's not the polite thing to do, you'll get knocked on your ass a lot."

Despite his passive nature, Ted resolved not to be the one knocked on his figurative ass this day. His anger had outweighed his fear of it. Many years of thinking back to Taylor's mistreatment of kids was raging inside him.

That does it, asshole. Today is the day I stop being a wimp.

"Mr. Taylor," Ted said, getting to his feet. "I'll be glad to explain,"

"What you will do, Theodore, is you will sit down until you are called upon."

"I don't think so," Ted said.

"Maybe you didn't understand me, McBride. Sit down."

Ted ignored him and went on. "The reason Hannibal took the Alpine route was—"

Just then the bell rang to signal the end of the class. Thirty kids bolted for the door and exploded from the room like a magnum load of pellets out of a shotgun.

"You wait right here McBride," Taylor said, closing the classroom door behind the last student to leave. Miss. Buckley stood by with her practiced stern expression; her penciled-on eyebrows raised.

"What do you mean by disrupting my class?"

Ted's lack of assertiveness had impacted every aspect of his life. But anger now canceled his passive nature. He no longer cared what anyone thought of him or approved of. It was time to stand up on his hind legs and fight back.

"What I mean," Ted said, "is that you don't have any right to do that to a kid."

Ted even startled himself with the outburst.

The teacher turned even redder than usual with anger. He grabbed for Ted's shoulder. When he did, Ted took hold of Taylor's arm. Using the man's own weight against him he sent him crashing into desks.

Now it was Buckley's turn.

"I'm going to get the principal," she said.

"Yes, do that," Ted said, calmly. "When he gets here you can tell us both what you two were doing at the St. Marks Hotel."

The angry Irish red drained from Taylor's face.

"Wha . . ." Taylor's mouth hung open. Ted thought Buckley might faint.

"Your spouses might like to know, too. The idea of you two going at it is enough to make a person puke. It could traumatize a kid forever against sex."

"You don't know what you're talking about," Buckley said, clearly afraid.

"I'm curious. Which one of you gets tied up and which one gets flailed with a leather strap? Or do you take turns?"

While Ted was looking at Buckley, Taylor seized the opportunity and charged again. This time it was Ted who was flung against the chalkboard.

It took a moment to recover. By then Taylor, who outweighed the teenage Ted by more than a hundred pounds, was coming at him again. Taylor was easily deflected. Before the man knew what had happened his feet had been swept out from under him with a side kick and he was in a painfully twisted arm lock.

Ted's anger had now turned to murderous rage. "Move and I'll break your arm."

"Let me go," Taylor said, gasping for breath.

"No," Ted said, applying more pressure. "I'll tell you how it's going to be from now on. If I ever hear of either of you pulling a stunt like that on a kid again, I will destroy you both. That should be clear enough even for a couple of mental peewees like you."

"I—"

"Got it?"

Buckley started to say something.

"Sit down!" Ted said. To his surprise, Buckley did as she was told. "Think of me as your personal time bomb. Do something to a young person like you just did to Tommy and I could go off at any time."

"That's blackmail," Taylor said through the pain.

"You bet it is. It's one despicable human trait colliding with another. Now do you see what it's like to be helpless? You do the same thing to kids, you freak. Tommy's self-esteem is low to begin with. What you do to these young people will affect them for the rest of their lives you fat piece of garbage."

Ted released Taylor's wrist and turned to leave the room. "Just remember what I told you," Ted said, his back to the teachers.

Taylor jumped to his feet and charged again. He connected and spun Ted away from the door.

What happened next could not have worked out any better if Ted had planned it.

"I'll kill you, you little bastard." he screamed, just as Principal Arthur Bitting came into the room.

Taylor grabbed Ted by the neck and shoulders, bounced him off the wall and sent him sprawling to the floor.

Ted had spotted Bitting before Taylor did and simply did not fight back. He doubled over and turned in what he considered an Academy Award winning performance . . . complete with groans and yelps.

Brando was never this good.

"Ralph!" the principal shouted at the outraged teacher. "Stop it! What are you doing?

Taylor spun around, wide-eyed, to face the principal.

"This young man needs some discipline," Taylor said, wheezing and sweating as though he had just run a marathon.

"You call choking and beating a student and screaming profanities at him 'discipline'?" The principal was fuming. "Are you all right, Theodore?"

Ted put a hand to his throat and nodded.

I've taken worse beatings than this in my kickboxing classes.

The principal helped Ted to his feet. "Do you need the nurse to look at you?"

"I'll be fine, sir," he said, pseudo-weakly, rubbing his neck and shoulder, wheezing out a pathetic little cough.

"Tell me what happened, Theodore."

Still amazed—and a little unsettled over his own Dr. Milquetoast-to-Mr. Hyde transformation, Ted gave the principal the Reader's Digest condensed version. "Mr. Taylor and Mrs. Buckley were ridiculing Tommy Hammaker," Ted said. "I complained about it. He started knocking me around. Mrs. Buckley was cheering him on."

The principal glared at Taylor in a way that said more than words could have expressed. Then he turned back to Ted. "You may go now, Theodore," he said quietly. "I would appreciate if you would not mention this to anyone."

Ted nodded and closed the classroom door quietly behind him.

Damn, that felt good.

Ted's response to the cruel teacher was completely out of character for the man he had been just a short while ago.

As he walked home, Ted was thinking that one of the worst days in all of high school the first time around had turned out to be the best.

The day was not over yet.

CHAPTER 15

IT WAS A BEAUTIFUL SPRING AFTERNOON. All the more exquisite for Ted's having handed out a measure of justice to two sadists who apparently believed humiliating students was a higher calling than educating them.

Ted was enjoying watching migratory birds as he walked home from school. They were reestablishing themselves on return from their annual trip south, filling the sky and populating trees leafing out along the streets of his hometown.

Clouds created by warm updrafts colliding with the cooler upper atmosphere hovered over a stretch of the Appalachian Mountains a few miles from town. The summit was several thousand feet above the Susquehanna Valley floor as the ancient range snaked through Pennsylvania's midsection. The rolling landscape continued northeastward. Time-worn ridges swooped down where the Susquehanna River had cut a swath, then rose again on the opposite shore.

A cat raced across Ted's path, chasing a rat into a thick stand of sumac that covered an empty lot where only a few years earlier Ted and a small band of junior buckaroos rode broomstick broncos in pursuit of imagined renegade Indians.

He recalled those times when his nemesis lay in wait for him on the way home.

It occurred to Ted that Jimmy Deavers was again not at the place where he could usually be counted on to ambush Ted and make his early years so miserable.

Where are you, you little creep?

After what he had witnessed on the street in front of Jimmy's house the previous evening, Ted was less inclined to destroy the scourge of his early years.

Farther along, the bully was, indeed, hidden in weeds and waiting for him. The boy was smaller than Ted remembered.

"Hey faggot," Jimmy called out."

Ah. There you are.

"Go away Jimmy."

"Why would I want to do that, homo?"

"Because I don't want to hurt you."

Jimmy stared in apparent disbelief at what he heard. Ted turned his back on the boy and continued down the path.

"You're the one's gonna get hurt," Deavers said.

If Ted had been residing in his future body at more than double Jimmy Deavers' weight it might have been like a mite on a moose. However, inside his fifteen-year-old frame Ted was a closer physical match with the boy. Jimmy suddenly collided with him and sent him to the ground. Books and papers went in all directions.

Not again. Two fights in one day . . .

"That hurt," Ted said.

"It was supposed to hurt, dumb-ass."

Ted was dusting himself off when the boy charged once more, yelling as he ran.

With advance notice of a new attack, Ted was ready for him. He stepped aside. Jimmy shot right on by and skidded to a halt. When Jimmy turned back toward his prey, surprise turned to fury.

God, he's persistent.

The outraged kid launched another charge.

When Jimmy reached him, Ted delivered a neat kick to the boy's midsection, knocking him backward. Before he could recover, Ted had Jimmy in a painful neck and arm lock.

All the anger and fear Ted had carried with him through the years was focused when he spun Jimmy around and punched him in the face.

How do you like that you little toad?

Since leaving Carbonville, Ted had spent his entire life cringing at the memory of attacks by Jimmy Deavers and others like him. So many times over the years he had thought about incidents like this. Ted had dealt out punches to Deavers in his imagination that he had not been able to deliver for real. He realized that retaliating against Jimmy was less a matter of strength and skill than it was of resolve. After all, he was going to be hit anyway, why not get hit . . . while hitting?

Anyone who had ever been bullied as a child could testify that the dark memories remain deeply embedded for a lifetime. They become part of the total person. A kind of Post Traumatic Stress Disorder had plagued Ted from being terrorized by the boy now struggling to break free.

"Let me go you sonofabitch," Jimmy screamed.

It was hard to tell whether Jimmy was angrier or more surprised that his traditional victim had retaliated. Blood began to ooze down Jimmy's lip and chin.

"You broke my nose."

"I doubt it," Ted said. "Jimmy I'm not going to let you do this anymore. There is no reason for you to take your frustrations out on me. I've never done anything to deserve it."

"You hit me."

"You've hit me hundreds of times," Ted said. "It's about time I got in a punch or two. You've done this ever since I can remember. Explain it to me."

"Because you're weird."

"Weird. Just because I'm not exactly like you? Because I get good grades in school? Because we don't have the same interests? Because I haven't fought back until now? How is that being 'weird'?"

Deavers was close enough to the ground to reach a good-sized rock with his free hand. Before he could throw it, Ted landed another light punch to the boy's face. Jimmy dropped the rock. Then he did the last thing Ted would ever have expected. Jimmy Deavers, master intimidator of his childhood, began to cry.

Oh, crap.

Regret swept over Ted. The memories that had jabbed at his psyche were now at war with his inner adult. Now that he had the long-delayed opportunity to best the boy in a fight, Ted realized something he should have known years earlier.

He's just a kid.

Without releasing him, Ted said gently in the boy's ear, "Jimmy, I saw what your dad did to you last night."

The boy took in a sudden breath and tried again to break free. "You're crazy."

"The more you squirm, the more it's going to hurt, Jimmy."

The struggle continued. As predicted, Jimmy's pain intensified, although Ted applied no more pressure than necessary to keep him from getting up.

Ted said, "I saw your dad hit you when you took out the trash."

"Ow! You're hurting me."

"I don't want to hurt you, Jimmy, I want to help you."

Actually, I want to break every bone in your freakin' body you little shit, but let's be mature here Ted.

"I don't want your goddam help. I don't need anybody's help."

"Yes you do. You're in a bad spot. I can show you how to make it right."

"It's none of your business."

"Jimmy," he said, trying to be patient, "why do you act stupid. You seem like a pretty smart guy."

The boy stopped wiggling for a moment. "I got two Cs and three Ds on my report card the last time. You call that smart?"

"You're not dumb. You're lazy, disorganized, unfocused, and unmotivated. You get poor grades because you give up. Stop it. I want you to give up . . . giving up."

"Mind your own business," Jimmy said, still trying to get free.

"I'm making it my business because you've been bullying me ever since I can remember. I have a stake in changing your behavior."

Jimmy said no more. Perhaps because even he could not clearly define why he had chosen Ted as his enemy.

Risking further injury, Ted let him loose.

"I'm not going to hit you again." Then Ted added, "Unless you force me to."

To his surprise, Jimmy just sat there rubbing his nose, smearing blood on his hands and face. Ted gave him his handkerchief.

"What's the use?" Jimmy said, wiping away the blood. "I'll probably end up working on the railroad just like everybody else in this crummy town."

"If you believe that, then that's all you'll ever be. Let me tell you something, Jimmy. Here is a sad truth. Most of us have parents who want the best for us . . . some more than others. If we're lucky we may have friends we believe are looking out for our interests. In many ways they are. But, you have to understand that your future, your success, whatever becomes of you in life is entirely up to you. We are alone in this world."

A pretty heavy load to put on a kid.

Ted let that notion sink in for a moment.

It had been Ted's experience that hardly anyone takes advice. They have to learn the hard way. But Jimmy might be desperate enough to listen to something that could change his life.

"Jimmy, if you hope to amount to anything, it is completely up to you. Stop waiting around for someone else to hand you success or failure. Stop blaming others for the things that don't work out. *You* have to work them out."

If anyone could understand how being abused as a youth could affect someone well into adulthood, it was Ted McBride.

"My dad will keep beatin' me up," Jimmy said.

"You can't think about that," Ted said. "Right now, just think about your own future. If you want things to change, change them. If you want things to be different you have to do something different."

Christ, I'm turning into Arnie.

"Stop hiding behind the way things have always been," Ted said.

Where have I heard that before?

Jimmy kept looking down at the ground. "I can't wait to be old enough to quit school."

Exasperated, Ted put a hand on Jimmy's shoulder.

"You really do work hard at being an idiot, don't you? School is your way out."

"Bullshit. It's boring. The teachers are assholes."

Ted had to think about that for a moment.

"I have to agree with you about some of the teachers," Ted admitted. "There are some good ones, too. If you asked for help, they'd go out of their way to give it to you."

"Aw, I can't do it."

"You can do it. You will do it. I'm going to help you."

Jimmy shook his head. "No."

"You didn't hear me, Jimmy. You *are* going to do this if I have to drag your skinny ass up the hill every morning and down the hill every evening."

Jimmy looked as though he might respond to the threat. He thought better of it when Ted cocked his head, curled his fists and aimed an evil eye his way.

"Why would you help me? We never got along before."

Ted knew Jimmy didn't get along with anyone. His alienation because of his treatment at home had shut out all friendly interactions.

"It was you who didn't get along with me," Ted said. "I've always been willing. But we'll put all that behind us now."

It took a monumental effort for Ted to say the words: "Let's start over. I'm not going to do anything for you. You're going to do it yourself. If I catch you loafing I'll kick your butt up one side of Riley Street and down the other."

The suggestion of force was familiar ground for Jimmy, though Ted regretted making the point in that way.

The kid has enough violence in his life without my adding to it.

"Meet me right here tomorrow morning," Ted said. "We'll go to school together and get started on your future."

"Aw, man. . . I don't know—"

"Tomorrow, Jimmy," Ted boomed. "Be here or I will hunt you down. Do not test me."

Jimmy still had a surprised look when Ted started down the path toward home and didn't look back. Ted took it as a positive sign when no stone hit him. He had never felt more empowered in his life.

CHAPTER 16

JIMMY WAS WAITING FOR TED THE NEXT DAY as he had been instructed. But on this particular morning Jimmy was relaxed, even subservient.

"Did you think about what I said?"

"I still think it's no use," Jimmy said.

Jimmy had a new bruise on the side of his face. Ted knew their confrontation the previous day had not caused it. "Want to talk about how you got that bruise?"

"What do you think?"

"Where are your books?"

"They're in my locker at school."

"Jimmy. They're not doing you any good in your locker. Today you write down your homework assignments and bring the books from those classes home with you."

"Mmmff," he said, hunching his shoulders.

"Jimmy."

"Okay," he said, shoving his hands in his pockets and looking at the ground.

This is one hard-headed kid.

When the two traditional enemies arrived at school together it drew some stares, but no one said anything.

They climbed the stairs and turned right.

"Why are we going this way," Jimmy asked.

"We're making one stop before you go to your homeroom."

Jimmy shrugged and trailed after Ted.

When they arrived at Mrs. Simpson's room, Ted motioned for Jimmy to go in.

"What for?"

"Because we're putting you on a success path, starting right here."

Jimmy entered the classroom reluctantly. Mrs. Simpson was at her desk.

"Good morning boys," she said, looking at the mismatched pair.

"Sorry to bother you Mrs. Simpson," he said. "I wanted to ask for some advice and a favor."

Mrs. Simpson smiled, "I'm sure there is nothing you could ask that I wouldn't be happy to grant, Ted."

Whoa! Would I love to put that to the test.

The woman was only slightly older than the 1960s version of his own mother, but younger than his 21st-century self. Ted shook his head and recovered from the thought.

"Jimmy is lagging behind in his education," he said. The boy squirmed with embarrassment, looking very small.

"Yes," she said. "He certainly is."

"Jimmy thinks he's dumb."

The teacher was obviously surprised. "Is that true, James?"

Jimmy just shrugged. He looked as though he would like to be somewhere . . . anywhere else.

"Well, two of us in this room apparently don't believe it," she said.

Jimmy's face brightened. He was not accustomed to hearing anything positive from a teacher.

"I notice, however, that you are a genius at thinking of ways to get in trouble."

Jimmy was busy looking at the floor.

"Mrs. Simpson," Ted said. "I wondered if you might have some suggestions as to how we can get him headed in the right direction."

The teacher thought about it for a moment. "You would have to do your part, James."

"Yuh," he mumbled.

"You would have to radically change some behaviors I've observed. Do you understand?"

"Um."

"Do you understand?" she said again with more force.

Ted was not in the mood for Jimmy's hesitation and gave him a bump with his hip.

"Yes ma'am," Jimmy said.

"All right then. Come back here before you go home this afternoon. We will see what it takes to fill in any gaps and what study materials will be needed. Ted, I assume you are willing to help?"

Ted nodded. "My family is moving away at the end of the term, but I'll absolutely be here for him until then."

The bell sounded to warn students to report to their homerooms. Jimmy turned away from the teacher's desk. Ted nudged him impatiently again and mouthed 'thank you' to the boy.

"Thank you Mrs. Simpson," Jimmy droned.

"You're welcome."

As he left the classroom, Ted thought once more of Mrs. Simpson's unfaithful husband and wondered if he might help her in some way.

At the end of the school day Ted went to each of Jimmy Deavers' teachers and asked for the boy's homework assignments. He knew Jimmy would have neglected to do it himself.

He found the boy and steered him back toward Mrs. Simpson's classroom.

"Where's your list of homework assignments, Jimmy?"

"Um . . ."

"You didn't write them down, did you?"

"Uh . . . nuh."

"Well . . . surprise." Ted said and handed him the list had had put together after checking with Jimmy's teachers. "Tomorrow you do it for yourself." Ted shook a finger at Jimmy, wordlessly implying he expected compliance.

Ted was not really angry, but he made it appear so to Jimmy.

Mrs. Simpson questioned Jimmy to see where she should start in bringing the boy up to his grade level.

In the unlikely event that Jimmy were to study on his own at home, he would have no peace with his father nearby. So Ted stayed with him after school. He gave up some of his band practice time to help the boy with his English homework. Jimmy fidgeted and looked out the window as Ted played drill sergeant and made him pay attention.

"Do you understand the rule?"

"Uh huh," he said.

"Okay, what is it?"

"Um . . ."

"Jimmy, you haven't been listening; 'I before E except after C'. Repeat it."

Jimmy repeated the spelling rule that he should have learned many grades ago. Ted made him give examples until it was certain he had it firmly in his mind.

If an award for patience were ever warranted, Ted thought he had certainly earned one. And, if he had been keeping score of the changes he hoped to make, he might have chalked up a potential point for his side.

CHAPTER 17

THE NEXT DAY JIMMY FAILED TO SHOW UP at their regular meeting spot. Ted searched the kid's usual haunts, found him and practically dragged him to school. Ted knew it was going to be a challenge to get the boy straightened out.

The information Jimmy could get out of a more complete education and the discipline he would develop along the way were important ingredients in building a life. But those alone would not be enough to give Jimmy a start on his future.

Ted had some other ideas along those lines.

Charlie Freeman was practically running down the hallway as Ted was headed for his homeroom.

"Teddy." Charlie shouted, "Taylor resigned."

Resigned, my ass.

"You're just trying to make me feel good Charlie."

"I'm serious. A note on the bulletin board says 'personal reasons'. Buckley's gone, too."

Score another one for McBride . . . and the crowd goes wild.

"What's her excuse?"

"The announcement says she has to take care of a sick relative in Lancaster."

Ha! Given the choice of quitting or going to jail for abuse of a poor, defenseless student.

"I heard you had a run-in with both of them yesterday," Charlie said.

Ted had an anxious moment, afraid that somehow word had leaked out about the scuffle.

Crap!

"Where did you hear that?"

"Ted, the whole school knows how you mouthed off at those two jerks."

Ted was relieved the full story had not gotten around.

"Oh, that."

"'Oh, that', he says, like it was nothing."

"They exercised their right to be jerks, I objected, they didn't like it, I got a nasty tongue-lashing and went home. End of story."

Somehow Ted's lying to Charlie didn't seem like lying.

"Funny they both left at the same time," Charlie said.

"Maybe I scared them away," Ted said, working up an evil grin.

"Right. Maybe her and Taylor ran off together," Charlie suggested.

"Charlie," Ted said as the boy started off to his own class, "you have taken a beautiful moment and made me want to puke."

No one would ever believe a fifteen-year-old boy had waited forty years to get revenge.

Chapter 18

Without his teacher's knowledge, Ted had decided to gather some information. It was mid-afternoon on Saturday when he picked up Mr. Simpson's trail as the man was coming off his railroad shift. Ted had learned that Simpson worked the seven a.m. to three p.m. shift. He was carrying his mother's Polaroid camera.

He followed Simpson on foot to a residence on the south side of town. He got a shot of him entering the house and he wrote the date, time, and address on the margin of the photo. Ted knew the woman who lived there. Not personally, but by reputation. She was a favorite subject of village gossip and made Vikki Deavers look like a saint by contrast.

What on earth is this man thinking?

Ted found a spot in a cluster of shrubs where he could not be seen by his quarry, nor would he be noticed by neighbors. After several hours of watching it became apparent that Simpson was not coming out again. It was more likely he would be spending the night there, possibly even living with the woman now that he had been evicted by his wife.

Ted ended his surveillance and went home.

The next morning he returned to his lookout spot. He didn't have to wait for long before Simpson emerged with his work gear. Ted snapped another Polaroid picture and watched the man head back to the railroad.

On Monday, Ted handed Mrs. Simpson a manila envelope with the pictures and notes he had taken.

Looking at the material she said, "How did you know . . .?"

". . . that you were filing for divorce? I didn't, actually. But I thought that if you were, you might need some ammunition."

Ted could see that Mrs. Simpson was pained.

"Oh, Mrs. Simpson, I'm so sorry. I wouldn't hurt you for anything. I just wanted to help."

"No, no . . . Ted, it's all right. It's just that it seems strange that a boy your age . . . my student . . . is involved in . . ."

". . . such a personal matter? Ahh . . . I could kick myself."

"But what you have found out will certainly be valuable . . . and I thank you."

"I hope you won't feel embarrassed. And I would like for you to think of me not just as your student, but as a friend who is concerned about your welfare."

The teacher was obviously uncomfortable talking about her marital situation, but she nodded. "My husband and I no longer live together. In the case of a contested divorce, under Pennsylvania law I would need specific grounds such as desertion, bigamy . . ."

". . . adultery."

She looked even more intently at Ted. "Yes," she said. "Adultery."

"So, he's denying it and you need to prove it to a judge's satisfaction in order to end the marriage and get what you are entitled to in the settlement."

"How did you—"

"I looked it up." Ted could not tell her he had gone through a similar situation himself, although his divorce was not contested.

"Once the court approves," she said, "it takes two years of living apart after the filing before it can be final."

"You should probably have a lawyer verify what I've discovered," Ted said. "A lawyer makes a better witness than a fifteen-year-old kid."

"Sometimes," Mrs. Simpson said, "I have to wonder if you actually are only fifteen, Ted. You certainly are the most mature teenager I have ever known."

"Thanks, Mrs. Simpson. But I guess I still have a lot of growing up to do."

Ted realized the truth of the statement. He did have a lot to learn. Call it "maturing" or call it "enlightenment," finally learning things a reasonable person should have known all along. Although Ted had always been sensitive to others, he was becoming even more attuned to people than before his adventure.

If Ted was adding to his own knowledge, there was someone else who also needed to be taught a lesson.

CHAPTER 19

IT WAS LATE WHEN BLAINE DEAVERS ARRIVED HOME from a night of drinking. A streetlight along Riley Street cast long shadows across the front yard and sidewalk.

From behind a hedge, one of the shadows walked up behind Deavers. In an eerie voice somewhere between a whisper and a growl the shadow said, "Welcome home asshole."

Startled, Deavers spun around and squinted through the semi-dimness. The intruder was wearing a dark hooded jacket and a mask made of a nylon stocking. The smell of liquor was strong, even from ten feet away.

After the initial shock, Deavers recovered some of his usual bluster. "That's *Mister* Asshole to you."

"If you want a 'mister' out of me, you'll have to earn it."

"Who the hell are you?"

"I'm someone who is going to give you a sample of what you do to your wife and son."

"You think so, huh?" Deavers said, with a slight slur and a nervous laugh.

The challenger was about the same size as the man who was making Jimmy and Vikki Deavers' lives miserable.

"If I hear that you have hurt them again, I will ruin your health. You got that?"

"That right?" Deavers seemed a little less intimidated. "Well, why wait?"

"Why, indeed," he said, taking a step closer.

Bullies hate it when you do unto them what they do unto others. Therefore, Golden Rule, Subsection One-A would have to be applied.

"I knew talking to you wouldn't do any good. So I've decided to communicate in a language you can understand."

"Whoever you are you sonofabitch, you can mind your own goddamn business."

Deavers reached out, only to find his arm swatted aside.

Most men would certainly agree that testicles rank really high on the list of least favorite places in which to receive a swift kick, such as the one delivered to Deavers' groin. There is little doubt that a well-placed foot puts the kicker in charge of any situation.

The man was on the ground, moaning in pain.

Deavers' attacker hunkered down, took the man by the collar and, with a gloved fist, landed a volley of quick, crunching punches to the face. He then went nose-to-bloodied nose with him, as though daring him to retaliate.

The prostrate abuser squawked through his aching nose and mouth. "I'b gud-dah caw 'd cops od yuh."

"Good luck in identifying me. Be sure to tell them how your wife and son always have cuts and bruises on their bodies."

Blaine Deavers was whimpering.

"If I ever find out you have beaten Jimmy or your wife again, there is no place you can hide from me. I will find you and I will hurt you."

"Yaw-reddy hurt be y'sonabish," he groaned.

"No . . . no . . . you don't understand," His living nightmare spat at him. "I don't mean I will make you hurt. What I'm saying is . . . I will *hurt* you. I will break bones,"

He grabbed Deavers by the collar and punctuated each point with another blow to the face.

"Your closest relatives won't recognize you."

WAP!

"I will make you bleed."

WHAM!

"Your hearing and vision will never be the same."

SMACK!

"You will have to be fed through tubes. You will spend the rest of you life walking with a limp. You will prefer death to life with the pain I will inflict on you."

The spooky lighting may have helped.

Deavers seemed appropriately terrified, but a man with a history of violence and a need to dominate was probably harder to convince than most.

"Let's be absolutely certain you understand me. I know how guys like you operate. Someone takes the control away from you and you take it out on the family."

A few more vicious, rapid-fire punches were delivered for emphasis, carefully calculated to leave visible marks around the eyes and face for all to see in the coming days.

"If you hurt them again, I will materialize in the night"

Words failed Deavers. He had peed himself.

"If you doubt me, I will be happy to give you a demonstration right now." He started to bend Deavers' elbow in the opposite direction from what nature intended. With little effort, the joint could have been hyper-extended and the limb rendered useless for months.

"Nuh, . . . pweeth," He pleaded, staring, wide-eyed.

The grip was released. It had been an empty threat because the family depended on Deavers' railroad earnings. Permanently injuring him right now was not a real option.

"If I find out you have hurt Jimmy or Vikki, I will know about it. I guarantee it will be the most painful day of your miserable life."

Genuinely traumatized, the man was left sobbing on the ground as his attacker walked away, pulling off his disguise on the way home, just four doors up Riley Street.

Theodore Winston McBride, you should be ashamed of yourself for feeling so good.

CHAPTER 20

At breakfast, Ed McBride was slightly more communicative than before. Ted's father had actually said 'please' and 'thank you' several times during the meal.

Baby steps.

Ted hoped it might evolve to an actual conversation. It had better be soon, though, because time was running out.

When he met up with Jimmy on the way to school, Ted was still feeling elated from the night before.

"How's it going Jimmy?"

The boy seemed nervous. "My old man's been avoiding me," he said. "His face was all messed up when he got home last night and he smelled of piss and booze."

Ted's pal Arnie would have insisted that playing dumb wasn't much of a stretch for him. Ted covered bruised knuckles with his book bag.

"Don't complain. His avoiding you is a good thing."

"Good, but strange," Jimmy said. "Mom and I figured he got into a bar fight. But that doesn't explain why he didn't take it out on us the way he always does."

"You know what they say; 'never look a gift horse in the mouth.'"

Jimmy looked puzzled at the analogy.

Ted continued. "It means if someone gives you a horse for free, accept it without checking the horse's teeth to find out how old he is. You got a freebie. Enjoy it."

Jimmy turned to Ted and looked him straight in the eyes.

"Teddy, did you have anything to do with that?"

Ted thought he did a pretty good job of looking surprised at the question.

"Me?" he said. "What could I do? I'm just a kid."

CHAPTER 21

A FLOCK OF BUTTERFLIES WAS HOLDING A CONVENTION in Ted's stomach when he trailed behind Marlene Sutton from a distance as she walked home from school. He was absolutely convinced the girl had a problem. He believed he knew what it was, but he had no evidence beyond personal experience in observing similar behaviors. He was determined to find out what was troubling her.

The girl lived in a neighborhood where at least half of the homes were run-down. Hers was among the seedy half. It occurred to Ted that Marlene's empty-headed high school girlfriends were probably not aware of where she lived. If they had been, it is likely they would have taken a different view of the stylish Marlene they knew. Ted knew that she worked weekends at a women's clothing store in the city. The earnings and a store discount would explain how she was able to afford decent duds.

His observations of Marlene's rapid shift between arrogance and anxiety set off alarms in his head that there could be something wrong in her life—most likely in her own household. The sinister-looking man he had seen at her house all those years ago added to the conviction.

Marlene's home was still five blocks away. Ted walked faster, until he was within shouting distance.

"Marlene."

She turned only slightly in his direction. Seeing Ted, she continued walking.

"Go away." she shouted over her shoulder.

"Marlene, I want to apologize for what I said last week."

She whirled around. "You made a fool of me in front of my friends. Now you say you're sorry when it's just the two of us."

"If it will help I'll say it again when that whole crowd is there. Meanwhile I wanted to talk to you alone."

"You were mean to me," she said, turning away from him.

"Because you've always been . . . aw, hell . . . no matter what the reason, it was inexcusable and I really am sorry."

"I don't have anything to say to you," she said and resumed walking even faster than before.

"Well I have a lot to say to you and I think you should listen."

"Get away from me," she said and picked up the pace.

Ted was experiencing a moment of doubt. But, at the risk of being completely wrong and looking like an idiot, he decided to take a daring leap. He stopped walking, took a deep breath to calm himself. He let the air out slowly and said, "Marlene, I know what's happening to you at home."

Marlene stopped suddenly, churning up a small cloud of dust on the dirt path. From twenty paces away Ted could hear her gasp. She put her head down and didn't look directly at him.

A shriek came out as a whisper. She said, "What do you mean?" She turned slowly toward him. The panic was obvious. "You don't know anything about me. Nothing is happening to me at home."

The sudden tension in her body all but confirmed Ted's suspicions. "I just know," he said.

"No you don't," she said frantically, her voice trembling. "You're making that up. Now get away from me."

She continued walking even faster.

"I know quite a lot about you Marlene . . ."

Based on Marlene's reaction, Ted felt more certain than ever he was right. It gave him confidence to act as though he had the whole story and could see what it would reveal.

"I know someone has been doing things they shouldn't."

Marlene gasped and stopped again, drawing her books up close to her chest, not turning toward him. She was holding her breath to the point that Ted was afraid she would faint.

"How could you—"

Bingo.

Marlene began to run away from him, shouting at him as she made a dash for home.

"Leave me alone," she screamed.

Ted ran ahead of her, blocking the path.

"No one told me, if that's what you're afraid of," he said. "Nobody else knows about this. It's just that I've seen it all before. I had a student—" He stopped, realizing he was being his adult self again. "Let's just say I do know and go from there."

"It's a lie! If you don't stop—I'll tell the police you've been following me."

"Good idea. We can ask them to investigate."

"No—"

He knew the last thing Marlene would want was police involvement. Not because she would not want the abuse stopped and her abuser punished, but because everyone would find out about it.

"Even if it was true, why should you care?"

He was alongside her now.

"I'm offended at the injustice. I don't like to see a good person being wasted."

"You're wrong," she said, less forcefully than before.

"I know that someone close to you is robbing you of your youth. If something isn't done about it they will rob you of your adulthood, too."

The distressed girl did not confirm what Ted had said, nor did she offer further denials.

"You have to let me help you, Marlene."

Ted was now certain the self-confidence he had seen every day was an act she could only have pulled off in the school environment.

"What do you get out of it?" she said.

Ted was stunned at the suggestion. "What do you mean?"

"I've seen you looking at me."

Except for that one recent incident when she spoke to him at school, Ted had not been aware that Marlene had ever noticed he existed. That had troubled him in his original past, but Ted was not the smitten young boy on this day.

"That was the old Ted," he said. "The new Ted sees you as a person who is not just a pretty girl, but someone in trouble."

Marlene slowed and turned to him. She placed a hand on his chest. "You mean you don't like me?"

"Stop that!" he said, pushing her hand away. "Girl . . . don't you know there is more to you than sex?"

Marlene blanched at the word and drew back. "Try telling that to—never mind."

"Who?"

"Nothing."

"You've got to trust someone, Marlene. Otherwise this will continue."

She dropped her book bag, covered her face with both hands and began to sob.

"Tell me," Ted said.

"It doesn't matter. Nothing is going to change. Why should I trust you, Teddy?"

"A fair question," he said. "But if you don't trust someone the problem can't be solved. So it may as well be me."

Marlene picked up her book bag, pushed her way past Ted and continued toward her home.

"Marlene, stop running away. You have to let me help you."

The girl was in a box. Ahead of her was the intolerable home situation. Behind her was someone who knew her secret. Neither was acceptable, yet she had to make a choice.

Again Marlene stopped abruptly and stood quietly for a moment, hugging her books.

Then she said, "My own mother doesn't want to hear about it."

Marlene would have a thick wall of embarrassment to get past before she could fully confide in him. Still, Ted sensed she was beginning to trust him. Perhaps she hesitated because she had been carrying the load for so long . . . or because she realized she was trapped and Ted had shown the first sign that there could be a way out of it.

Ted handed her the neatly pressed white handkerchief his mother had put in his pants pocket that morning.

"I tried to tell her," Marlene said at last. "She defended him . . . wouldn't even let me finish . . . said it was my imagination. She called me a flirt and said if anything like that really did happen it would be my own fault. Why am I telling you this, Teddy? It will be all over school by tomorrow."

"No it won't," Ted said. "This is between you and me. What about your father?"

"He left us five years ago. He was the smart one in the family. We never heard from him after he went away. Since then she's had a string of boyfriends. Joel holds the record. He's been here for about two years."

"Tell me about Joel."

She started to walk away. "I don't want to talk to you any more Teddy." she said, obviously still afraid for what could happen to her . . . and that she had already told him too much.

He ignored the plea. "Your mother's boyfriend is behaving . . . inappropriately . . . toward you."

Marlene turned to him, horrified at what both surely knew was a vast understatement.

". . . and you are feeling alone and helpless," he said.

Ted could identify with feelings of being alone. He had been isolated from his peers in his own youth and not well regarded by his father.

Marlene searched Ted's face, possibly for some sign he was not a danger to her. "Teddy, please stop this."

"Too late, Marlene. We've gone this far and there is no turning back. Let me guess. He's supporting you and your mother. She is afraid he'll leave. You're caught in the middle."

She was breathing in desperate gulps. "Joel brings in some money when he's working . . . when he hasn't been drinking . . . which is rarely . . . and he . . ."

Ted filled in the blank, ". . . behaves inappropriately."

"Teddy," she pleaded, "if this ever came out I couldn't face anyone at school and my mother would throw me out of the house."

The best thing that could happen to you, girl.

Ted had seen Marlene at the supermarket once with a sullen older woman who must have been her mother, although the woman was the opposite of her daughter in appearance and manner.

Anger was doing a tap dance on Ted's stomach lining. It was an emotion he had denied himself for so long. He seemed to be making up for lost time in that department. Marlene's mother was obviously more concerned about her own survival than for her daughter's welfare. In Ted's modern world the woman would have been arrested and charged with child endangerment. Her daughter would have been taken away from her and the resident pervert would be in prison. In this era the victim would become a social exile.

"I know it's hard for you to trust anyone right now," Ted said. "But you've got to get out of there."

"You can't be serious. I don't have anywhere to go."

"You will."

Although I don't have a clue where.

"Meanwhile," he said. "Neither of us will say anything about this."

It was plain to see she felt trapped. She seemed to be wrestling with the need to trust someone if she ever hoped to get out of an intolerable situation at home.

"The important thing now is whether it's safe for you to go home."

"He's leaving today. He's going to his parent's place in Philadelphia and won't be back until next Friday."

That would give Ted more time to find a solution.

"Have some faith, Marlene. We will solve this together."

She wiped away the tears and tried to make herself look presentable before she faced her mother. "He said he would kill me if I told on him. You can't imagine how I feel right now."

Ted knew she was in a box. Now that someone else knew about it, her entire world, such as it was, was threatened with collapse.

He felt the tension as he took her by the hand and was surprised when she didn't pull away.

"I hate it," he said, "when someone says 'I know exactly how you feel'. No one can ever know that. What I do know is you are scared and you can't get out of it by yourself. I can only assure you that I will do my best for you. Marlene, I don't want anything from you. And you don't have to worry that this will get around."

She still looked afraid. Given the way most teenagers gleefully shared every scrap of gossip they picked up, it was understandable. He was experienced enough with human nature and social dynamics to know that those who posed as Marlene's friends would turn on her. Those who envied her would delight in bringing her down.

Ted knew Marlene had no more reason to trust him than to trust any of the empty-headed types she considered her friends. Having no choice surely added to her desperation.

She was being denied her youth. He swore to himself that he would not let it continue.

Ted took advantage of the occasion to explain about Charlie Freeman and warn her of his sly way of faking disinterest.

"You have to know that Charlie wants something from you that should be saved for someone who deserves it."

She seemed disappointed to hear that Charlie had dark motives.

"I guess there's nothing much left to save."

"You haven't given anything, Marlene. It was taken from you. That means it doesn't count."

He sensed a growing tension in the girl as they got closer to her house.

"Oh, God," she said as they turned the corner at her street.

The man Ted once thought was Marlene's father was putting a suitcase in the trunk of his car.

Ooo. This could be fun.

"You can't go with me," Marlene said.

Ted continued to walk with her.

"Please, Teddy. I'm begging you."

Ted brushed aside her protests. He continued walking. When they were standing beside her mother's boyfriend, the man looked up at them.

"Who the hell are you?" said the man Ted had seen in his previous past.

"Name's Ted. What's yours?" he said, although he knew it could only be the monster, Joel.

"My name's none of your goddam business," he said, anger radiating like waves of heat from an asphalt roadway in mid-summer. "And you don't need to be sniffin' around Marlene neither. Now what you're gonna do is you're gonna turn around and get the hell outta here and stay away from her."

Ted had felt irritation at times in his life, but the rage he was experiencing now topped anything in his experience. He'd had his fill of bullies and was not about to back down from this one. Ted stepped forward. When he was within Joel's reach, he locked eyes with the man.

"Or . . . ?"

"What do you mean 'or'?" Joel demanded.

"I'm to stay away from Marlene," he said, with venom in his words, "or . . . what?"

Joel went silent momentarily, possibly in amazement that he would be challenged by someone so young.

"Or I'll pound hell outta you and rip your head off. That's 'or what' . . ."

Ted smiled. If he had been timid in his future life, he could feel it fading like ocean waves receding from a beach. The pendulum had swung far to the opposite direction.

"And while you're doing all this 'pounding' and 'ripping,'" Ted said, taking still another half step toward Joel, "what do you suppose *I'll* be doing?"

Joel's jaw dropped and much of the macho showmanship dissolved.

"Uh . . ."

"Because if you think I'm going to just stand here and take it, then you need to rethink your strategy."

Ted knew the man could neither appear to be afraid in front of Marlene, nor could he back down. But he was apparently not sure enough of how he would come out in a fight with this boy who exuded such self-confidence. Thus, he did the only thing he could do.

"Well, just consider yourself warned," Joel said, and reached for the door to his car. "Now get out of my way, I'm in a hurry." He got in and drove off, leaving a patch of rubber behind.

Ted was actually disappointed, although he knew an outright physical confrontation could ultimately have cost Marlene dearly if she continued to live under the same roof with her tormentor. As it was, Joel would need to restore some of his dignity when he got back. Ted knew he had to get her out of there before then.

"Teddy," she said, "that was amazing. I've never seen Joel looking afraid before."

"What bothers me is that he could take it out on you."

"He won't be back until the end of next week."

Ted considered whether he needed to take immediate action.

"Do you want me to go in the house with you?"

"No! Teddy, if my mother sees me with you she'll yell at me and call me a tramp."

If anyone deserves that label it's her mother.

"All right, I'll leave. He wrote his home telephone number on a scrap of paper and handed it to her. "If you need me, call anytime . . . day or night."

"Promise me," Marlene said. "Promise, promise, promise you won't tell anybody about—"

Ted could not think of any way to convince the girl that no one would ever hear about her secret from him.

"I know you have trouble trusting, Marlene. But I want you to know that I will be looking out for your interests. You can be absolutely certain this will not get around."

She looked at him as though about to say something more, but could not seem to find the right words. Ted took that to mean she accepted his promise. Or, perhaps, that she had simply resigned herself to her lack of alternatives.

As he walked home Ted thought about the newly-acquired intensity of his feelings. For many years he had denied most emotions. It was like those times when he waited in a long, slow line. He just stuffed all of his feelings down inside, allowing himself to go numb, enduring until it was his turn. If Ted's life had been put on an oscilloscope he assumed it would have registered a slightly wavy line. Since he came back to his adolescence, that same scope would show a jagged line of ups and downs.

Ted knew there was only so much a teenager could do to help Marlene. As far as anyone could tell, that's what he was. He would have to enlist the help of an adult who would be sensitive to the dilemma. Someone who would hold it in complete confidence and help find a safe place for her.

Without having changed a single molecule, this fantasy *'woman'* of Ted Mc-Bride's youth had morphed into a child.

Marlene would be safe for the moment, but he could not afford to waste any time. He had some serious planning to do.

CHAPTER 22

ON HIS WAY TO LUNCH WITH CHARLIE the next day Ted spotted Marlene and her friends at their usual spot. He gave her a wink. She smiled weakly in return. Ted could see she was afraid and confused. A wink would have to hold her for now.

The cafeteria noise level was typically in the range of the combined decibels generated by Niagara Falls and World War II. That was not completely unpleasant, since it also helped to drown out Charlie Freeman's stream of ill-considered philosophies and harebrained 'facts'.

Ted was clearly able to hear Charlie above the din when the boy leaned over and said, "I'm gonna make my move with Marlene."

Ted was appalled at the idea of Charlie imposing himself on the troubled girl.

"What's that mean?" Ted asked.

"She has suffered enough," Charlie said. "It's time I made a real woman out of her."

Anger surged through Ted once more. He said nothing, but he was boiling inside.

Ted caught up with Marlene on her way home from school.

"Marlene, I know you've always been fascinated with Charlie Freeman, but I need to tell you something."

"You already told me that, Teddy. I don't think of him like that anymore"

"Good. But today he said it was time he made his move . . . time to make 'a real woman' out of you."

She turned around quickly. "He actually said that?"

"Just thought you should know."

Marlene said only, "hmmm."

Thinking of his reactions to Charlie and to some of the other teens he was dealing with, Ted realized that in his adult life he had always found it easier to be force-ful with young people, such as his son, than with adults. There was no penalty if he got firm with kids and they got upset with him. With adults, especially his father, he had suffered the pain of disapproval and rejection. Ted decided that from this day forward—in his past and future lives—he would try to be more patient with the young—at least those who deserved it—and he would not allow adults to put their priorities above his own.

CHAPTER 23

WHEN CHARLIE MET UP WITH TED ON THE WAY to their first morning classes, they passed by Marlene's group. Ted noted that she was dressed somewhat more conservatively than usual. Not exactly demure, but not the in-your-face sex bomb either.

"Hi Teddy," she cooed as they passed by.

"Hi Marlene," he said. "You're looking especially lovely this morning."

"Why, thank you Teddy," she said, staying focused on Ted, never acknowledging Charlie. Charlie looked so bewildered, his mouth was still hanging open when the two of them were halfway down the hallway.

"What the hell just happened?" Charlie said.

"What do you mean, Charlie?" Ted said, trying to look innocent.

"Marlene didn't even say hello to me, but she practically slobbered all over you."

"Well, Charlie," Ted said, "maybe you just don't know how to treat a 'real woman.'"

Ted decided he had to move faster on the Marlene project.

He went to his English teacher's classroom. Ted knew he could absolutely trust Grace Simpson.

"Mrs. Simpson, there is a female student who needs help. There's only so much I can do about it. It's going to take an adult to get her out of her predicament."

"Of course, Ted. I'll help in any way I can."

"I can't stress enough how important it is to keep this between you and me. I know I can count on you to keep what I'm about to tell you in confidence."

"Absolutely."

"We can't even let the police know about it just yet . . . and the school administrators must *never* hear of it."

She agreed and then listened as Ted explained Marlene's situation. She was clearly startled at what she was hearing . . . and probably uncomfortable talking about such a subject with a young student.

"That's terrible," she said. "It's important to get her out of that house as soon as possible."

"A safe place has to be found for her."

"Let me worry about that," she said.

"Okay. Meanwhile, I'll look into how to get that man out of circulation."

It was almost time for Ted's evening talk with Arnie. He walked up Riley Street and found a quiet spot in a wooded area that would one day be the site of an apartment complex.

A full moon shone brightly through the haze drifting in from the railroad. It was the same moon Ted had observed in the 21st century, except it did not yet have American astronauts' footprints on its surface and their abandoned equipment scattered across the moonscape.

A cool breeze felt good against Ted's face. Leaves rustled and there was the soft twittering of birds settling in for the night in the trees above him. Mrs. Foster's lilacs were in full fragrance, mingled with the smell of diesel fumes from the railroad. A dog barked in the distance and there was the constant sound of trains. Streetlights emitted a different kind of illumination from the mercury vapor lamps of his future that would pollute the atmosphere and blot out the stars.

He sat down in the weeds, out of view of the occasional passing car. The nearest occupied building was several hundred feet away.

He did not have to wait for long.

"*Teddy?*"

"Yes Arnie. I'm here."

"*I can't see anything.*"

"I'm in the woods."

Ted turned toward the street so Arnie could see lights through the trees.

"*Oh. I was afraid we had a glitch.*"

"Not in the system, although life in my revisited youth has some glitches needing attention."

"*No doubt. How was your day m'boy?*"

"Bizarre, as usual. How's that guy on the mud bed doing?"

"*As healthy and relaxed as I've ever seen him.*"

"Be sure to keep him that way. Arnie, do you remember the high school dream girl I spoke to you about?"

"*Of course I—Teddy—!*"

"No, no. . . she's the abused girl I mentioned before. She has changed into a child from my adult perspective."

"I should hope so."

"The kid is in trouble. Her mother's boyfriend is molesting her."

Ted could hear Arnie gasp all the way across the cosmos.

"Rat bastard."

An understatement if ever there was one.

"I think I have part of the problem almost solved," Ted said. "Now I'm working on the justice part. I could use some information."

"Fire away."

"I have to find out what child abuse laws apply in these pre-enlightened days."

"I'll do what I can."

"A-S-A-P Arnie. The child is in distress."

"I'll get back to you A-S-A Possible, lad."

"I'll talk to you tomorrow night . . . or even before that if you learn anything. Break in anytime during the day. I'll find a private place where we can talk."

"See you then. Over and out."

CHAPTER 24

ASIDE FROM THE USUAL OBNOXIOUS BEHAVIOR of some of the kids and teachers, the day was moving along relatively uneventfully. Until Arnie called Ted during algebra class.

"Earth to Teddy."

Surrounded by students, Ted was not in a position to respond.

"Ahem," Ted said. One can say 'ahem' at any time. People think it's the clearing of one's throat.

"I copy your 'ahem' my child and I will be standing by."

"Putz," Ted said, covering it up with a cough.

"I heard that."

The bell sounded. The next period was study hall, a concept that, by the 21st century, would largely be abandoned.

Ted took a detour to the boy's restroom and checked all the booths.

"All right . . . it looks clear."

"Okay, Teddy. I checked the state legislature's website. It was and still is a second degree felony for an adult to have sexual contact with a person under the age of sixteen. If the assailant is four or more years older than the victim, it's statutory rape . . . even with consent. If the victim is under fourteen years old, the penalties are even tougher."

"Rats. Marlene is fifteen."

"It's still a major crime," Arnie said. *"Wait. You have to find out how old she was when the abuse began."*

"That's it. Arnie, you're a genius. Why didn't I think of it?"

"Because I'm a genius and you're. . . well. . . you."

Ted ignored him.

"I think it's been going on for awhile."

"*The dirtbag is facing a felony rap.*"

"I love it when you talk like Sam Spade."

A voice behind Ted said, "Who are you talking to?"

He whirled around to see a boy who had entered the rest room unnoticed. Ted flashed a glance for Arnie's benefit.

"*I see him,*" Arnie said.

"Oh. I was just practicing a line from a poem."

"I didn't know there was a poem about Sam Spade," He said.

It took Ted a moment to think of an answer.

"Not all poetry was written in the 18th century, you know."

Apparently satisfied, the boy went about his business.

It was taking so long to wash his hands until the intruder finally left that Ted thought he might rub the skin off.

"*Quick thinking, Teddy. You're becoming quite an accomplished liar.*"

"Sad to say, the skill is serving me well. It explains why young people often lie. It keeps them out of more trouble than the truth. Or at least defers punishment."

"*Being a kid isn't for the weak. What do you want me to do?*"

"I need the legislative numbers so I can refer the information to the powers that be, whoever the hell those are."

Ted wrote the information on a paper towel and stuffed it into his pocket.

"*Let me know how it works out.*"

"You bet. I'd let the whole world know if it wouldn't hurt the girl."

"*Yeah. What people think of you is especially important at that age.*"

"Why Arnie, you actually are a sensitive soul."

"*Ha. I got sensitivity I ain't even used yet, buddy.*"

"See ya."

"*Later dude.*"

In 1960s-speak, a 'dude' is a city guy on a western ranch. In 21st-century jargon, 'dude' is an unlikely form of address to be coming out of the mouth of Professor Arnold Hoffmeier.

Ted had a brief moment of calm, enjoying the thought that he might be able to get Marlene to safety. But he was going to need some more help. He knew of only two people he could completely trust in that regard; Mrs. Simpson with Operation Marlene, the other with Operation Teddy McBride.

At the first opportunity he sneaked out of school and hopped on a bus to the county seat.

The District Attorney's office was in a red brick building with a Civil War era look to it. A sign on the wall outside the office listed several deputy DAs. The dark interior of the building had the same old-time feel to it, with a musty smell unique to buildings of that time.

After giving the receptionist a brief outline of the problem, Ted was directed to a waiting area down a long, dimly-lighted hallway with wainscoted walls, high ceilings and pebbled glass windows on office doors. They looked like something out of a 1930s detective novel and Ted half expected to see "Private Eye" painted on the glass. Instead it read, "Stanley Remley, Deputy District Attorney."

Ted was the only person waiting when a small, fat man opened the door. He looked more like an accountant than a lawyer.

Pigeon toes and crossed eyes. What was Mother Nature thinking?

"Mr. McBride," he called out, looking around the room over the top of the thick lenses of his steel-framed glasses. His gaze finally settled on Ted.

Ted took an immediate dislike to the man.

"That'd be me," Ted said.

"Are you accompanied by your father?" Remley asked.

"No, I'm the Mr. McBride with the problem."

If doubt were gold, Ted figured Remley could have afforded the redecoration his ratty little office desperately needed. He gestured for Ted to take a seat.

"We don't often get teenagers as complainants," Remley said, taking his seat behind the desk.

"Probably because most adults don't give teenagers much respect or a lot of credit for intelligence."

Remley just stared at the young man before him.

Ted continued. "Young people either deal with problems on their own or suffer in silence."

The deputy did not respond immediately.

"All right," he said finally, leaning back in his chair. "Tell me how I may help you *Mister* McBride."

"Actually, it's about a fifteen-year-old girl whose mother's boyfriend has been sexually molesting her for some time."

He gave Remley the legal information to help him look up the applicable law . . . not including Marlene's name and address.

Ted noticed the man was not writing anything down. The officious attorney did one of those steepled fingers, pursed lips kind of looks that are popular with bureaucrats when they want to give the impression they are thinking.

"Uh huh," Remley said, at last. Then more silence, implying a thoughtful pause. Ted was beginning to think the receptionist out in front was more familiar with the law than this cretin with the diploma hanging on the wall of his office.

"You know, Mr. McBride," he said, with a dash of sarcasm, "a lot of teenage girls have a bad habit of flirting, then complaining when the men—"

Ted jumped to his feet. "Mr. Remley, you are pissing me off."

If a kid had said something like that to the adult Ted he would probably have gotten his back up. Remley did.

"What do you mean. . . coming in here—"

"Look, if this is not of interest to you or is beyond your understanding, your authority or your legal expertise, please just let me know. I'll find other ways to handle it."

That got his attention. "Other—"

"The newspapers are always eager to cover stories like this. Especially when they find out officers of the court aren't doing their job."

Remley again ran through his little inventory of self-important poses and pauses.

"Wait here," he snapped. He pulled himself to his feet and waddled out of the room.

Oh, shit. Now you've done it McBride.

A few minutes passed. Ted could hear a murmur in a nearby office. Then a raised voice . . . and silence. Finally, footsteps clopped down the hallway. Remley returned to his desk. He was followed by an attractive young woman.

"Mr. McBride?"

He nodded.

"I'm Senior Deputy District Attorney Margaret Tuttle. Would you follow me please?"

She led him to an office similar in size, but with a friendlier décor. She pointed to a chair.

"Mr. Remley says you threatened him."

Covering his ass.

"You could say that. I told him there was a problem. He didn't show much interest or offer a solution. He even suggested it was the victim's fault. I told him if a resolution was beyond his capability I would have to find other ways. I'm sorry I went about it in such a heavy-handed manner. The problem persists and I am determined to solve it . . . with or without the help of this office."

Ted continued to amaze himself at his transformation from dove to hawk.

For a moment he thought the young attorney was going to give him a repeat performance of Remley's time-consuming, off-pissing gesticulations. To his surprise, she softened.

"If you'll pardon my observation," she said, "I see a boy, but I hear self-assurance and language usage uncommon for someone your age."

Uh oh. There I go again.

Thinking fast, he said, "I'm fifteen years old and live in a household where parents don't talk down to their children. In other words, they treat me like a person and I've become one. Please call me Ted."

She sat back in her chair and rewarded him with a smile.

"As I understand it. . . Ted. . . a young girl in your acquaintance is being sexually molested by an adult male."

"You got it." He gave her the details as he had interpreted them. "I recognized the signs, confronted her . . . scared the wits out of the girl . . . she finally admitted it . . . and I told her I'd get help."

"Recognized the signs? How did—never mind. You've come to the right place. I'll need to know her name and where she lives."

"Whoa. Slow down."

"I can't help if I don't know who she is."

"You must understand the situation. I would need absolute assurance this would be handled quietly and with discretion."

"Being a public matter, that would be the hard part."

"Look, I can appreciate your position. You are a public official, the public is constantly breathing down your neck. It would be a feather in your cap to make it known that you had gotten a monster out of circulation."

The young woman pursed her lips and sat back in her chair.

"Surely you don't believe I'm that superficial, Ted."

Ted had to think about that for a moment. Especially considering his experience with the bureaucratic slug down the hall.

"Okay. Sorry. Let's look at it from the viewpoint of a teenage girl. She has no resources to go anywhere else. She's scared. Her standing among her peers would be destroyed if this got out, even though she is entirely guiltless. Having been a teenager yourself not so long ago, you surely are aware of what a reputation means to someone that age."

The young lawyer got a faraway look in her eyes, perhaps remembering her own adolescence.

She appeared to be giving the concept thoughtful consideration. She nodded and said, "all right. Here's how we'll handle it. You will set up a meeting with the girl."

Ted started to protest.

"Wait. . . wait . . . it sounds like she trusts you as much as she trusts anyone. Let her know I won't cause her any harm. There are community resources available."

"If you mean Child Protective Services? Forget it."

"We don't call it that, but that's the idea."

"No way. I'll find a safe place for her."

Tuttle cocked her head and narrowed her eyes. He realized she might be suspicious of a teen male's motives.

"No . . . no . . . I have some friends . . . good, trustworthy *adult* friends."

"Not that I don't believe everything you've told me, Ted, but you must understand that I have to investigate this."

"Of course," Ted said and gave her the information, including everything he knew about Joel Snyder. That in exchange for assurances she would keep a low profile for Marlene's protection.

"You will have to move quickly on this," she said. Ted agreed to set up a meeting with Marlene on neutral ground.

"You will hear from me as soon as I can put it all together," Ted said.

As he passed Remley's office on the way out, the man flashed Ted a nasty cross-eyed look. Ted stopped, turned toward him and returned a glare that changed the man's scowl to something close to fear.

Ted was really enjoying this new assertiveness. He left the office with more hope than when he arrived. The logistics and legalities of removing Marlene's abuser from her life could actually be underway. Marlene's mother would probably cooperate . . . or at least not get in the way. Especially if threatened with prosecution for having looked the other way. If all went as expected the boyfriend would do hard prison time among men who did not like his kind. Child abusers and rapists were at the very bottom of prison social rankings.

It felt strange to Ted to face situations he had not dealt with . . . or even recognized . . . in the original version of his youth. The experiences he had gained as an adult were allowing him to see things that would not have been noticed by most teenagers. It was not likely young people would have shared their troubles with him in his adult form as they now did in his guise as one of them.

I wonder what I may have been blind to in my own son.

It also made him wonder about the ingredients in the human recipe. Part environmental, certainly. A pinch of chemistry and a dash of genetics. A heaping tablespoon of good or bad luck; right place, right time. Maybe even a sprinkle of magic that is sometimes called the 'spark of life' that powered the human engine; synapses snapping between neurons in the brain in a certain order and combination as unique to each individual as a Ford is to a Chevy or an elephant to an orangutan. That could help to explain why children in the same family who had been subjected to roughly the same influences had turned into entirely different personalities. It was well known that a family that could produce a great humanitarian could also spawn a murderous psychopath or that a president of the United States could have a bum for a brother.

Forces were at work that had put Marlene Sutton into an intolerable situation. Ted surrendered to the reality that he could not cure the world of all of its ills. He would just have to attack one ill at a time. That would start with finding a way to bring some stability to the life of a troubled young girl.

The first priority was to find a safe place for Marlene. The next would be to punish the molester. The unfairness of the man's actions stuck in Ted's craw like a large pill that would not go all the way down.

CHAPTER 25

MARLENE AND TED RODE A BUS to the county seat. Ted waited outside the deputy DA's office while Marlene told her story.

When they came out of the room, Margaret Tuttle said, "All right, Ted, it looks like we have a good case. With what Marlene has told me about Joel, we should be able to learn more about him."

"Okay. What's next?"

"Find a safe place for Marlene," Tuttle said, putting her hand gently on Marlene's arm. "She's long overdue for some relief from her ordeal."

"I will get things moving right away," he said.

The McBride home would not do. Even if his father approved, it would look bad to have a girl of Marlene's age and record of flirtiness living in the home of a boy known to have mooned over her since the fifth grade.

He would have to go back to his partner in intrigue.

Ted waited until the last of the students had left Grace Simpson's classroom to tell her about his visit to the DA's office.

Mrs. Simpson said, "We'll make room for her at our house until there's a better option."

"Wow. I never expected you to personally take on the responsibility."

"She's in trouble. It is the fastest solution. It's settled."

And that was that.

All Ted could do now was wait.

CHAPTER 26

THE END OF THE SCHOOL YEAR WAS LITTLE MORE THAN a month away. With freedom just out of reach, frustration among the students was increasing, like steam building in a pressure cooker. Summer vacation would have to come soon or an explosion was assured.

Ted knew he would have to take a radical step if he hoped to overcome certain drawbacks that came with being a kid. He would need assistance to get himself on an adult level to handle some of the other challenges he faced. At the same time he could not risk letting his secret get out to the wider world.

I need adult help, but not just any adult.

John Wilson was in his late thirties. He had a permanent crease between his eyebrows that was consistent with unfulfilled dreams. Wilson might have resented that Ted had a clean slate and a real shot at achieving what the science teacher could not afford to pursue. But the man was Ted's biggest supporter.

Conscious of Wilson's personal problems, Ted had come up with a plan. From long experience with his close teacher-student relationship, he trusted Wilson. Plus, he knew the man had the kind of curiosity that would be helpful for what he had in mind.

After the last student left the science classroom, Ted approached the teacher, who had resumed work on an elaborate math problem on the chalkboard. He was obviously doing it for his own enjoyment. The complexity of the equation clearly indicated the man was in an intelligence category well above his pay grade, although Ted had spotted an error in the calculation.

"Mr. Wilson."

Wilson looked up briefly from his work. "Yes Ted," he said without enthusiasm.

"I wondered whether you had looked into computer technology."

"I'm aware of it," Wilson said, "I haven't given it serious inspection."

"You should check it out," Ted said. "Computers are the future."

"It sounds interesting, Ted," he said. "But I have enough trouble dealing with the present."

"Look, Mr. Wilson, let me make a long story a lot shorter."

Ted took a bold step. He picked up the eraser and chalk and made the correction on the math problem.

"You are obviously bored out of your mind," Ted said. "Teaching young people who couldn't care less about the subject can't be very fulfilling for you."

Wilson looked with open mouth at what had been done to his calculation and at what Ted had said.

"How did you—"

"Okay," Ted continued. "Your boredom is a given. You're trapped in a place you have not been able to get out of and you hate it."

"Ted," he said, apparently bewildered that a mere boy was able to correct such an elaborate equation. "What gives you the idea I'm unhappy in my profession?"

"Who wouldn't be? A lot of these kids are here because the law requires it and because their parents will need someone to blame later if their little darlings don't succeed in life. I sometimes think public schools are actually nothing more than camouflaged child care facilities. Parents park their kids here while they go off to make a living doing the things they resent doing for young people who don't appreciate it. I don't see how anyone could take satisfaction from trying to teach the chronically disinterested."

Ted thought of the little spider trapped in the kitchen sink at his apartment: take one step forward, slide two steps backward.

"That's somewhat simplistic," Wilson said.

"Mr. Wilson, it is obvious you are an intelligent man." Ted rapped a knuckle on the math problem the teacher had been working. "And that I am an intelligent . . . teenager. You, sir, are in a rut."

Ted had often wondered why Wilson was not teaching math rather than science, which was clearly far beneath his potential. Possibly because teaching math at the high school level would be more frustrating for the man than teaching something that didn't mean as much to him.

Wilson sighed. His shoulders slumped as he packed papers into his briefcase. "Not that it's any of your affair, but sometimes a man's rut is too deep to climb out of."

"Well, I'm not in your particular rut, so why don't I try to help you find alternatives."

"Ted," Wilson said, "This is really not your concern. You're just . . . why you're just . . ."

". . . a kid? Ted said. "Things are not always as they seem."

"No offense, but you don't have enough experience at anything, let alone the ability to analyze someone else's life."

Ted looked him straight in the eye. By now he had completely abandoned his teen-speak persona. "You need to go to Pennsylvania State University and apply for any teaching position in the math field."

"Ted, I can't just—"

"Mr. Wilson, you should learn all you can about computers and quantum mechanics while you're there and eventually switch to teaching them."

"Why would—"

"I'm going to tell you some things that will occur in coming years. I don't want you to think I'm crazy or a pathological liar. What I'm going to say is the absolute truth, although I'll admit that even I still have a hard time believing it."

"Please don't tell me you can look into the future, Ted."

"I wouldn't tell you that. Not exactly."

"Thank goodness. You had me—what do you mean 'not exactly'?"

All right. Here goes.

Ted closed his eyes for a moment, took a deep breath and looked around to be sure no one else could hear. He said, "Mr. Wilson, I *am* from the future."

The silence in the room might have been compared to a remote canyon, far from the sounds of rushing highways, jet planes, and roaring rivers.

Ted continued. Wilson looked like a man who did not know whether to keep listening . . . or to run for his life. "You see before you a fifteen-year-old boy," Ted continued. "But I am actually a fifty-five-year-old computer science professor at what will become the Penn State University's Harrisburg campus."

Wilson slammed his briefcase on the desk. "That does it!" he shouted. "Get out of here!"

Considering the violence he had experienced in recent days, Ted was not going to let a little outburst like that bother him."

"Let me prove it to you."

"How could you possibly prove it? The future hasn't happened yet?"

"That's true. For you the future is yet to come. For me it . . . it already has."

"Now you're really scaring me."

"Please don't be afraid. I'm not crazy or homicidal. I believe I can show you."

"How—"

"Give me a minute."

The only way to confirm that he was from the future was to give Wilson some information about something that had not—in the teacher's world—happened yet.

"Okay, Mr. Wilson," he said, again picking up a piece of chalk. "I'll give you the evidence you need to prove I am not insane, delusional or on some mind-altering drug."

Stunned, Wilson watched as Ted wrote the word 'ARNIE' on the chalkboard in thick capital letters.

"What's an 'Arnie'?"

"Not a 'what', a 'who,'" he said. "Professor Arnold Hoffmeier is a colleague of mine."

"Colleague?" Wilson sniffed. "Ted, fifteen-year-old boys don't have colleagues. They have classmates. . . buddies."

"True. But fifty-five-year-old university professors do."

Wilson looked as though he might bolt from the room. Anyone but a brilliant man involved in science probably would have.

Ted's 21st-century pal would have the sound turned down until their usual meeting time. But he probably had the visual monitor running and he . . . or his associate . . . would be able to see the printed letters.

Ted stared at the name on the board.

"What are you doing, Ted?"

"I'm trying to attract someone's attention," he said, keeping his eyes riveted to the board.

"By looking at the chalkboard?"

"I'll explain soon."

Meanwhile, in the 21st century, Harold, Arnie Hoffmeier's lab assistant, happened to glance at the monitor.

"Professor Hoffmeier," he said. "You should see this."

Arnie looked at the screen and saw his name displayed on it.

He sat down at the console and turned on his microphone.

"Teddy . . . are you calling me?"

"Yes, Arnie."

The suddenness of Ted's reaction startled the teacher.

"Who are you talking to, Ted?" Wilson said.

"Shh . . . wait a minute." Ted held up a hand in the hope he would stay calm. "Thanks for getting back to me, Arn."

"Teddy, is someone there?"

"Yes, Arnie. My science teacher, John Wilson, is here." He turned toward Wilson to let Arnie see him.

"Oh, Ted. You didn't—"

"Yes I did, although I haven't convinced him yet of what's going on."

Wilson sat wide-eyed and disbelieving as Ted spoke to someone who was not there.

"Teddy, I have a bad feeling about this."

"No need for apprehension Arnie. I trust Mr. Wilson completely. I have to persuade him that I'm from the future."

The teacher's look was one of fear mixed with curiosity.

"This is a really bad idea Teddy."

"Well, you'll just have to trust me that it will be okay. I want you to find something for me that happened tomorrow. *My* tomorrow, not yours."

"Arggghhh!"

"I'd like for you to Google the date or check the city newspaper archives and find something significant that hasn't happened here yet."

"This could really make big problems, Teddy."

"Let me explain something to you, Arnie. And I'll be telling Mr. Wilson at the same time because I've never told him before. He has been a great friend to a kid who has no real friends. I survived childhood in large part because of John Wilson. I trust him absolutely. Don't give it another thought. Besides, who's Mr. Wilson going to tell? People would think he's nuts. Right now he probably thinks *I'm* nuts."

"Aw, man . . ."

"Do it, Arn. Get that information for me. Everything will be okay."

Ted could hear keyboard chatter and knew Arnie was doing as he asked.

While he waited Ted turned to the teacher. "I don't mean to scare you Mr. Wilson. This is the only way I can prove—"

"Teddy."

"Wait . . . Arnie's back. Yes Arn."

"Tomorrow afternoon . . . your tomorrow . . . Congress will pass a bill regulating—"

"No, no. Too dull—too general. Congress is always passing a bill to regulate something. I need an incident that will stand out, close to home. Something that is not possible to predict today."

More keyboard sounds as Arnie surfed the Internet for a significant event.

"*Okay Teddy. Tomorrow morning, according to the newspaper archives, a small plane crashed—will crash—in a field west of Carbonville, on a farm owned by a Gustav Wimple. The pilot and passenger survive with minor injuries. The plane had—or will have—the left wing torn off and a bent propeller. The two occupants have to walk from the crash scene to get help.*"

"Let me repeat it," he said, turning to Wilson. "A small plane will crash west of Carbonville tomorrow morning . . . Gus Wimple's farm . . . no serious injuries. A broken left wing, bent prop. Pilot and passenger have to walk for help. Okay. Thanks Arnie."

"*Your teacher looks ill. I hope you know what you're doing Teddy.*"

"Yes, he does look kind of pale. It'll be okay, Arnie. You worry too much. I'll talk to you again at the regular time tonight."

John Wilson was in a severely flummoxed state.

"You heard," Ted said. "Now we wait."

"This is insane," Wilson said.

"Of course you would think I'm certifiable, Mr. Wilson. But please withhold judgment about my sanity. I'm trusting that you won't tell anyone about this."

Wilson's jaw was still at half mast. "If I told anyone," he said, "you would probably deny it and they would call me a madman. You can bet your life I won't say anything."

"Okay, I'll see you tomorrow," he said. "If nothing else, I hope to prove there is the prospect of a better future waiting for you."

"I don't see how that's possible," Wilson said.

"Improving your life would be a small accomplishment compared to time travel, wouldn't it?"

Ted had a few ideas he would have to give some more thought.

CHAPTER 27

IT WAS JUST BEFORE LUNCHTIME THAT CHARLIE FREEMAN came tearing down the hallway. Ted was standing with John Wilson at the door to the teacher's classroom.

"Teddy," Charlie said. "I just heard that an airplane crashed out at Gus Wimple's place."

Wilson got the same message.

"How about that," Ted said, at the same time making eye contact with the teacher, who was looking stunned at the news. "Anybody hurt?"

"Not too bad. The pilot and another guy got out okay," Charlie said. "The plane was banged up though."

"Huh," Ted said. "You'd sure need both wings and a propeller if you hoped to fly it."

"What?"

"Just kidding Charlie."

"Teddy, I didn't say anything about the wing and propeller. How did—"

"Just a wild guess," he said. John Wilson knew it was not a guess.

When Charlie left, Wilson motioned Ted into the room.

"Ted . . . I don't understand—"

"I told you yesterday. You didn't believe me."

"I still don't know what to believe," Wilson said. "It's not possible. It happened just as you said."

"I hope you don't think I sabotaged an airplane, causing it to crash at exactly the spot I said it would."

"No. . . no . . . I just—"

"Look, Mr. Wilson. I know how hard it is to accept all this. I'm still wrestling with the idea myself. A short time ago I was teaching computer science, living in a city that won't be as it was when I left it for another four decades. Then a genius friend of mine got me involved in a project that brought me here."

"But . . . you're a teenager—"

"Sure looks like it, doesn't it?"

Wilson looked thoroughly confused.

"It won't go on forever," Ted said. "Thank heavens, because I would truly hate to re-live my entire teen years. I can't stand half these kids and I want to do violence against a couple of teachers. Once the experiment is completed, my 21st-century self will be reawakened. The fifteen-year-old Ted McBride will return to normal after my family moves away from Carbonville. No one will be aware of the change because I'll be living miles from here when it occurs."

"Those close to you would notice . . . your parents."

"Yeah . . . I'm working on that. Meanwhile you could help me greatly."

"How?"

Ted thought of the mind-numbing blather he had to endure from Charlie Freeman every day.

"For one thing, I'm tired of having to modify my speech with kids. It's just a notch up from baby talk. It's a pleasure to speak on the adult level."

"You've got to tell me more about this."

"I've told you all I can. Even that you must keep to yourself or it could cause great problems."

"Who would believe it anyway?"

"There's that, of course. Anyone you told about it would treat you like one of those people who claim they were picked up by aliens in a UFO."

Wilson shivered at the prospect of being shunned, his credibility and his career destroyed.

"All right," he said. "But how do I figure in all this?"

"Being a kid comes with a whole set of problems," Ted said. "Much of what they say is pretty off-the-wall and based on imagination more than experience. As a result, adults don't take them seriously when they actually do have something to contribute."

"Not much I can do to change that."

"You could speak for me. You can do some things an adult can do that a teenager can't."

Wilson thought it over before commenting. "Such as?"

"For starters, I need some information about rural land availability and prices of large tracts not more than ten miles west of Carbonville. No real estate agent would talk to a kid about that. I'm not interested in active farmland, just scrub acreage . . . relatively flat, weedy patches not being used for agricultural purposes. Close to main roads. The bigger, the flatter, the better."

The idea came to him when Arnie told him about the airplane crash in a vacant field. In years to come, the Wimple property would no longer be a cow pasture. Gus Wimple would have died long ago and five-hundred families would be living in look-alike houses on the site.

"All right. I don't understand why," Wilson said, "but I'll take a drive out there and have a look. A friend of mine is a realtor. I'll get him to check out property prices."

As horrified as Ted was about urban sprawl in his own future, he knew expansion was inevitable. He would take all precautions against defiling productive farmland.

Ted almost dreaded his evening talk with Arnie, but steeled himself for another Arnold Hoffmeier lecture.

"Teddy."

"Hi Arn."

"I'm very concerned you let your science teacher in on our secret."

"He's a good man, Arnie. I'm making an investment in his future . . . maybe the world's."

"Since it's already been done, I'll have to have faith that it works out."

"I need some more information."

"Oh dear. All right . . . shoot."

"Check on past stock performances. Find me two inexpensive stocks that increased significantly in price overnight in this time frame; one the day after tomorrow, the second the day after that."

"Why on earth—"

"To generate a pile of cash quickly for a couple of humanitarian projects I'm working on."

"I'm getting a bad feeling again."

"It will work out just fine, Arnie. Just find me two stocks and get back to me as early in the day tomorrow as possible."

Arnie finally caved in. He agreed to let Ted know the following morning.

CHAPTER 28

JOHN WILSON LOOKED AS IF HE HADN'T SLEPT the previous night. He flagged Ted down in the hallway.

"I checked out properties," he said. "Three tracts of the type you described had 'For Sale' signs on them. Why did you want to know about land for sale?"

"Mr. Wilson, one day land is going to be worth lots of money. I recommend you buy it."

"Buy land? Ted, I don't have a loose nickel to spare."

"Okay. We have to find some money to use just for a couple of days."

"Don't look at me. My entire life savings is only a little more than two-thousand dollars in stocks and bonds."

That's a relief. Now I won't have to do anything illegal.

"Good. Then you already have a brokerage account."

"But Ted—"

Ignoring what he knew would be a protest, Ted quickly gave Wilson an overview of the plan to generate money, make him more financially secure and free him from his mundane existence.

"Here's what we'll do . . ."

"But—"

"I'll let you know in greater detail later. Meanwhile, if you can gather up the cash, I have work to do."

When Wilson was finally able to get a word in edgewise he said, "Ted . . . I can't afford to lose that money."

"Not only will you not lose it, Mr. Wilson, you will make a lot more with it. Don't forget who you're talking to."

Wilson could hardly quibble over the safety of his savings when it had just been proven that Ted McBride could look into the future.

They would decide the next step after the raid on the New York Stock Exchange was completed.

It was mid-morning before Arnie called with the information Ted needed. He had found two low-priced stocks whose value would rise significantly from one day to the next.

The plan was presented to John Wilson.

"I want to believe you, Ted," he said. He had cashed in his assets after their talk that morning. "You have to understand the financial position I'm in. I absolutely cannot afford to lose that money."

"I do understand," Ted said. He pointed to the New York Stock Exchange listings for the day. "I propose we take the two-thousand dollars and buy five-hundred shares of this four-dollar West Virginia coal mine stock. The company will announce a fat, long-term coal contract during the trading day tomorrow. The stock will briefly soar to sixteen-dollars a share for long enough to sell it at a profit."

"It's frightening, Ted," Wilson said, clearly stressed over the prospect of losing his savings.

"There's a rainbow here Mr. Wilson. You can't get the pot of gold if you don't head for the end of it."

"Okay . . . okay . . . I'll make the call to my broker. If it doesn't work, you will be responsible for my death because my wife will kill me."

CHAPTER 29

THE SOARING RESULT OF THE STOCK MARKET INVESTMENT the next day was no surprise to Ted, but John Wilson looked pale and exhausted when they met.

"Good lord," Wilson said. The sale of the mining company stock had given him a hefty profit. "It worked, Ted."

Ted was elated that something seemed to be working out for this man he so admired.

"Yes it did. Now for Phase Two."

Wilson let out a long sigh and leaned against the classroom wall, his eyes to the heavens. Sweat was forming on the man's forehead.

Ted knew the success of Phase One had not entirely eased Wilson's apprehensions as they entered the next step.

Now they had eight-thousand dollars to work with.

According to Arnie's information, a small West Coast aircraft company would announce it had won a bid to design and build a new U.S. Army jet fighter plane. News of the contract would increase their newly purchased one-thousand shares of eight-dollar aircraft stock to thirty-six dollars a share.

Wilson made the call to his broker.

As predicted, the stock price soared the next day. The sale brought Wilson's new fortune up to thirty-six thousand dollars . . . an amount equal to as much as a quarter of a million dollars in 21st-century spending power.

"It would not be smart to keep the winning streak going," Ted said. "Someone at the brokerage house may wonder how you did that. Some government agency could get curious and demand answers. They'd accuse us of insider trading."

Ted knew they wouldn't be able to prove anything illegal, but the two guerilla investors certainly did not need to call attention to themselves.

"Too bad they won't have a state lottery until 1972," Ted said. "We could really score big with one of those jackpots."

"Lottery? Lotteries are illegal."

"Just watch," Ted said. "Meanwhile, not a bad couple of days work, Mr. Wilson. What did your wife have to say about you investing the money?"

"Uh . . . Ted . . . I didn't tell her," Wilson admitted. "I feel awful. I'd never kept anything from her before."

Ted understood Wilson's feeling of guilt, but considered the greater good.

"Machiavelli said, 'the end justifies the means.'"

"Well Machiavelli can go to Hell."

"No," Ted said. "That was Dante."

The teacher did not look convinced. "My wife knows where I keep the key to the gun cabinet."

"The next phase should take care of your guilt—and your health."

"Not again. I don't think my heart would hold out for another cliffhanger."

There was no help for the lie by omission. However, Ted believed he could bring Wilson back to even money on the official record.

"Okay, here's what I propose," Ted said. "We put the original two-thousand dollars back where it was . . . in some stocks I have in mind. The rest will go into as many of those properties as what's left of the money will buy."

Ted gave Wilson a list of stocks he knew would increase in value in the coming years and advised him to hold onto them, no matter what.

Wilson's normal color was returning.

"Now," Ted said. "About that land. I'd like for you to buy some of it for yourself and reserve some for a young friend. He is not doing well and I would like to give him a leg up on the future."

"Tell me his name and I'll try to help him."

That was a bonus Ted had not expected.

"His name is Jimmy Deavers—"

"That little rascal—"

"I think you will see some changes in the boy. It will be worth the effort."

"One more thing," Ted said. "This is kind of awkward for me, but I need some money to cover the cost of some other things I have to do while I'm here. Those could add up to a lot more than a dollar-a-week kid's allowance can handle. I'll return anything that's left over before my family moves away next month."

"Will five-hundred dollars cover it?"

Ted was amazed at Wilson's generosity. "I doubt I'll need anywhere near that much," he said. "But it would be nice to have it in reserve."

There was no way to predict how much it would cost to rescue Marlene Sutton.

Considering what was yet to be done, the next few days could be a roller coaster ride.

Ted had to make some calls.

CHAPTER 30

By THE TIME HE ARRIVED HOME AFTER SCHOOL, Ted had already made his decision to take still another bold step . . . even if it meant again breaking a promise to Arnie Hoffmeier.

"Teddy," Alma McBride said. "Unless my eyesight is failing, I thought I saw you walking with Jimmy Deavers this morning."

"Your eyesight is fine, Mom. Jimmy and I have come to an agreement."

Her look split the difference between quizzical and skeptical. Given his history with the bully, puzzlement was a natural reaction.

"What sort of agreement?" she said.

"He has agreed not to lay in ambush for me. I have agreed not to break every bone in his body."

Skeptical edged out quizzical by a wide margin.

"Actually," Ted said, making no effort to camouflage his adult mode, "I confronted him with some of the things that made the boy the way he is. I will help him improve his grades in school and get him on a success track."

"That's generous of you Teddy. Especially considering how terrible he's been to you."

"Because it's not his fault," he said, now completely abandoning the simplified 'teen-speak' he had been so careful to use. "It's not fair that the rest of his life should be wrecked because he has a sadist for a father and a floozy for a mother."

"Teddy!"

"Okay, maybe it's overstating the situation where Vikki is concerned. You have to admit Jimmy is handicapped because of his home environment."

Alma McBride stared at her son.

"There's something I wanted to talk with you about, Mom. Emily needs her own room. A girl should have some privacy."

Ted's mother looked at him as though she were seeing a stranger.

"A day bed off the living room doesn't qualify. All I need is a place to sleep and read and keep a couple of things."

Alma's mouth was hanging open. Ted reached over and gently pushed her chin up.

"I propose that Em and I trade places," he said. "Even though it's only a short time until we leave here. The change would be symbolic more than anything but I think Em would appreciate it."

His mother was giving him that tuned-in look again. Her single eyebrow was rising.

Ted smiled, knowing what was coming.

Antenna alert.

"Teddy, I need to know what's going on here."

DEFCON four.

"Golly . . . gee whiz . . . gosh . . . whatever do you mean, Mother dear?"

"Teddy . . . ?"

DEFCON three.

Ted smiled. "Kids don't tell their mothers everything, you know."

Alma's magical lone eyebrow went all the way up.

"Teddy—" she said again, foot tapping, arms folded, single eyebrow raised.

DEFCON Two. At least she hasn't hit me with my full name yet.

"Theodore Winston McBride!"

Uh oh. DEFCON One.

That was how his mother handled cold winter mornings when it was time for school and he absolutely did not want to get up. The coal-burning furnace in the cellar was always stoked for the night. By morning the house had cooled considerably. The down comforter felt so good pulled up around his neck. On the third try to get him up his mother would call him by his full name and loudly suggest from the bottom of the stairs that if he didn't get his rear in gear he would find his mattress turned upside down on the floor, with him under it.

Judging by his mother's raised eyebrow, it looked as though Ted could be in the market for a symbolic mattress dumping.

Oh well.

He had already decided what he was going to do. Now was the time.

"Okay . . . here's the deal, Mom . . . and you're not going to believe it."

Her arms had gone full-blown akimbo and her foot tapping had reached a bongo tempo.

"You're behaving like an adult," she interrupted, "doing unexpectedly mature things. Not that I object to maturity, Teddy. But this is totally out of the blue. You're not due to be a grownup for another ten years or so."

"I don't know how to tell you this, Mom, but most people don't actually grow up until they are in their late thirties and early forties. Some people mature in some ways, but not in others . . . and some people never get there at all."

"I don't understand what is happening, son."

"It would be best if you sat down."

She plopped into a nearby chair. A larger-than-normal crease had formed between her eyebrows.

"Tell me," she said, obviously expecting something terrible, rather than the something impossible that he was going to tell her.

How in the world do you tell your mother you're from the future?

"Mom," he said. "I'm from the future."

"Wha—"

"I am actually a fifty-five-year-old college computer science professor with a son, your grandson, Tim, who was fifteen years old when I left the 21st century for this visit."

"You—"

"You know I've had an interest in computers. In the next forty years the technology will have advanced to the point where time travel is possible."

"Are you telling me you are from forty years in the future?"

"Yes I am."

"Well, I knew there had to be a logical explanation," she said with a nervous laugh.

She was always great at humoring me.

"You're probably thinking I've gone mad."

"Son," she said after careful consideration, "why don't you let me make an appointment for you with Dr. Gruenwald."

"The psychologist?"

"He's done a wonderful job with Marge Bowers' son, Terrance. The boy has stopped his late-night screaming out of the attic window . . . almost entirely. I'm sure a little talk with Dr. Gruenwald and you will be just fine."

Ted felt a deep sigh coming from down there where deep sighs come from. He put his hand on his mother's arm. He could feel her trembling.

"Mom, on July 20, 1969, an American astronaut named Neil Armstrong will be the first human to set foot on the moon."

"No. You can't possibly—"

"Cataract surgery will be done in the doctor's office. A patient's clouded lens will be replaced and they will go home an hour later. Damaged hip and knee joints will be replaced routinely. Many of the several hundred forms of cancer will be curable or treatable. Organ transplants will be commonplace—"

"Stop, Teddy," she said. "Please."

But Ted decided to go on. "Deoxyribonucleic acid, or DNA, is a material in the body that dictates all aspects of every living being's physical self, from the color of their eyes to the diseases they are susceptible to. It is as unique to humans as fingerprints and will even be used to tie criminals to crimes."

Alma McBride stared at her son. He had gone this far, he figured he may as well lighten up a bit.

"In the 1980s General Motors will stop building those fake exhaust ports into the hoods of Buicks. They'll bring them back on some models in 2003 and—"

"Stop it. Don't do this son."

He couldn't let her be this stressed.

"On Tuesday I told my science teacher there would be a plane crash Wednesday on Gus Wimple's farm. As you know, that happened. If you doubt what I'm telling you, ask John Wilson. I've entrusted him with the same thing I'm telling you. I know you're afraid for me right now, Mom. I understand how my explanation may not be within the normal range of rational."

She had stopped shaking.

"It is important that you not tell anyone about this. First of all, they'd think you were a nut job. Second, it would complicate my temporary stay . . . in my teenage form. Third, it would get in the way of some really important things I must do while I'm here."

Ted could not recall ever seeing his mother entirely speechless before.

He continued. "When I'm finished here the young Ted McBride will once again be his fifteen-year-old self. The fifty-five-year-old Ted McBride will fade back to the 21st century where he told you he was going to be out of town related to his teaching job. I needed to tell you this. If I didn't you would wonder about the change after I got back to being a goofy teenager."

Ted decided it would be wise to stay quiet while Alma thought it over. She continued to stare, antenna extended, all super powers in hyper-drive, looking into the eyes of her son who appeared to have lost his mind just since breakfast.

"It's been worth the trip to see you looking this young again, Mom."

That made her notice. "You mean I'll still be around then?"

Success. Mom's lost tongue has been located.

Ted knew his mother would not be as hard to convince as his science teacher had been. He had never lied to her and she had always trusted him.

"What else can you tell me, son?"

"We should probably leave it right there, Mom." He said, although there was one more message. "And there is something else. You must encourage Dad to give up smoking and to see a doctor."

That made her sit up in her chair. Now she looked really scared.

"What I mean, Mom, is that research is being done on thoracic aortic aneurysms. It would be a good idea to have Dad examined."

"How—" The words were slowly sinking in. "Do you mean he's—"

"Do that for me . . . for Dad . . . for Emily."

"You *do* know something."

Ted had not seen such concern since he was six years old and got a fishhook stuck in his finger.

"If he doesn't do this he won't have much of a future. That's all I will say."

She sagged against the back of the chair like a balloon losing air.

"I'll call Dr. Engle right away—"

"No," he barked with an intensity that startled them both. "Dr. Engle is good for giving tetanus shots and for treating measles and mumps. You have absolutely no idea how limited his knowledge is."

"He's been our doctor since—"

"Mom. . . Dr. Engle was Grandma and Grandpa Patterson's family doctor. He delivered *you*. He probably hasn't opened a medical book since his internship. The old man is not far advanced from when physicians didn't know enough to wash their hands between patients. I'll find a specialist in Harrisburg. Then you make an appointment for Dad. You will have to tell the doctor about the research. They've known about aortic aneurysms for many years. That's what killed Kit Carson in 1868. That was before they learned how to correct them with an operation. They can now, although it isn't widely practiced yet and it's not totally without risk. But doing nothing is not an option. The local specialist probably won't be entirely familiar with it. You will have to direct him to experts in the field."

"Ted, you must tell me how you know all of this."

"It's far too complicated. You just have to believe me."

I'm going to have to get firm with my own mother.

Arnie had looked into where the scientific studies were being done in this time period.

"The Mayo Clinic in Rochester, Minnesota, is a leader in developing techniques to manage ruptured abdominal aneurysms. I've written down the information for you. They can direct you to someplace where the procedure is being performed."

She no longer looked at him as though she believed he had gone insane. Ted was banking heavily on her trust.

"I'll make the appointment," she said. "It will be hard to get him there without a good explanation."

Ted had already thought of that.

"Tell him you heard that dark circles under the eyes is an indicator of heart irregularities. Say you're concerned for his health and that you would like to have him around for awhile. Don't let him talk you out of it, Mom. You know how hard-headed he can be. This is genuinely a matter of life and death."

"Oh, Teddy . . . I've always known you were smart and you had a bright future ahead of you. I never dreamed you'd bring the future here."

"Don't feel alone, Mom. It's still got me a little spooked."

The next day Ted located a specialist of some proven skill for the day. He hoped Arnie was not monitoring. He had not planned to tell Arnie that he had let his mother in on the big secret. After all, he couldn't be preserving his dad's health and, at the same time, giving his best friend a stroke.

CHAPTER 31

THINGS WERE MOVING SO FAST AROUND HIM that Ted was feeling the need for some stress relief. Music had always soothed him.

A year before the great adventure began, the band Ted had joined along with some fellow university teachers, played at local clubs, weddings, parades, and such. The group called itself "The Syncopated Professors." Ted had suggested "The Dow Jones Average Industrial Band," but the guy whose idea it was to form the group said it was too many words to fit onto Harley Campbell's bass drum head.

It seemed like a good way to break up his routine, so Ted decided to join them. He had driven up to his mother's farm to dig his old trombone out of a closet.

"What do you want that old thing for?" Alma McBride had said.

"Some of the guys at school are forming a Dixieland band. I thought I'd get back into it."

Ted knew his mother would approve of one of the few musical genres that had successfully survived across the generations. Even Ted's own teenage son could not help tapping his foot when he put a Dixie tune on his stereo which, at the boy's urging, Ted had stopped calling his 'hi-fi'.

"It certainly is corroded, Teddy," his mother said of the instrument that had not seen daylight since her son's final day of high school.

"Poor people have corrosion on their trombones, Mom. People like us have patina on ours."

Ted had to admit it was pathetic looking.

"It certainly has lost its shine in forty years," his mother said.

"Haven't we all?"

The challenge was to make what was going on inside his head come out the other end of the horn.

Helping Jimmy Deavers with his homework had made Ted late for after-school band practice. Through the walls of the band room he could hear the others warming up. The sound grew louder as he pushed open the door.

"Well, Mr. McBride, so good of you to join us," John P. Krauss said. The band director carried himself as though he believed he was in the league of John P. Sousa.

Over the years, Ted had forgotten how rude many grownups were to kids. He was in his early twenties when he first began to feel he was treated as an equal by adults. He wondered if he had done the same thing to young people. Krauss was one of those for whom it was useless to make excuses. Ted offered none.

He took his seat in the brass section and looked at his tuba player neighbor's music stand to see what was up next. He put up his sheet music, although the material was firmly in his head.

The director raised his baton, the signal to start "Stars and Stripes Forever."

Several bars into the piece, Ted thought, what the hell. His teen lips were tougher than his adult lips had been, giving him wider tonal range. He took off in a jazz riff not quite on the beat or on the note and made what he thought were some interesting triple-tongued twists and turns around the piece.

"Hold it." Krauss shouted. "Hold it." All the musicians stopped. "McBride, is that you doing all that squawking and squeaking back there?"

Ted nodded. "Well, yes. . . but I call it improvising."

"Just play the notes, McBride," Krauss said across the heads of the players in the front row. He held up the sheet music and shook it. "Those notes are not anywhere on this page."

"Gee Mr. Krauss, most band directors reward their instrumentalists for creativity."

"That's not creativity, McBride, it's cacophony, do you know what cacophony is?

"I'm a tea drinker, myself," Ted said, "but a c-cup of cacophony would be much appreciated, th-thanks."

The tuba player snorted so loudly that Ted thought the boy might inhale the instrument.

"It's noise," Krauss said, slamming his fist down on the lectern. "Just play the blasted notes as they're written funny man."

"Okey-dokey," Ted said. Being disrespectful was not in his nature, but he thought he could afford to be humorously smug. Any penalty would be meaningless since, according to the calendar on the band room wall, the McBride family would soon be leaving it all behind. Besides, he was enjoying the confidence that had eluded him for so long.

As the band members took it from the top, Ted played along with the music as written. He wondered if, like a horse that sleeps while standing up, it were possible to doze off with a trombone in his mouth.

Mercifully, the band practice ended.

"Yo. McBride . . . wait up," Eddie Stolsfus called out.

Eddie played a mean tenor sax.

"What's up Eddie?"

"Me and a couple of other guys have a little group that plays together."

"Yeah? What do you call yourselves?"

Eddie looked puzzled. "We call ourselves four guys who get together at my place and play music. What else?"

"Like the "Mountainaires" or the "Polka Dots" or some such."

"Oh. No. We just do it for fun. Never thought of turning pro. Maybe some day."

"Are you guys any good?"

"Pretty good and getting better," he said. "We're practicing tonight. How'd you like to make a fifth? We could use a trombone and you sounded great."

"I'm not sure I'd be a reliable fifth, Eddie. I have a lot going on and we're moving away at the end of the school year."

"Well, it's one of those things where you can be there when you can be there and not be there when you can't . . . be there."

"Okay then. Sure."

That evening Ted rode his bicycle to Eddie's house for the session. Eddie's dad had finished off the basement with insulation and knotty pine paneling. Ideal for sound suppression and neighborhood tranquility.

The trumpet player occasionally hit a sour note and the piano player's fingers didn't always land exactly where the sheet music said they should, but Ted thought the boys did a decent job. More than that, he was enjoying the opportunity to cut loose outside the rigid high school band structure and take a break from the responsibilities he had taken on.

Eddie switched from saxophone to clarinet for a rousing version of "When the Saints Go Marching In" that left them all breathless and sweating.

"Eddie, you've underrated the group," Ted said as they were putting their instruments away. "That was great."

"Felt good, didn't it?"

"John P. Krauss would have rolled over in his grave if he was dead and that might have killed him."

"That's not creativity, McBride," Eddie said. "It's c-c-cacophony."

That got a laugh from the boys, who had each suffered rebukes and indignities at the hands of the school's tight-assed band director.

It occurred to Ted that he was not only taking liberties with the musical notes, he was not following the figurative notes or the beat typically imposed on this entire segment of his life. That also felt good.

Ted tied the trombone case on his bicycle rack with cotton clothesline rope and wished with all his might that someone would hurry up and invent bungee cords.

CHAPTER 32

Grace Simpson got Ted's attention as he passed by her room.

"Now is the time to get Marlene out of her house," she said. "Before that man returns."

As anxious as Ted was to find a safe haven for the girl, he was surprised at the speed with which Mrs. Simpson had made the arrangements. She told him she talked it over with her daughter and Alice had agreed enthusiastically, even without knowing the full story.

"When . . . how—"

"Right after school today," she said and explained her plan.

A light rain was falling when Ted caught up to Marlene on her way home. Lightning flashed over the distant mountain. Thunder boomed down the valley as a storm rolled toward the town along the Appalachian ridge.

If he had approached Marlene earlier in the day he knew she would have been distressed for the entire day and everyone would have known something was going on.

"It's moving day, Marlene," he said, coming up behind her.

She spun around, looking surprised and afraid.

"You're leaving home today," he said. "I'll go with you. You can pack while I explain to your mother."

"My mother? No, Teddy, you can't—"

"You have to understand that she's part of the problem, girl."

Surely Marlene had figured that out for herself. But, even a bad mother is still your mother. If you didn't have that, there wasn't much left to hold onto.

"I don't have anywhere to go?"

"Yes you do. You'll stay with one of the kindest people I've ever known."

The approaching black storm cloud and the cool breeze that preceded it amplified the chore waiting for him at the Sutton home. Nevertheless, Ted was determined to get the girl to safety.

"I'm scared, Teddy."

"Of course," he said. "We can't let fear stop us. Let's get moving."

Ted was feeling some apprehension, but was determined to press on. They picked up the pace. As they neared Marlene's house, the rain was coming down in sheets. They both ran through the deluge.

"My mother is going to have a screaming fit," Marlene yelled over the sound of the rain.

"And right after that she will co-operate," he said, with more confidence than he actually felt.

"She'll jump all over me about it," Marlene said. Both were eager to get in out of the weather, but Marlene hesitated going into the house, obviously afraid of what was coming.

They made it to the porch.

"While I'm talking to your mother," Ted said, "you pack the basics to take with you . . . enough clothes for, say, a week. We can pick up anything else later, with an adult present if there's trouble."

"What will I tell her?"

"One thing you will *not* tell her is where you're going."

"How—"

"Because Joel would no doubt find out and come looking for you. What he has been doing is a crime of violence and control. When denied that he is likely to take it out on you and your mother . . . and the friends I'm asking for help. I can't risk that. Now let me handle this."

The first thing Ted noticed upon entering the Sutton household was the smell; a sour combination of stale cigarette smoke and rancid cooking odors that permeated the drapes, carpets, and the mismatched furniture's upholstery. Marlene apparently isolated her school clothes from the rest of the house because he had never noticed those smells in her presence.

The house was a perfect match with the woman it was Marlene's bad fortune to have assigned as her mother.

Ted stepped into the entryway. Mrs. Sutton stared at them. "What are *you* doing here?" she snapped at him.

The woman was missing an upper front tooth. She wore a grease-stained housecoat that fell open, revealing a dirty slip with strings hanging down from it. She may have been pretty at one time, but years of smoking, drinking, overeating, physical abuse, and despair had erased all that. Mrs. Sutton possessed few social graces and had absolutely no sense of style.

There was a greenish-yellow bruise below her left eye, possibly the fading result of a punch delivered by an angry right-hander.

"What I want," Ted said, "is a better life for your daughter."

"What are you talking about?" she demanded.

"Go, Marlene," he said.

The girl practically ran down the hallway to her room.

"Who do you think you are, coming into my house, ordering my daughter around?"

"Mrs. Sutton," he said, "I'll make this real simple for you. Your boyfriend has been molesting Marlene."

The woman took in a breath, but quickly recovered. "You're a liar."

As the storm raged outside, the storm inside was picking up intensity.

Ted's patience was taking a beating. "It's a fact. Furthermore, you know it."

"I don't believe you," she said without conviction.

"Denying it won't help. I'm taking Marlene with me."

"You can't just walk in here and tell me you're taking my daughter away."

"If you make trouble, I guarantee I will see that you are charged with allowing her to be abused."

The woman suddenly looked less certain than when Ted first arrived.

"Joel's gonna want some answers when he gets back," she said.

"Tell him whatever you like." Then Ted had another thought. "Or tell him nothing at all. If I were you, I'd plan to be somewhere else when he returns."

"How'd you like it if I called the cops and told them you kidnapped my kid?"

Ted smiled at the idea. What was it about the guilty parties that made them think getting the law involved would work out well for them?

"I'd like it just fine," he said, taking a step toward her. "Because that would give me the perfect excuse to turn you in for child endangerment and watch them haul you off to jail."

The woman jumped back as though she had been struck in the face.

"I'm her mother," she said, wide-eyed and close to crying. "I have a right to know where my daughter is going."

"If you don't know where she is, he won't be able to beat it out of you. I doubt that he's a man who takes 'no' for an answer."

She raised her arms. At first Ted thought she was positioning herself for a physical attack on him. But her hands went to the top of her head, the way some people do when stressed.

"Now here's how it's going to be," Ted said. "I am taking Marlene to a place where she will be safe. It will be her decision if or when you ever see her again. I'm guessing that won't be until you learn how to be a mother who can be trusted with her welfare. I haven't seen any evidence of that."

Ted knew Marlene also had a few things to learn. First, that sex is supposed to be pleasurable. But not at the hands of someone not entitled to the privilege. She had to understand that unauthorized interference with nature's gift is not acceptable . . . that it was the trespasser's fault, not hers.

Marlene stood listening to the exchange, two suitcases in hand.

"I'm ready," she said.

"Marlene," her mother said. "How can you do this to me?"

"Do this to *you?*" Marlene said, practically screaming. "I told you about it . . . not in so many words. You knew what I was meant, but you didn't believe me. You were too busy looking out for yourself. I should be asking how you could do that to *me.*"

Marlene was sobbing as Ted picked up her suitcases. He led her outside, leaving her mother behind, looking defeated.

When they got to the sidewalk she said, "I'm so scared."

It had stopped raining. The sun sparkled off wet surfaces and cast strong shadows.

"There are better days ahead," he said. "I don't just mean the weather. Think of this as the storm before the calm."

Ted looked behind him to be sure Marlene's mother had not followed them. He did not want to give her any hint as to where he was taking her daughter.

They walked around the corner, out of view of the house. A car was waiting.

Marlene spotted the driver, who reached across and opened the passenger side door.

"Mrs. Simpson?" I had no idea—"

"Hello Marlene," the teacher said. "Get in front with me."

Marlene hesitated.

Ted said, "Go on. Get in." He put her bags in the trunk and climbed into the back seat. "I enlisted Mrs. Simpson's help. I told her the basic facts about the problem you were having at home. You can share any details you want. Up to you."

"You'll stay with Alice and me, honey," Mrs. Simpson said. She put a comforting hand on Marlene's arm. "For as long as it takes to keep you safe."

Marlene had once again taken on that trapped look . . . stuck between an intolerable home situation and her difficulty with trusting anyone.

Sensing Marlene's fear, the teacher patted the girl on her arm.

Grace Simpson had added further to the reasons she was on Ted's very short list of favorite people in both of his worlds.

Why, he wondered, couldn't he have met her in his own time? Of course, there was this little matter of the time-space continuum thing.

CHAPTER 33

ALICE WAS WAITING IN THE LIVING ROOM WHEN MARLENE entered the Simpson's home. She was smiling.

Marlene looked nervous as she scanned the room, no doubt feeling out of place. She had only known Mrs. Simpson as her English teacher . . . and barely knew her daughter at all, beyond passing Alice in the school hallways. Despite the Simpsons' willingness to help her, Marlene had little experience with the family.

From Ted's perspective, however, entering the Simpson home sent a warm wave of welcome flowing over him. It was a house filled with pictures, knick-knacks, and furniture of no particular era or theme. It was a collection of items that reflected the openness and acceptance of the Simpsons, themselves.

Family mementos included a plaster of Paris impression of a hand. It sat on a lamp table with the words, "Alice Simpson, Age six-and-one-half" printed in a child's block letters. Framed Alice Simpson artworks were proudly displayed in quality frames on the walls. They ranged from stick figures drawn when she was a small child to more recent depictions of people, animals, and objects that demonstrated emerging artistic talent. The girl had artfully channeled her frustrations onto paper and canvas. By framing and hanging the work, Alice's mother had reinforced how much her daughter was valued.

Noticeably absent from the displays were pictures of the errant husband-father. It would take some time before he could be forgiven for his transgressions . . . if ever.

In any other home the assortment might have come off as a hodgepodge. In this one it told the visitor, 'come on in and make yourself at home'.

Ted wondered if the comfort he was feeling was shared by Marlene. He assumed that, despite the terrible conditions Marlene had been living under, there had been a kind of perverse comfort in the familiarity of it. Despite what now appeared to be the promise of something better, it was understandable that the unknown would still be unsettling.

Knowing the Simpsons as he did, Ted was certain any apprehension would not last for long.

"Welcome home, honey," Mrs. Simpson said, putting an arm on Marlene's shoulder. Alice picked up one of Marlene's suitcases and took the girl by the hand.

"Mrs. Simpson," Marlene said. "Alice. . . I don't know what to say."

"Don't thank me yet. I'm not a great cook."

"Yes she is," Alice said. "Come on Marlene, I'll show you your room." Alice turned and walked toward the stairs.

Marlene leaned over and whispered to Mrs. Simpson, "Does Alice know?"

"No," she said quietly. "I told her there were problems at your home. She would never ask on her own. I will say, however, you could not have a better confidante than Alice. I'll leave that to you."

"Marlene," Ted said. "I would trust Mrs. Simpson and Alice with my life. Anything you tell either one won't go anywhere."

Mrs. Simpson refused Ted's offer of money toward the cost of having another mouth to feed.

Ted thought he should get out of there before the girl talk started. With a wave, he walked toward the door.

"Come back here young man," Mrs. Simpson called to him.

"You're not gonna make me sit in a corner are you, teacher?" he said with a laugh.

"Far from it Ted . . . you're my hero," she said, giving him a hug.

"Mine too, Marlene said, joining the hug. It was not the faux sexpot Marlene or the fantasy girl of Ted's youth. It was a simple, warm expression of gratitude from one friend to another.

A three-way hug was very nice.

Alice ran back down the steps and hopped into the tangle to make it four.

As one proficient in the field of mathematics, Ted could say with some authority there was absolutely nothing the equal of a hug to the fourth power.

CHAPTER 34

TED HEARD HIS FATHER'S WOODWORKING EQUIPMENT down in the basement and decided he couldn't put off a confrontation with the man any longer. He opened the door to the cigarette smoke-filled basement that was his father's workshop-hideaway.

Ted was not sure what he would say after all these years. Ed McBride had continued to be critical of Ted and push him away. The last time Ted saw his father before he died, Ed still treated him as an unwanted child. The pain of rejection lingered.

When Ted cautioned his mother about his father's health problem he was not sure if he cared enough to head off the catastrophe he knew was coming. His main concern was for his mother and sister. They'd had hard financial times after Ed's death. For lack of money Emily did not get a college education. Ted had won a full academic scholarship and had a paid teaching assistant job. He went on to get his masters degree, then his doctorate. With college behind him he was making a decent living as a teacher. He helped his mother to the extent she would allow it. He even offered to help his sister, but Emily's feelings toward him were such that she did not want to be obligated.

Ted tried not to hate his father. He would certainly never have associated with any random individual who had treated him as coldly. Still, there was that biological connection, regardless of all that had happened.

If he had been physically beaten, he might have felt free to hate.

Ted paused at the cellar door. He let out a long sigh before he started down the stairs, remembering his father's attitudes of long ago.

But university computer science professor Ted McBride was not a child on this day and he resolved not to allow himself to be dismissed.

A length of wood turning on the lathe was becoming a spindle for the back of a partially assembled rocking chair sitting on a table along the foundation wall.

Although the wood was unfinished and the chair back pieces were not yet completely fitted together, it was clear that a beautiful, artfully-crafted piece of furniture was coming to life. There was a gentleness in the subtle curves of the work, reminiscent of Shaker pieces, yet unlike anything Ted had ever seen before.

Why hadn't I noticed this the first time around?

Ted had never thought of his father as a gentle person. Nor had he been aware that Ed McBride had any creative talent.

Blue smoke from Ed's unfiltered Lucky Strike circled upward, into his eyes, contributing to the dark circles under them.

"Yes?" Ed said over his shoulder, not turning to face his son. "What is it?"

"Just wanted to see what you were doing," Ted said. He had to fight back feelings that had eaten away at him over the years. He gave up on any close relationship long before he went out on his own. The hostility continued until Ed's death, just a few years from the *Now* Ted was experiencing.

In those final years, Ted viewed any effort on his part to patch up the relationship as unproductive. Yet there was some oddity in human nature that nagged at children and made them continue to hope they could please their parents, no matter how remote . . . and even cruel . . . they may have been. The hopes and regrets often went on long after a parent's death, well past the point when the child was no longer a child and resolution was no longer possible.

"I don't see much of you," Ted said. "I'm just getting out of bed when you come home from work . . . and I'm in school all day."

"Well, that's the graveyard shift for you." Ed said curtly. He returned his attention to the project. "It pays better, but it doesn't leave much time for anything else."

The bitterness was evident in his words and body language. Ted pushed onward.

"I guess it's a pretty hard job. Dangerous, too." Ted had heard stories of railroaders injured and killed on the job.

Ted's words seemed to take his father by surprise. Ed reached over and shut down the lathe. As it spun to a stop he took a long drag on his cigarette and inhaled deeply before he answered.

"Sometimes it's physically hard," he said. "Sometimes it's dangerous. Mostly it's boring as hell. That's probably the hardest part."

"We've never talked about your work."

Ed looked more closely at his son than Ted could recall his ever having done before.

"I've often wished I could do something different for a living," Ed said. "There aren't many choices for a man with only a high school education. No work except the railroad."

Ted let the words settle. He was surprised at the ease with which the conversation had gone from hostility to an actual exchange. Ted realized he had never considered Ed's side of the story. Ted's own experience as a parent were similar in some ways. He often felt as though he was laboring for an unappreciative family. The difference was that there was some enjoyment to be had in Ted's chosen field. There was certainly no physical danger in what he did for a living.

Ted found himself asking questions he had not had the courage to ask years before. He realized the answers could have changed both of their lives.

"I never appreciated the sacrifices you've made for us," Ted said, surprised that he genuinely meant it. "I've taken you for granted."

For a moment Ted thought he might have seen moisture in his father's eyes. Ed covered it up with a deep drag on his cigarette.

"We've never talked like this Teddy."

"Dad, we hardly talk at all in recent years. Even when we did speak it was mostly criticism. Mostly you've treated me like something you're stuck with."

"Am I like that?"

"Yeah, you are," he said without hesitation.

Neither said anything for awhile, each silently inspecting the other.

Ted took a closer look at the chair his father was giving birth to. Wood was being transformed into something more than furniture. It was aesthetically pleasing; sturdy, yet not clunky. The elegant curves were the result of a keen eye and a skilled hand.

"You say you have often thought of doing something different for a living." Ted said, running his hands over the smooth wood. "You could turn furniture making into a business."

"No time," Ed said.

"You're working on something now. If you didn't have to work on the railroad, those hours could be spent on what you like doing. You could just as easily build something for sale as for recreation."

"Nobody outside the family has ever seen my work."

"Maybe it's time to let the world know there is a new artist in town."

Ed actually smiled at his son. Ted could not remember the last time that had happened.

"Teddy, you've grown up and I've missed it."

He had missed more of Ted's growing up than he could possibly have imagined. The son was actually older than the father.

"You've had a lot on your mind, Dad. You should change to a less stressful line of work."

"The choices are the same as always," Ed said. "You work on the railroad or you sleep under a bridge. No, I'll take my pleasure from my woodworking as a hobby."

". . . and resign yourself to a life of quiet desperation." Realizing he was again sounding like an adult, Ted quickly added, "Henry David Thoreau wrote that in 'Walden'. We had it in literature class."

"Are you sure you're only fifteen years old?"

Ted considered briefly how much he should tell him, but rejected the idea.

"A different line of work would be healthier," Ted said. "And a lot safer."

"I already have a job. You and Emily have the job of growing up to be good citizens. Mine is to earn the living while you do that. Some day it will be your turn."

Ed McBride had no way of knowing that Ted had already learned that lesson.

In the days following their cellar session it became a priority for Ted to spend time with his father. To his amazement, Ed showed him how to use some of his workshop equipment. When his father occasionally became impatient, Ted was quick to point it out.

Ted began to actually look forward to Ed McBride's arrival from work each day, joining him for breakfast and brief conversation. Their time together was not without abrasive moments, but both were learning to put those aside. Ill feelings that had accumulated would take some time to heal. Each had made a start.

Learning some of the secrets of converting wood into fine furniture was a small part of the time Ted spent with his father. The real value was in Ted's getting to know this unhappy man as one who had put his own life on hold for the benefit of his family.

The solution to Ed's quandary had been right there in front of him. Just as John Wilson was afraid to take chances with his life savings for fear of losing what he already had, Ted's father was not able to make the leap that could change his life.

CHAPTER 35

IT WAS SATURDAY AFTERNOON. Ted was helping his mother in the kitchen when his father approached him.

"Teddy," Ed McBride said, "you wouldn't happen to know where the rocking chair is that I just finished."

"Yes I do," he said. "I stole it."

Ed looked intently at his son and Ted could see the anger building.

"Until this morning," Ted said, "it was sitting in a shop in the city that specialized in fine furniture."

An older boy with a driver's license and a pickup truck had helped him take the chair to the store.

Ed McBride looked at his son with disbelief. "You had no right, Teddy—"

"I did have a responsibility, though."

For a moment Ted thought his father might strike him.

"We're going there right now and get it back," Ed said.

"Too late. It's not there any more," Ted said. He reached into his shirt pocket, took out an envelope and handed it to his father.

"What's this?"

"Open it," Ted said.

Ed hesitated. Then he snatched the envelope from his son's hand.

He tore open the flap. Inside was a crisp new fifty-dollar bill. Ted had gotten it at the bank in exchange for the worn, smaller denominations the furniture store manager had given him.

"What is this money for?"

"The store owner sold the chair just minutes after I got to the place," Ted said. "The buyer couldn't believe his good luck."

Fifty dollars in the 1960s was equal to five or six times the buying power in Ted's future time. It was a good percentage of what his dad made on the railroad for a week of risking his neck.

"It's proof you could change your life if you wanted to."

"You sold my rocking chair? For fifty dollars?"

"More than that, actually. The store got a commission."

"I was going to give that chair to your grandmother."

"I guess you'll just have to make another one for her. Then you'll make more chairs and other furniture for people who know quality when they see it. By the way, the store owner wants more chairs. I told the guy the artisan—that's what I called you—the artisan makes very few of them and is particular about who he sells his work to. He has to be sure they get a good home. If people think not everybody can have something, everybody will want one."

"You should have asked me."

"You would have said no. I would not have been able to convince you that your work had merit. Dad, you have a skill that could change your future. You have a chance to do something you enjoy doing . . . and that won't risk your life and health."

The anger was fading noticeably as Ed seemed to be considering the possibilities. Ted wondered whether his father had ever seen a fifty-dollar bill before, let alone held one in his hands that actually belonged to him.

"Do you forgive me for taking your chair, Dad?"

Ed McBride smiled. "My son is a thief."

Ted smiled, too. "I'm sure you mean that in the nicest possible way."

CHAPTER 36

Ted had phoned the county's Senior Deputy District Attorney to bring her up-to-date about Marlene's being in a secure place. Margaret Tuttle was given Marlene's former address and the approximate time Joel Snyder was expected to return from Philadelphia.

"We'll take it from here," Tuttle told him.

"I should be there to identify Joel."

Tuttle agreed and told him where to meet the deputy.

Ted was apprehensive as he waited with Sam Hoffman, a large, slow-talking plainclothes sheriff's deputy. They sat in an unmarked car parked within sight of the Sutton home. A second deputy was inside the residence, hidden from view.

Marlene's mother had taken Ted's warning seriously. She was not at home on the day Joel was scheduled to return.

"You see," Deputy Hoffman said, "people think police work is all shootin' and car chases and like that. But most of what we do is just like this; sittin' in a hot car waitin' for bad guys to show up."

"And sweating," Ted said, mopping a flood of perspiration off his face.

"Yeah, we do a lot of that, too. And going door-to-door asking questions. The movies got it all wrong."

"You sure have to have a lot of patience," Ted said.

"You could sit here for three minutes or three hours or three days."

Just then a car Ted recognized went by and pulled up to the curb in front of the Sutton home.

"That's our guy," Ted said.

Joel got his suitcase out of the car and went inside.

Ted and Hoffman hurried to the house and stationed themselves in the yard just in time to see Joel come blasting out the front door. He apparently spotted the inside deputy and took off.

They stood directly in line with the fleeing man's escape route. Ted stuck his foot out and sent Joel sprawling. It didn't take much effort to trip someone whose upper body was angled so far forward of the lower half. The man landed on his hands and face, skidding on the rough sidewalk, straight into the size twelve shoes of Deputy Hoffman.

The lawman looked down at the pathetic creature whose nose looked as though it had been raked with a rasp.

"Beats me why they run," the big man said. "We always get 'em. Coulda saved himself an extra charge of resistin' arrest . . . and a skint nose."

As Hoffman handcuffed him, Snyder looked back at Ted with undisguised hatred. "You? You bastard," he screamed. "What business is this of yours?"

Ted laughed. "You're right. It wasn't my *business*, Joel," he said. "It was my *pleasure*."

It would be several years before police would be required to read the Miranda perp speech to suspects. So Deputy Hoffman simply said, "Mr. Snyder, you are under arrest on suspicion of child molestation and child endangerment."

"This isn't over," Snyder shouted as he was being shoved, not too gently, into the unmarked car.

"Deputy Hoffman," Ted said, "maybe you can explain to Joel just how 'over' it is."

"I will be very happy to, young man," the lawman said. Turning to Joel he said, "It's *over*, dipshit."

"That should cover it," Ted said.

As it turned out, Snyder was not Joel's real name. A fingerprint search revealed his identity as Joel Sanders, a parolee with a criminal record that included, to no one's surprise, sexual abuse of a minor.

The law required convicted sex offenders to report their whereabouts after their release, which Joel had not. Then there was the matter of the regular check-ins with his parole officer as a condition of release, which he had also neglected. Mr. Snyder-Sanders had compounded his crimes as well as his sins. Violating parole and adding to his record as a pervert meant he would be going away for a long time.

While awaiting trial, Marlene's abuser would be restrained behind heavy steel doors. Two-foot-thick stone walls at the county jail would keep him nicely separated from the civilized world until he could be tried, convicted, and sent to state prison where he would be guarded by ill-tempered men who outweighed him by a considerable margin and were highly skilled in dealing with his ilk. He would serve out the remainder of his previous sentence even before he began serving whatever sentence a judge imposed for any new convictions.

Ted had been assured that a deposition by Marlene would be sufficient for the trial. Joel's lawyer could make any challenges to her testimony in private. Marlene would not have to appear in open court. Because of her age, her name would not be made public.

Even with Marlene's tormentor gone, living in her mother's house would still not have been the best environment. Her mother would no doubt continue her lifelong habit of hooking up with losers. The cycle would continue. But it would go on without the child she had permitted to be damaged.

With some reservations, Ted allowed himself to believe that at least one of his targeted problems had been solved . . . or was in the works.

But time was running out and there were still some fences to mend.

CHAPTER 37

He had always described her as a 'royal pain in the ass'. Still, Emily was his sister and he was no longer fifteen years old. Not inside his head, anyway. Therefore, the responsibility was on Ted to overcome youthful hostilities that drove them apart into adulthood.

She was sitting in the living room with her nose in a book.

"Hi baby sister," he said.

"Huh?" she said, puzzled, scrunching up her face.

"Just checking to see how you're doing."

The difference in their ages put her well out of his peer group. They had little in common beyond genetics, parentage, and shared living space. They had always irritated each other. Not unusual among siblings mismatched in age and gender.

"Why do you care? You've never cared how I was doing before."

"Yes," he said. "And shame on me."

In hindsight he realized that he, as the eldest by five years, had an unfair head start on the affections of parents and grandparents. There had been time for the elders to accumulate more pictures on the mantle of first-born Ted than of second-born Emily. Ted had been a cute baby with naturally curly hair. His sister started life as a bouncing baby prune. She had facial features all the wrong size and erratically arranged. Ted was already beginning to lose the cuteness and would eventually lose most of the hair. Emily would one day grow into her face, fill out in all those feminine places and become what guys would later regard as a 'hottie'.

For Emily it was not unlike trying to catch a train that had already left the station. Although she would never admit it, she was jealous. Ted resolved to try to repair the damage.

As basic as it sounded, self-improvement could not begin any sooner than right now.

"Howzabout a movie this Saturday?"

She looked at him in complete disbelief.

"Are you sick Teddy?"

"Feel fine. You?"

"You hate taking me to the movies."

"Oh, you must mean because ever since you were six years old and Mom made me take you with me and you talked all the way through the show and you wouldn't listen to me and I yelled at you for getting too close to traffic . . . stuff like that?"

Emily did not have a reasonable answer, so she resorted to her old standard.

"You're not my boss."

"You were my responsibility. I always worried about you."

"You didn't have to yell at me . . . or hit me."

She had him there. It certainly wasn't the adult thing to do. He admitted he should probably have been more understanding, even then.

"All right, I won't yell . . . or hit. Now, how about that movie?"

"You usually go with that awful Charlie Freeman."

Yeah, why was that?

"I guess I just felt the need for the company of someone I preferred to spend time with. Charlie isn't on the list. So . . . how about it?"

Still looking dazed, she said, "Um . . . well . . . okay."

"And you get to pick the movie."

They rode the bus to the city together. Emily's choice of a film was one that he wondered in the years since why anyone would ever pay actual money to see it. He had the feeling someone sat in a movie company's cafeteria and wrote the dialog on napkins. Ted had seen it before. It starred a lot of people who would be dead by the 21st century. The film ran . . . will run . . . constantly on late night cable TV in his future existence. But employing all the technical expertise in the world would not make it anything but a really lousy movie.

Of course, the film wasn't the object.

To his amazement he only had to ask her once not to talk during the show. Rather than poke her as he might once have done, he just put his arm around her, leaned in, kissed her on top of her pigtailed head, gave her a squeeze, and simply said 'shhh'. To his utter flabbergastment, Ted did not hear another chirp out of her all the way to the end of the picture.

"You were great," he told her later, as they walked back to the bus stop.

She reached up and took him by the hand. That had never happened before.

"I guess this means you're not going to run out into traffic and I won't have to bop you."

She giggled and nodded at the same time.

It had been a good day. Ted found himself starting to like this little girl who once bothered the crap out of him.

Their relationship through the years had only gotten worse, reaching toxic levels by the time she was in her thirties. Ted knew that if he had waited until Emily was older for him to make an effort to change their relationship it probably would not have worked. By then her bitterness would have been too locked-in for her to change. At just ten years old, Emily was more flexible. It was easier for Ted, too, since this was the youthful version of the woman he had become so estranged from.

Ted wondered how he had missed opportunities to improve his little sister's childhood and beyond. All it would have taken was an occasional hug, a kind word, and some generosity on his part. From this vantage point he could see how easily a life could be ruined by the things he did . . . as well as the things he did not do.

Later that evening, Ted was reading when Emily showed up at his room.

"What's up Em?"

"I gotta do my homework. Can I borrow a pencil?"

"Sure," he said. "They're in my top desk drawer."

She gave him a confused look.

"You don't need to ask," he said. "Just help yourself anytime you need a pencil."

Emily went to the desk timidly. In that previous life Ted had defended his property as though it were important.

"Anything else you need?"

Unaccustomed to brotherly support, she hesitated.

"Do you think . . ." she said, ". . . you could help me with my arithmetic?"

Now there was a surprise of jaw-dropping proportions.

"That's the first time you've ever asked me for help."

She shrugged.

"I guess I haven't been as nice to you as I should have been."

More shrugging.

"Get yourself over here, girl. Let's work on it."

Her eyes went to high beam. She hopped onto the bed beside him and they spent a delightful time that even managed to squeeze some arithmetic in among the laughs.

Their mother heard the laughter and looked in on the miracle taking place.

The experience probably helped Emily with her studies, but arithmetic was the least of it for both of them. It began to change how he regarded his little sister. It seemed to have done the same for her.

Even smart guys don't always do the smartest things.

CHAPTER 38

CHARLIE AND TED WERE WALKING TO THEIR MORNING CLASSES when a spitball struck Ted on the back of his head. One of Ted's traditional enemies, a large, tough-looking boy named Wally Baumgardner, walked by, laughing hysterically.

"I'll see you after school, faggot," Baumgardner shouted.

"Not today, Wally," Ted called after the boy. "Make an appointment with my secretary."

Wally stopped dead, his mouth went to half mast. So did Charlie's.

"Christ, Teddy," Charlie said. "He's gonna beat the crap outta you for that."

"He's going to *try*, Charlie."

"Are you crazy?"

Ted chuckled and they walked on down the hallway.

Wally was a mass of muscle and meanness. He hung out with other chronic losers and preyed upon those who were small or lacked confidence. The original Ted had been a tailor-made candidate for Wally Baumgardner's abuse. Wally had flunked two grades on the way to his sophomore year. That put him two years behind in school and two years ahead of his classmates in physical growth. He could legally have quit school if his parents would sign for him. But they apparently preferred knowing he was someone else's responsibility for at least part of every day.

Baumgardner was the type who would jump off the low end of the seesaw when someone was on the high end. He had been caught torturing a cat the previous summer. A serial killer in the making.

Wally got perverse pleasure from intimidating Clark Erickson. Clark was a frail boy whom Baumgardner delighted in calling names that implied an unacceptable sexual preference.

When Clark was at the drinking fountain, Wally would push the boy's face down into the spouting water. "Sorry Miss Erickson," Baumgardner would call out for all to hear. Clark would simply mop the water from his face with a handkerchief, resign himself to the taunt and slink away.

The bully often lobbed rubber band-launched paper wads at the back of Clark's head. Occasionally he would walk up behind him and bump the back of the boy's knees with his own knees and then give him a push.

"What's the matter, Miss Priss?" Baumgardner would say when Clark's legs buckled and he fell down. "Can't stand on your own two feet?" Then he would laugh loudly, not caring whether anyone in authority heard him, daring them to expel him from school. He didn't want to be there anyway. Clark was not inclined to fight, nor was he physically capable of defending himself against someone so large and so devoted to violence. Wally knew Clark would get no help from others who were afraid they would also become targets. Even some of the teachers were reluctant to challenge him.

In his adolescence, Ted had been among those who suffered Wally Baumgardner's assaults.

Clark was the only male student in the Home Economics class. The course included knitting. Ted happened to be near the school entrance at lunchtime when Baumgardner spotted the knitting needles and yarn jutting out of Clark's tote bag. He snatched them away.

"Only girls and sissy boys knit," Baumgardner taunted. He held the materials out of reach, dancing around in cruel imitation of Clark's mannerisms as the boy tried to get it back.

It was too much for Ted. He knew that in the future Clark would commit suicide. The man who was currently living inside teen Ted's head could not allow the abuse to continue.

Ted walked behind Wally and bumped the back of the bully's knees the way he had seen it done so often to Clark. An extra push on the back of the lummox's shirt sent him crashing to the rough dirt. Wally was so surprised that he just sat there, stunned.

Ted took the knitting materials out of Wally's hands and handed them to Clark.

"What's the matter little girl?" Ted said, facing Wally and walking around the boy. "Can't you stand on your own two feet?"

A crowd was gathering.

Unaccustomed to anyone ever doing anything but backing away or quivering in fear, Wally lost what was supposed to pass for a smile and struggled to stand up.

"Oh . . . my goodness," Ted said, shrinking back in mock fear, hands to his cheeks. "Wally is getting to his feet. Whatever shall I do now? Dear me . . . you're not going to hurt me are you, Wally?" Then Ted walked up to the bully and gave him a lightning-fast double slap to his face.

Baumgardner started to reach out with his right hand, but Ted pulled the arm aside with his own right hand. At the same time, he wrapped his left arm across the front of the boy's neck and, with his left leg behind Wally's right leg he pushed him to the dirt once more. As Wally lay there, Ted bent down, grabbed him by the collar and slapped the boy twice across the face again with a sound that reverberated throughout the school grounds.

Baumgardner's eyes darted left and right, apparently looking for support from among the onlookers. He got none.

Ted slowly circled behind the young thug and whacked him hard on the back of his head. "You're not gonna cry, are you Miss Baumgardner? Boo-hoo," Ted taunted. "We expect more from our mouth-breathing, knuckle-draggers, Wally."

Two male teachers walked by. Mr. Collins took a step toward the boys, apparently to try to break up the confrontation. But Ted looked up to see that Mr. Ballard held up a hand to stop Collins and shook his head to warn the teacher to stay out of it.

None in the gathering crowd had ever before seen Baumgardner looking afraid. Ted wanted to batter Wally's face so his own mother would not recognize him, but the boy had lost more status by being slapped than if he had been punched. Ted settled for several more weak slaps and a curled fist promising more.

Remember Ted, you're an adult.

Ted shook a finger at him. "I've often suspected you were a coward, Wally," he said, growing very serious. "Now stand up. Let's see what you've got." But Wally stayed where he was, rubbing his reddened face.

"Stand up, Baumgardner." Ted demanded. But Wally cringed and remained where he was.

Ted bent down, his face just inches from Baumgardner's face, his fist reared back as if to deliver an actual punch. Ted's eyes had fire in them as he stared without wavering and whispered, "Don't ever do that to Clark or anyone else again, Wally. I'll be watching." Ted gently patted Wally's cheeks and turned his back on the boy, like a matador daring the bull to charge. He joined Clark, who stood in awe of what had just happened.

The people Wally had expected to put on a show for were smiling and talking among themselves, clearly delighted to learn that the scourge of Carbonville High School had been given a large dose of what he had been handing out. The most timid among them would forever feel stronger. If Ted could conquer Goliath, maybe they also had less to fear.

"Clark," Ted said, loud enough for his new fan club to hear, "you knit?"

Clark nodded shyly.

"That's great. You think you could teach me sometime?"

Ted put his arm around the boy's shoulder. They walked together as the crowd stood watching.

"Thank you Mr. Ballard," Ted said quietly as he passed the two teachers.

"No, Ted," Ballard said. "Thank *you*."

It was refreshing for Ted to see that there were adults who appreciated seeing the bully get long-deserved lumps.

When they got inside the building and away from others, the dispirited boy said. "Aren't you afraid you might catch it, Teddy?"

Ted looked directly at Clark.

"Which 'it' do you mean Clark?" Ted said. "About fifteen-percent of the American public is dyslexic; an estimated four percent is openly gay and ten-percent or so is left-handed."

The boy seemed to be considering a grin.

"Clark!" Ted blurted out, shrinking back in fake horror. They both stopped with a screech of sneakers.

"Wh—"

"You're not left-handed are you?"

"No," he said.

"Boy, that's a relief. I was afraid you meant I'd come down with a case of left-handedness."

Some of the boy's stress had lessened and he risked a small smile. It soon faded. "I've never told anyone about . . . you know . . ."

Ted looked around to be certain no one else could hear and said, "I'm honored that you would confide that in me, Clark. Now let me tell you something. '*It*' is not catching, nor do you need to feel ashamed. These kids are reflecting their own parents' prejudices. Some Christians are busy putting their noses into other people's business instead of doing the good their religion requires of them. They make judgments that are not theirs to make. They've decided that when something is not average, it's abnormal . . . even evil. Don't believe it. You're a good young man. Preference has no bearing on goodness. Build on that. Make a life for yourself.

"Until the world wises up it's going to be tough for you. There are others out there who also believe there's no one else in the world like them. Find them and be happy. Nature makes mistakes, Clark, but that describes Wally Baumgardner, not you. Don't let misfits like him destroy your life."

Clark smiled weakly.

Ted patted the boy on the back and said, "If you need someone to talk to, I'm here. And no one but you and I will ever know what we talked about."

Clark nodded slowly and went off to his class.

Ted knew the boy was grateful that someone had stood up for him publicly. But the sting would no doubt linger because of attitudes held by those who had decided he was somehow inferior.

"You haven't gone queer on me, have you, Teddy?" Charlie Freeman said.

Ted knew what Charlie was talking about, but decided not to respond.

"That business with Clark," Charlie said.

"Clark is a good kid, Charlie."

"He's a fairy, Teddy. I'm thinking of nominating him for prom queen."

"Well, even if that were true, it has nothing to do with the quality of the person. Sometimes I have to wonder where the hell your values are, Charlie."

"I don't understand you, Teddy. The past couple of weeks you're . . . different. You need to get your head on straight."

"One of us sure does," Ted said.

Charlie didn't get it and never would. His lack of ethical development was firmly entrenched, like a cancer that had spread too far to be cured. His downward spiral was as irreversible as Wally Baumgardner's. Charlie was in a 'me' mode; dedicated to making up for all he lacked in his own life, even if it meant he had to diminish others.

Charlie shook his head and went away, their relationship never to be the same. Ted wondered why he had not figured that out way back . . . now.

After school Ted spotted a crowd of young people along a wall outside the building. He took a closer look and found Wally Baumgardner with his back to the bricks. George Warren, Alf Miller, and Mickey Wolfson, three of Wally's traditional victims, were on the edge of violence. The victims had become the victors as the pendulum swung wildly the other way.

None of the boys had touched Wally, but it was clear the big oaf sensed pain was imminent. The worms had turned.

As much as he believed Baumgardner deserved the worst his victims could dish out, Ted was more concerned at the moment for the turned worms.

"What's going on, fellas?" Ted said, stepping through a gap in their audience.

"Hey Teddy," George Warren said with respect in his voice. "Wally jumped Mickey, so we jumped *him*."

"I guess you needed a refresher course, Wally," Ted said, leading the boys away from the cowering bully.

Wally used the break to his advantage and fled. The crowd of onlookers quickly dissipated.

"I'm worried about you guys," he said.

Surprised, Alf said, "Worried about us? You should worry about Baumgardner."

"I'm worried about him too, but for public safety reasons," Ted said. "Look, he's a bully and a rat and he deserves some of what he's getting now. But revenge will hurt you more than him."

"Teddy," George said, "Wally was beating on Mickey. We ganged up on him. He has pushed us around since the third grade. Isn't it time we did some pushing?"

The sentiment could not entirely be denied, but Ted's personal experience told him otherwise.

"Self defense is one thing, but you can't let yourself become what you hate in Baumgardner."

"He has it coming."

"Maybe. But you don't"

"Huh?"

"You deserve to have one less bully in your life. You have that. You found out that guys like Wally are mostly full of wind. But you have the right idea about getting a lot of you together against guys like Wally."

"You mean we should gang up on him?" Alf said.

"Not in the way you probably mean it, but there is strength in numbers. It's important that you never be the aggressor."

"What then?"

"If you hear of someone being a victim, you and your fellow former targets should get together and surround the guy."

"We're not fighters," George said.

"Of course not, and it is unlikely you will ever have to fight. If you did, it would be over in seconds. Picture a couple of dozen fists pounding on one guy who has only two fists. Collectively you're an overwhelming force that only an idiot would take on."

"There are at least a dozen guys that Wally and some others like him have pushed around," George said.

"And a dozen against one is pretty scary odds, isn't it? Look at what three of you just did. Imagine what it would be like with all those."

"Kind of like . . . like . . . vigilantes," Alf suggested.

"Yes," Ted said, "but without the lynching."

George thought about that for a moment. "I kinda like the idea of the lynching," he said.

Ted knew pretty much how the boy felt, having been a victim of Wally Baumgardner himself.

"But this way you won't have to do anything except be united. If those thugs think they'll suffer the wrath of the Carbonville Vigilantes, I doubt they'll try anything like that again."

Ted knew the boys would continue to enjoy their newfound power before returning to their gentler ways. He thought it would be interesting to see how it played out. Meanwhile, the incident gave him an idea. He had some shopping to do.

CHAPTER 39

THE NEXT DAY TED BROUGHT A BOX TO SCHOOL. He found Alf Miller and handed him the box. It contained a dozen whistles of the type police use. Alf looked inside, then at Ted, confused.

"What are these for?"

"Give one to each of the vigilantes. Make it clear to them that they are only to use it when they're actually being threatened. When they hear that, they all come running."

"What if we're in class when we hear a whistle?"

"Drop what you're doing and head for the trouble spot. I've cleared it with the office and the principal is going to pass the word to the teachers."

Ted had spoken with Arthur Bitting and received the principal's blessing for the strategy. Bitting was easily convinced that bullying was a problem and applauded Ted's creative solution. Still, he cautioned that Ted should emphasize to the boys how important it was that the bullied not become bullies.

Alf grinned. "Thanks Teddy," he said, and took off running, anxious to get the nuclear response plan into action.

Principal Bitting came out of his office. "Ted," Bitting said, "could you come in here please?

A woman was seated next to Bitting's desk. She was rough-looking and seemed uncomfortable in what were probably her best clothes. It was as though she was not accustomed to being in a formal setting . . . like someone who wore her best outfit only on Sundays and squirmed until she could get back home and into her grubbies.

"Is that him?" the woman said when she saw Ted. "Is that the one who attacked my son?"

"Attacked your—tell Mrs. Baumgardner what happened, Ted."

"Oh, sure," she said, "you don't think he'll tell it the way it happened."

"If Ted's version is not sufficient, Mrs. Baumgardner, there are fifty other students and several teachers who witnessed the incident. I'll be glad to bring them in if you like. Go on, Ted."

"Wally was bullying another boy who is much smaller than he is. I stepped in and stopped him."

"My boy came home all scuffed up and his clothes dirtied," she said. "Mr. Bitting, I want this little bastard punished."

Bitting was having trouble keeping a straight face when he said, "Yesterday's incident was to be the last in a long history of violent episodes by your son. Not only will I not punish Ted, I am expelling Wally."

"Expelling him? The way he tells it he was setting some queer kid straight when this boy jumped him for no reason."

"I can see there is nothing I can say that will make you see the situation the way it really was, Mrs. Baumgardner, so that's the end of it. Wally is out."

"If he's not in school I'll have to stay with him at home. I can't be doing that. I gotta work for a living. He has to be in school."

"You are correct. He does have to be in school. Just not *this* school."

"What's that supposed to mean?"

"State law requires that every child must get an education. Unless he has parental permission after the age of sixteen to withdraw, he has to attend school until he is eighteen years old."

"All right, then," she said. "That means you have to keep him here."

Bitting shook his head slowly. "Not at all," the principal said. "Just because he can no longer attend this school does not mean he doesn't have to go to classes somewhere. Possibly you can find a private institution that will take him."

"I can't afford something like that."

"That is not our concern."

"He's seventeen. He can legally quit school."

"With your permission, that's true."

"That means he'll have to . . . I'm not gonna . . . he can't . . . I'll sue you, that's what I'll do."

"It's been tried before, Mrs. Baumgardner," Bitting said. "You will end up spending money for a lawyer who will tell you what I just told you . . . that others have sued and lost. You don't have a case."

"We'll just see about that," she said, jumping to her feet. "And I'll sue this bully while I'm at it."

"Mrs. Baumgardner," Ted said, "I don't know whether you noticed, but Wally is twice my weight and nearly a foot taller than I am. Do you think any court in the land will believe I bullied your son?"

The woman stormed out of the office and slammed the door.

"Ted," Bitting said. "I would be extra careful out there until this cools down."

"Mr. Bitting. Wally is the one who needs to be careful and I think he knows it."

CHAPTER 40

IT WAS EARLY EVENING. TED WAS HELPING EMILY with her homework when the telephone rang.

"Teddy, it's for you," his mother said.

He rarely got calls and had a moment of apprehension when he thought it might be Marlene.

"Ted, this is Deputy District Attorney Margaret Tuttle."

"I planned to call to thank you for what you did," Ted said, keeping his voice low. His mother knew nothing about the Marlene project.

"I'm afraid I have some bad news," she said. "Joel Sanders has escaped."

The news hit him like a physical blow. His heart rate shot up considerably.

"Dear God. What happened?"

"At his arraignment this afternoon," she said. "The bailiff and a jail escort were waiting for the judge to enter the courtroom. Sanders knocked the bailiff down and broke a chair over the deputy's head. He took the handcuff key and bolted from the courtroom. I called you as soon as I heard about it."

"Damn." he whispered.

"The bailiff has a broken arm. The deputy is in the hospital with a serious concussion. But Ted, that's not the worst of it."

"What could be worse than having that monster on the loose again?"

"Joel took the deputy's revolver," she said. "He's armed."

Ted felt as though he might pass out. He was concerned for the Simpsons and Marlene. "What's being done to find him?"

"That's part of the reason I'm calling you. I know he's angry that you had a role in his arrest and he might come looking for you. I have deputies on their way to Carbonville to look for him."

"If he were smart," Ted said, "he would want to get as far away from this area as possible."

"A smart person would," she said. "But we're talking about Joel Sanders. There was a report of some men's clothing being taken off a clothesline near the jail and a car was stolen in the same neighborhood."

"So, he's out of his orange jail jumpsuit," Ted said. "He is very likely headed this way. I'm not afraid for myself, but he might go after Marlene and the people who are taking care of her if he can find them."

He gave Tuttle the Simpsons' address. "I'll meet your deputies there."

"No . . . no . . . Ted," she pleaded, "don't—"

But Ted did not hear the rest of it because he had already hung up and was racing for the front door.

"Teddy," his mother called out. "Who was that? Where are you go—"

Ted didn't take the time to answer. He was out the door. He jumped on his bicycle and pedaled madly through the semi-darkness in the direction of the Simpson home. Ted was not certain if Joel could have found out where Marlene was staying, but he wasn't taking any chances. She and the Simpsons could be in danger.

"Teddy."

"Arnie, I can't talk right now. Something really important has come up."

"I'll check with you later," Arnie said and clicked off.

Ted's leg muscles burned as he pedaled furiously along the town's hilly streets, but he kept going. His lungs struggled to keep up with the physical exertion. The Simpsons lived two miles away, several hills in the distance. Calling on primal instincts, Ted continued to strain at the upper edge of his physical endurance.

Katydids and crickets chirped a cadence, counting off each stoke of the pedals as Ted sped along. Night bugs slammed into his face and glasses.

Ted considered—hoped—that he might be overreacting, but he couldn't risk underestimating the enemy. Onward he raced, passing through warm air currents at hill crests, cool patches in the low spots.

All he could think of was the possible danger his friends might be in . . . and what he would do to Joel Sanders if the man harmed them.

Ignoring his burning lungs and the pain that throbbed in his legs, he was thankful to be living inside the physically fit body of a fifteen-year-old.

Thank God for gym classes.

He could feel his pulse thumping in his temples. He pressed onward. The distance seemed greater than he remembered it.

Even though he was in excellent physical condition Ted thought his heart might burst through his chest. But he did not dare stop.

Finally Ted arrived in the Simpson's neighborhood, out of breath and aching as never before.

It was dark except for dim streetlights and points of light from homes along the street. Ted approached with caution. Rather than come up on the house from the front, he had taken a side street that brought him several houses away from the rear of the Simpsons home. He laid his bike down and made his way quietly on foot to the back porch.

Looking through a window, he could see Mrs. Simpson, Alice, and Marlene sitting at the dining room table. They were laughing, playing a game of Scrabble.

As he was about to knock on the door Ted felt, more than heard, a presence behind him.

"Don't say a word," said a voice from the darkness. Joel had been crouched behind the shrubbery and was pointing a gun at Ted.

"Ah," Ted said. "Mr. Snyder—or Sanders—or whatever you're calling yourself these days."

"I'm calling myself pretty smart," Joel said. "I tailed the bitch here after school. I figured if I waited around long enough you'd show up. That's a bonus for me you little punk. Now I'll take care of all of you at the same time."

Joel's facial injuries were still visible where he had made a three-point landing on the sidewalk when he was arrested.

"You won't get away with it, Joel."

"Sure I will. Nobody to stop me."

"The police know you're here because they figured you were stupid enough to go for revenge rather than leave the area. Who do you think they'll be looking for if anything happens to us?"

"Where I'm going, nobody will ever find me."

"I would not want to be in your shoes for anything right now."

Ted suddenly turned toward the window and started to yell a warning to those inside. He did not get a single word out before fireworks went off in his head and everything went wobbly. He was only half aware of screams when the door was kicked open and he was dragged into the house.

Ted's consciousness slowly returned to normal, although he had a killer headache. He was laying on the floor in the Simpson's living room.

Grace Simpson was helping him to a chair. "Are you all right, Ted?"

"I'll live," Ted said.

"We'll see about that," Sanders said, pointing the weapon at him. "I wanted you to be awake when I gave you what you deserve. Then I'll take care of the little tramp and the rest of them."

"Why?" Ted said. "They haven't done anything to you."

"Witnesses, idiot."

Ted nodded. "Oh, sure . . . why didn't I think of that?"

Seated deep in an overstuffed chair was not the best position for springing into battle. What happened next felt like a gift.

"Stand up you sonovabitch." Joel demanded. "I want to show you what happens when you stick your nose in other people's business."

Ordering Ted to his feet was Joel's first mistake. His second mistake was grabbing for Ted's shoulder to turn him around, presumably to be shot in the back of the head.

Before Joel was even aware of what had happened Ted deflected the man's left hand, snatched the weapon from his right hand and planted a balled up fist into the man's trachea.

Joel's hands went to his throat. He gasped for air and dropped to his knees, wheezing desperately. The blow was enough to disable him, but Ted added a kick to side of the head as insurance.

Marlene was already on the phone, calling the police.

Ted uncocked the weapon. "Mrs. Simpson," he said, calmly handing her the gun butt first, "Would you hold this, please?"

Joel lay in a moaning heap. Ted flipped him onto his stomach and used the man's belt to secure his hands behind his back. He used his own belt to bind Joel's feet.

"Your poor head," Mrs. Simpson said, holding a wet washcloth lightly against the bleeding knot that had formed on the side of his head.

"I'm so sorry, Mrs. Simpson," he said. "I put you all at risk."

"It was not your fault in the least, Ted."

Joel was only half conscious when a sheriff's deputy arrived, handcuffed him and returned Ted's belt to him. Ted turned the revolver over to the deputy and helped him toss the prisoner into the back seat of a waiting cruiser with little regard for his comfort.

"Do me a favor, deputy," Ted said. "Keep him locked up this time."

The deputy looked very serious. "He'll be wearing leg irons at his next arraignment," he said. "Maybe a straight jacket, too. And now we have a new list of offenses to add to the others."

"You hear that, Joel," Ted called out to the prisoner. "They're getting a nice little room ready for you over at the state prison. Where you're going you'll have lots of friends who just love your kind."

Joel muttered something incoherent.

Marlene's worst nightmare had become her tormentor's own worst nightmare.

"Where did you learn to fight like that?" Mrs. Simpson said, continuing to work on Ted's injury.

Ted substituted a groan for an answer and she did not ask again.

After he got the Simpson household settled in, Ted jumped on his bike and started for home.

"Teddy."

"Arnie! You've been watching?

"I saw it all. When you were racing along on your bike I knew something was wrong and I stayed with it. Pretty scary. You handled it well, Teddy."

"The video will give us something to watch on cold winter nights."

"You were right about the value of knowing then what you learned in all the years since."

"And you were right that memories evolve to something very different from the actual event. I never completely realized what a jerk Charlie was or that Marlene was a child having problems. It makes me wonder if I'm as smart as people say I am."

"It's not smarts, Teddy. It's experience. Witness bad stuff in your life and the next time you see it you know what you're looking at. As a teenager you had nothing to compare anything with."

"Yeah, well, who knows what all this means to the future . . . the one you're living in."

"I guess we'll find out when you return."

"You know, Arnie, I'm going to miss these people. I've gotten to know them in an entirely different way."

"'Parting is such sweet sorrow'. Romeo and Juliet. That Shakespeare guy knew some stuff, didn't he?"

"It will be like losing people I care for. But I'd do it all over again."

"It's getting close to time to bring you back."

"I still have a couple of things I have to do."

Ted knew his mother would want to know why he burst out of the house. He couldn't tell her the whole story, of course. He didn't let her see his head injury or she would have stroked out for sure.

"I was worried about you, Teddy. Taking off like that."

"It was something I had to take care of, Mom."

"Is everything okay now?"

"Better than okay."

CHAPTER 41

As the school year wound down, Jimmy Deavers' scholastic progress was slow. But each time Ted worked with the boy he could see improvement, both in what he was learning and in Jimmy's attitude toward study.

"Jimmy," Ted said, putting a hand on the boy's shoulder. "I've got some suggestions for you. First, you need to avoid hanging out with losers. Associate with winners and you will become a winner yourself."

"I don't really have any friends of either kind," Jimmy said.

"That's because you've mistreated so many people. You have to go to those kids and apologize and convince them you have changed. Besides, having no friends now could be a good thing," Ted said with a smile. "You can start from scratch."

"But who—?"

"You know Clark Erickson?"

"Teddy, you gotta be kidding . . . he's—"

"—a kind and intelligent person and not a threat to anyone. Whatever else you think you know about Clark, you have to realize that he is an outstanding example of what a sensitive human being should be."

Jimmy didn't comment, but it was clear he was not yet convinced.

"Okay," Ted said. "Now I'm going to give you the best financial advice you will ever get. Save your money."

Jimmy looked at him blankly. "I don't have any money to save."

"Oh, you'll have money, Jimmy. It won't be a lot at first because when you start out you'll be working at jobs that don't pay much. The trick is to keep improving yourself. Always keep moving up in earnings. Take courses. Continue learning and aiming for the next higher rung on the career ladder."

Ted thought Jimmy was listening to the words, but he wasn't sure the message behind them was getting all the way through that thick young skull. It was unlikely that Jimmy believed he would ever amount to anything.

"No matter how little money you make in your working life, before you do anything else, take out ten-percent and put it aside in savings or investments."

Jimmy stared blankly at Ted. "How can I live on ninety-percent of 'not very much'?"

"Hikers can live out of a backpack for indefinite periods with only the basics," Ted said. "Just adopt some of those ideas and you'll see how little you really need for survival. If you put it away and never have it, you won't miss it. If you have invested wisely, by the time you reach retirement age you'll probably have a million dollars paying you interest and dividends."

"I don't know nothin' about investing."

"Don't know 'anything' about investing," Ted corrected. "You'll find a financial advisor with a good success record."

"I don't even know what kind of job I could get."

"Think of something you like to do."

Jimmy thought it over.

"I like to build stuff. I made a doghouse in shop class once," Jimmy said with pride.

"Take any job you can get with a company that does whatever interests you . . . even if it's sweeping up floors and cleaning toilets. Summer is coming up. Maybe you can hire on with a local builder. Start looking now, before everyone else gets those summer jobs."

Ted spoke as an expert on the subject of preparing for retirement. He had not started taking his own advice until he was in his thirties. Once again, a bad example served as the best example. Still, he had put aside enough to assure his son of a college education and to retire in relative comfort.

"Jimmy," Ted said, "by 1960 the population of this country had grown by half again as many people as there were in 1920. By the time you are in your forties, the population will increase to more than twice what it is now. Those new people are going to need homes. If you own land to build those homes on, it will be worth a fortune by then."

Ted didn't tell him the benefits of going on to college. The boy was already overwhelmed by the prospect of passing high school English.

"You make it sound easy."

"Easy? Hell no, Jimmy. It will be the hardest thing you'll ever do. Always keep in mind that you will be working for two old people."

"What two old people?" Jimmy asked, wide-eyed.

"Yourself and your wife of the future."

Jimmy had his hands in his pockets and was looking everywhere except at Ted. "Teddy, I can't think about what's gonna happen next week and you already got me married . . . and old."

"Always think ahead, Jimmy. Life will have some unpleasant surprises. Not that you should spend all of your time worrying about the worst that can happen to you. If you did that you'd always be running scared, looking over your shoulder, never having any fun or getting anything done. But you do need to prepare yourself for the things that could happen. Things like health problems. Nothing will drain your resources like a catastrophic illness or injury. Take care of yourself as much as possible. You can buy health insurance, but prevention is the best and cheapest insurance you can get. Don't smoke, always have a healthy diet, get exercise even after you're out of high school and there's no gym teacher forcing you to play sports and run laps. Stay away from alcohol."

"That one's easy. I'll never be a drunk like my old man."

Ted wondered whether Jimmy would have the strength of character to avoid adopting his father's other worst traits.

"I hope you won't abuse your future wife and children either," Ted said. "It happens among people who were abused themselves."

"I would never—"

"Don't be too sure, Jimmy." Ted looked the boy squarely in the eye. "You turned your anger on me. One day you could become impatient with children of your own. You may be tempted to strike them. Don't be your father, Jimmy. If it ever comes to that, run to the nearest psychiatrist for help."

Considering Jimmy's lack of self-discipline, Ted was not at all certain the young tiger would change his stripes. Ted had done all he could. The rest would be up to Jimmy.

The clock was ticking toward Ted's return to his own time. He could not be sure he had positively impacted those lives he hoped to change for the better. He got the opportunity to do some of the things he had often thought he would like to have done. All he could do now was wait . . . and hope.

CHAPTER 42

WITH JUST ONE MORE DAY REMAINING in the school term, Ted said his goodbyes. He made it a point to put on a show of spending some time with Clark Erickson for the benefit of the passing multitude in the hallways. The two sat on a bench on the school grounds in full view of the other students as Clark showed Ted how to knit. It was a skill Ted knew he would never use again, but he enjoyed the effect the activity was having on Clark. He believed it was important for the boy to be seen as unthreatening. To Ted's surprise and delight, others. . . including some of the more macho young boys. . . joined in to try their hand, sitting next to Clark who, until recently, was someone most of them believed was best avoided.

Ted had formally introduced Jimmy Deavers to Clark. Each already knew the other, of course. But having them interact directly diminished Jimmy's fears and prejudices.

"Help him if you can, Clark," Ted said after Jimmy went to his class. "He's troubled, but I think there's some good raw material there."

Ted knew that after this day he would never again see the people of his hometown as he was seeing them now. And he would not be able to let them see him after he reverted to his teenage self because he would not be the same. The visit to the Simpsons would very likely be the last time he would ever see them again. That fact was both unbearable and inescapable.

Ted was again absorbed into the warmth of the Simpson home. The place was the perfect reflection of the Simpsons, themselves. While he had always thought of Mrs. Simpson as a great teacher, he had come to enjoy her as a friend. It made leaving that much harder.

"Thank you for all you have done, Ted," Grace Simpson said.

Ted nodded, afraid to say anything for fear of choking up.

Marlene looked more relaxed than he had seen her in the difficult recent weeks.

"If I'd had any sense," Marlene said, "I would have been mooning over you instead of that idiot Charlie Freeman."

Ted looked over at Alice. She nodded, apparently remembering a similar observation he had made about her.

"Well, now that you have some experience in that area you'll have a better idea of what to look for."

"I'm sorry you're leaving, Teddy," she said. She put her arms around his neck and kissed him on the cheek. In his previous past Ted would have been thrilled on a boy-girl level. In this dimension he was simply pleased at the success of the venture.

Ted glanced over Marlene's shoulder at Alice. She had her arms folded and her lips tightened. Tears streamed down her face. Ted read that as jealousy mixed with sadness. He went to her and gave her a long hug and a kiss on the cheek.

"Have a good life, pretty girl," he said and walked out the door with a lump in his throat the size of the Rock of Gibraltar.

There was still time for a visit with John Wilson.

"I'm not sure anymore which of us is the teacher . . . and which is the student," Wilson said as they walked along the quiet, tree-lined street in Wilson's neighborhood for the last time.

"You're what every teacher should be," Ted said. "I predict a great future for you."

"If anyone would know about the future, I guess it would be you."

Ted thought about his own future and whether any changes waited for him when he returned.

"Now I have to go back there and make a better life for myself," Ted said. "The old one wasn't that great."

"Did you accomplish what you set out to do here?" Wilson asked.

Ted did a mental tally of what he had wanted to do as opposed to what he had actually done.

"Several things I'm sure of," Ted said. "And a few we won't know about right away. . . if ever."

"Maybe they'll work out," Wilson said.

"John . . . do you mind if I call you John? After all, I am about twenty years older than you."

Wilson shook his head, amused at the absurdity.

"One of the things I'd hoped to bring about," Ted said, "was to get you out of your dead end life and into something more satisfying."

Wilson reached into a jacket pocket and produced two sheets of paper. He handed them to Ted. "I may have started on that."

It was copies of a job application and a resume.

"I applied at Penn State," Wilson said. "I have an interview up at the main campus next week."

Ted smiled as he scanned the forms.

"Okay . . . now I can add one more to my list of probable accomplishments."

"We'll miss you around here Ted. We don't get many time travelers in Carbonville."

"Not that we know of," Ted said.

That gave them both something to think about.

"For all we know, my friend Arnie is setting up a time travel agency, sending people out willy-nilly."

"Now you've done it, Ted. I don't think I'll ever be able to look at a kid again and not wonder whether I'm looking at a genuine young person or an older version in a young body."

Ted pulled out a wad of bills and held them out to Wilson. "I wanted to say goodbye and return the balance of your money."

Since Mrs. Simpson had assumed responsibility for Marlene and refused to take anything for it, Ted had used only a few dollars of the five-hundred he had been given.

"Keep it, Ted," Wilson said. "I'm way ahead of the game."

Ted was not surprised at Wilson's generosity. In fact, he had an alternate plan in mind for the money if the man refused to take it back.

"I assume you have decided what you're going to do with your new wealth," Ted said.

"I bought the stocks you recommended and the three tracts of land we talked about. There's money left over to pay the taxes on the investment profits and the property taxes for a few years. I'll just sit on that land until an appropriate time down the road."

"I assume you told your wife about your investments."

Wilson nodded. "I begged her forgiveness for playing with our savings without telling her. I didn't go into detail. She thinks I'm a financial wizard and forgave me when I told her it gave us enough for two properties to hold onto for our future."

"Two—I thought you said three properties."

"The third plot is going to young Deavers. I'll pay the taxes and hold onto it until he's twenty-one and then sign it over to him."

The man's generosity astonished Ted. Wilson could easily have kept it all. Instead, he remembered Ted's desire to help Jimmy.

"You will have to keep track of him," Ted said. "When Jimmy's out of school, he will be gone from his father's house fast . . . and as far away from that man as possible."

CHAPTER 43

RATHER THAN THE JOYFUL EVENT IT HAD BEEN WHEN he originally left Carbonville, moving day was a sad day for Ted. He had made friends he missed out on the first time. He was reminded of what he should have known all those years before. Being a teenager was similar to a salmon trying to swim upstream in rapids. He also realized that he would have to pay more attention to the world around him and its inhabitants and stop thinking so much about himself.

The McBrides were set to leave for the farm that afternoon. Ted and his father had finished loading a utility trailer with some items Ed did not trust the movers to handle carefully. The rest would be stored in Ted's grandmother's barn or added to her home décor.

But there was one more thing he had to do.

"Benny," Ted said to the town bookie, pointing to the larger of two cans filled with coins, "how much will you take for that one?"

Benny Hubbard had two metal containers with press-on lids like the one Ted's mother kept sugar and flour in. Each was filled to the top with coins. Benny would make change for his customers from them. When Ted delivered the man's mail, Benny would reach into one of the containers and fish out a quarter for him.

Benny put a hand to his chin and did a quick mental tally of the probable worth of the contents of the fullest one. "Without actually counting it," he said, "I'd guess there's about a hundred-dollars in this one."

Benny seemed surprised when Ted peeled off six twenties and handed them over. "The extra twenty," Ted said, "is in case you underestimated."

He took the treasure home.

Alma McBride was alone in the kitchen, wrapping the last of the dishes in newspaper and packing them into boxes. "Mom," Ted said, setting the heavy can on the table. "I'd like you to do something for me." He opened the container for his mother to see.

"My Lord, Teddy," she said, running her fingers through the coins.

"I want you to tape this shut and hide it somewhere at Grandma's and not touch it for at least thirty years."

"What on earth for?"

"Because it's full of coins with lots of silver in them. The government isn't going to put much real silver in metal money anymore. In years to come, the silver alone will be worth more than the face value of the coins. Many will be considered collectibles and have value beyond their precious metal content." He pulled out a Kennedy half-dollar and held it up. "This one alone will be worth more than five-dollars."

Alma McBride just shook her head.

"I also want you to take this," Ted said, handing his mother the balance of the cash he got from John Wilson.

"Teddy. Where in the world did you get this money?"

"Don't worry, Mom. I didn't steal it, if that's what you're worried about. It may come in handy in lean times."

She accepted the cash with no further explanation of how it had been acquired.

"I'm sure there is a good reason for telling me all this," she said.

She had turned on her sensors again.

"Because," Ted said, "I'm going to have to leave."

"Leave? Where are you going, son?"

"It's not so much a 'where' as the 'when' you mentioned."

"Oh," she said. "How—"

"I'll go to bed at the farm tonight. In the morning I'll be a regular kid again."

"Teddy, this is all so strange."

"You think it's strange for you? You're on the outside looking in. You should be inside my head looking out. It's really weird in here."

He could see her tension lessening, feeling more reassured.

"It's not like I'm dying, Mom," he said, giving her a hug. "I'll just be going back to being a teenage pain in the butt again."

Alma cocked her head. "Oh, honey, you've never been any trouble."

"You're the smartest, most sensitive mother there ever was. Part of the reason I had to tell you all this is because you're so smart."

"I still don't understand how—"

"My friend, Arnie, the guy who came up with this whole idea, will shut down transmission of my adult brain waves to my teenage brain."

"People will see the change in you."

"You're going to have to cover for me with Emily and Dad. Grandma won't notice because she has never seen me like this. Dad and Emily may notice a change. I've kind of slipped up around Dad and spoke 'grownup' when I should have been talking 'teenager'. No one else up there has seen me as I am now. Only you, Dad, and Emily."

"I'll work it out," she said, drawing herself up to full puff. "After all, I am the 'smartest, most sensitive mother there ever was.'"

"Well, there you go. One more thing. After the changeover don't mention this to me unless I bring it up. The teen me may not know much about what happened."

"Wonderful. I may have to wait forty years to talk to you about this."

"The best part is that we know we'll both be there. Gee, Mom, you don't even have to look both ways before you cross the street anymore."

"Oh, Teddy."

"You can sit in a draft without a sweater anytime you feel like it and you won't catch your death of pneumonia."

"You're making fun of your mother, aren't you?"

"I am not. Let me prove it to you. I'll go find a pair of scissors and you can run with them as much as you want."

CHAPTER 44

THE MORNING SUNLIGHT STREAMED THROUGH the windows of the old farmhouse kitchen as Grandma Patterson created one of her famous breakfasts.

Teddy McBride was just joining the family. His mother, father, and sister were already working on a stack of pancakes. In the center of the table within everyone's reach were all the delicious threats to life and health and challenges to dietary common sense: bacon, sausage, ham, eggs . . . as well as homemade bread and farm fresh butter and milk.

"Good morning sunshine," the old lady said cheerily as Ted sat down at the table.

"Mornin," he said, croaking out his first spoken word of the day. He had a chenille bedspread pattern on one cheek from sleeping on the spread's raised surface.

"Did you sleep well?" his grandmother asked.

"I had a really strange dream."

Alma McBride smiled.

Ed McBride looked up at his son. "You have the whole summer ahead of you. What's the plan?"

"Nothing special."

"Well, how about this," Ed said. He held up the morning newspaper. "Starting in two weeks, the Education Center is offering a class called 'Introduction to Computers'. Any interest there?"

The sleep instantly left Teddy's eyes. For a moment he thought he might not have heard his father correctly, given Ed's past objections to his desire to have a career in the emerging field of computers.

"I'll take your stunned silence to mean 'yes'," Ed said. "If you want to go, I'll drive you down to sign up." He handed Ted the newspaper with the registration information.

Alma McBride was wearing an amused smile that suggested she knew something the rest of the family did not.

Even Emily had become friendlier. She actually hugged her brother from behind when she brought pancakes to his end of the table. Ted had a vague recollection of resolving to be nicer to his sister. Apparently it had rubbed off on her, as well.

He thought that as soon as he got the sleep out of his head he would give it all some more thought. Meanwhile, he helped himself to a generous portion of the palate-pleasing artery-cloggers spread out before him.

It certainly had been an odd couple of months. Like a dream that was fading and he couldn't quite bring it back.

CHAPTER 45

THE LAST THING TED REMEMBERED before he felt someone lifting his eyelids was going to bed the previous night at his grandmother's.

A voice called out, "Professor McBride, are you in there?"

Ted opened his eyes and there was Professor Arnold Hoffmeier and his assistant.

"Arnie, Harold, how did you get to the 1960s?" Ted croaked.

"It's not the 1960s anymore, Teddy," Arnie said. "You're back home. It will probably take awhile to get reoriented."

"Oh. . . yeah . . . now I remember."

"How do you feel this lovely 21st-century morning, where dawn has just cracked?"

"Dizzy, groggy, foggy . . . and most of the other Seven Dwarfs."

"It'll pass when you start moving around."

Ted put his legs over the side of the bed and struggled to sit up.

That's a great beard." Arnie said, and held up a mirror. "You need a haircut, but you should keep the beard to cover up what nature left out."

Ted gave his friend a sour look. A stranger was looking back at him from the mirror. His hair was longer than he preferred, but someone had trimmed the beard stylishly as he slept.

"Ted Van Winkle," Arnie said. "You've lost that excess blubber around the middle. Looking good."

"Arnie," Ted said, putting his hands to his ears. "The ringing is gone." Ted had become so accustomed to not hearing the ever-present sound when he was in his youthful form that it took him a few minutes to realize that his perfect hearing had carried forward.

"The medical staff pronounced you in good health," Arnie said. "They packed up their equipment and left as you were waking up."

Ted tried to stand, but his legs had other ideas. It was as though they had no bones in them.

Arnie stifled a laugh. "We kept you exercised with a machine that moved your legs while you were asleep."

Arnie had planned well. The movement aided blood circulation but would not have fully maintained muscle strength. Ted would be in a weakened state until he became accustomed to having weight on his limbs again.

"It's going to be a shock to some family members in the 1960s that the old teen Ted is back," Ted said.

"Maybe not," Arnie said. "Teenagers are an odd lot to begin with. The casual observer may think it's just one more hormone eruption. They'll probably just roll their eyes and go about their business."

"I hope so."

"What do you remember about your time there?"

"I remember it all. Why?"

"Your memories of what happened during the visit may be clear, but what do you recall after you moved to the farm and reverted to the young Ted?"

"My memories after we moved to Grandma's are the same now as before I went back. Nothing has changed."

Arnie looked puzzled. "Strange," he said. "As you were waking up I Googled your old high school science teacher. Hundreds of references popped up about a John Wilson who taught higher math at the main Penn State campus for thirty years before he retired. He was a Quantum Mechanics and String Theory hotshot."

"So, he got out of his high school teaching job after all," Ted said. "Of course, he could have done that without my help. Even though I don't remember anything differently after we moved away, there could still have been changes."

"You may have a lot of surprises in the world you came back to."

"If there are changes to other people's lives, why wouldn't I recall any to my own?"

"We may never know the answer to that," Arnie said, "but it could have something to do with parallel universes."

Ted decided Arnie needed to know the whole story.

"I didn't tell you, Arnie. I let Mom in on the deal."

"Teddy!"

He explained why it was necessary to let her know.

"I told her she should never mention it to anyone, including me. In a way, I wish

I had told just one more person."

"Your English teacher, of course."

"Yeah. There was too much going on. It would have strained my credibility."

Arnie said he would not inform the university administration just yet that Ted had completed his part of the project. That would give him some time before he had to report back to his classroom. Until then he could look into what other changes may have occurred.

The possible scenarios tested the limits of imagination. Some people may have lived who had died. They would have had children who would not otherwise have been born. Those children had children—and on and on. Every action by everyone on Earth was multiplied by every move made by everyone else on the planet during his and her lifetime. That would have been multiplied again by how it affected everyone else. The resulting ripples from those altered consequences upon consequences were staggering to comprehend. If the concept of 'infinity' had been incomprehensible before, it was only because Ted had never seen a practical demonstration so close to home.

He decided not to take Arnie's advice about the beard. He would live with the face nature gave him. Using scissors and shaving gear he found in the lab bathroom, a thinner version of the old Ted was soon staring back at him in the mirror. He would get a haircut when he got back to the city.

It took an hour of walking around the lab before his land legs nearly returned and he had come completely out of the haze. His voice transitioned from froggy to something close to normal. Now he knew how astronauts must feel after months of weightlessness. It would take awhile to build up to full strength again.

"Before you go home," Arnie said, "let's get a little solid food into you."

The food court was buzzing as the early morning coffee and pastry crowd fortified themselves for the day ahead.

"You should probably have something light," Arnie said. "Like soup."

"To heck with soup. I'm dying for a donut."

As Ted reached for the last of the jelly donuts on the counter, a voice behind him said, "Hey . . . I had my eye on that one."

Ted picked up the donut and put it on his own tray. He turned to the man with a withering glare and said, "Then you should have gotten here ahead of me."

The man seemed chastened and backed away.

When they got to their table, Arnie said, "Our little boy is growing up."

"Don't start with me."

Arnie smiled. So did Ted.

"I've been thinking, Arnie. The government paid for this study. Aren't you afraid they'll misuse what you've learned?"

"I've thought a lot about that, Teddy. I made a decision that we should only give them the information it takes to *look* at the past, but not participate in it."

"Is Igor in agreement?" Ted said of Arnie's lab assistant.

"Absolutely, Dr. Frankenstein. *Harold* feels as I do that we can't have them tweaking every historical event to suit government's purposes. Can you imagine what life would be like with the changes they would make? I mean, look at what Congress has already done with the laws. Just about every aspect of American life is already either forbidden or mandatory. The politicians would nibble history to death."

After they finished their snack, Ted knew he had to go home. There was work to be done.

On the way to the parking lot Ted passed the sociology professor he had been so fascinated with. He nodded a scant greeting to her. Oddly, he no longer felt any great attraction. She, on the other hand, could not seem to take her eyes off him as he walked past with self-confidence he had never felt before.

Ted returned to his apartment. A call to his mother was first on his list.

"Teddy, I've been worried about you. Where were you?"

"Oh, here and there," he said.

"Well, come to dinner tonight and we can talk about it. There's a surprise waiting here for you."

"What's the surprise?"

"If I told you, it wouldn't be a surprise."

The motherly wisdom just kept on coming.

If Arnie was correct, Alma McBride would know exactly where her son had been. He would probably have to be the one to bring it up. Ted guessed his mother was playing it cool. He had known for a long time that he had a really cool mom.

Ted made a new dental appointment and scheduled kickboxing sessions with Abe Kirby at the YMCA. He also checked in with bandleader Clyde Butterfield about the upcoming schedule.

Ted found some clothes in the back of his closet he had not worn in quite awhile because they were too small.

I knew there was some reason I hadn't given these to the Salvation Army.

They were a good fit for the new and improved Ted McBride.

Before leaving for the farm he wanted to stop off for a haircut and then check up on some people to see how they fared in the years since his visit.

The area phone book had no listing for Grace Simpson. She would have changed her name if she remarried. Without her it would be impossible to find Marlene Sutton.

There was a James Deavers listed. Ted wondered if it could be the little terrorist he had known.

The phone was picked up in just two rings. *"Deavers."*

Ted said, "Is this James Deavers who used to live on Riley Street in Carbonville?"

"This is Jim."

"You may not remember me. My name is Ted McBride and—"

"Teddy. Remember you? Are you kidding? How the hell are you, man?"

"I'm fine. I was just thinking of you and wondered how you're doing."

"Better than okay and you can take a lot of credit for it."

"It's good to hear you've done well."

"Why don't you let me take you to lunch? We can catch up. Oh, man, this is great. How about today?"

"Name the time and place."

They agreed to meet at an upscale restaurant near the capitol.

CHAPTER 46

TED WAS APPREHENSIVE AS HE ARRIVED AT A COZY EATERY a half-hour early. A phone conversation was not quite enough to totally convince him of the miracle he had experienced. He had to actually see Jimmy Deavers in the flesh for absolute confirmation.

Ted used the time to look at oil paintings that lined the walls of the waiting area and dining room.

The name of the artist was a pleasant surprise: Clark Erickson. Some of the paintings had recent dates under the signature.

Clark had not ended his life after all, and he had turned his creativity to painting.

Ted was amazed at the range of feelings he was experiencing since his return. It was as though he had been reborn.

One painting in particular appealed to Ted. It was a fall rural scene, not unlike the family farm with its traditional red barn. He could not believe how realistic the artwork was. It had a quality that drew the observer into it. He felt it would be possible to reach out and dip his fingers into the stream depicted on canvas. The rich colors were as alive as those of any Pennsylvania October Ted had ever experienced.

Direct deposit of his university paychecks and no expenses during his two-month absence had swelled his checking account. Since he lived frugally, he certainly had the money. He could think of no reason not to buy it.

The hostess wrapped the framed painting and brought it to his table. He took it out to his car, locked it up and went back inside.

Ted noted that the man who breezed through the front door of the restaurant did not look much like the young boy Ted had known. Jimmy favored his father enough for Ted to recognize him. Jimmy would probably not want to be reminded of a resemblance to the monster that had made his childhood a nightmare. The skinny, unkempt kid had changed into a robust, well-groomed adult with a look of success about him.

"I guess I'd better start calling you Jim," Ted said. "Jimmy doesn't seem to fit anymore."

Jim shook Ted's hand vigorously. "Great to see you Teddy . . . Ted . . . I can't begin to tell you how grateful I am for everything you did for me."

Ted shook his head at the notion. "Mrs. Simpson was the prime motivator if I remember right. She moved away from Carbonville and I haven't been able to find her."

"I've been so busy with the business . . . and I hate to say it . . . I lost touch with her when she moved. Mrs. Simpson got me straightened out. She never let up on me the rest of the time I was in high school. If I got sloppy she'd practically drag my lazy butt into her classroom and get me going again. If I let down she'd make me feel guilty, saying how disappointed you would be if I didn't make something of myself."

"It couldn't have been easy for you, living in a house where you were abused."

"That problem went away when I went to work on a farm. Room and board and ten bucks a week. And, by the way, a dollar of that went into savings. When I wasn't getting beat up every day of my young life I could focus on self-improvement. After awhile, school got so interesting Mrs. Simpson didn't have to go looking for me anymore. She put some of the other teachers on my case, too. John Wilson got me hooked on science and math. He helped me get scholarships for college."

"College? Jimmy Deavers went to college? I never thought I'd hear your name and the word 'college' in the same sentence."

"Believe it or not. . . me. . . the guy who couldn't wait to be old enough to quit high school."

"Shows you what can be done when you bear down."

"What really made it click in for me," Jimmy said, "was that they showed me how each subject was relevant to real life. Proper English was important to communicating with people in business. Math was important as it applied to construction. History showed how we screwed up in the past and reminded us not to do it again."

"And here sits a Jim Deavers I almost don't recognize."

"And there was Clark Erickson," Jim said. "We became great friends. Still are. He was another one who pushed me to excel. The guy tutored me the rest of the way through high school."

"I just bought one of his paintings. Where is he now?"

"Where?" he said, pointing around the room. "Ted, he owns this place."

Ted was amazed. Not only was the boy he knew still alive . . . he had apparently thrived.

"I've got to say hello," Ted said, starting to get up from his seat.

"He's not here," Jim said. "I asked the hostess."

Disappointed, Ted sat back down. "I'll come back later."

"Another thing. John Wilson looked me up. It was soon after I turned twenty-one. I'd moved to the city. He came to my place and handed me the deed to a piece of property out west of Carbonville."

"Oh, why'd he do that?" Ted asked.

"You know exactly why, Ted. He told me you asked him to help get me started when I got older."

"Wonderful that he followed through and gave you that help."

"It made all the difference. I had been doing construction work, trying to get ahead. Owning that property made me work even harder. I learned the business inside and out and went for my contractor's license. I hung onto that land through some tough times. When I could, I bought more properties and put more money aside. John and I developed it ourselves a couple of years ago, when real estate was hot."

"You *and* John?"

"Yep. He also made a bundle in the stock market. I thought I ought to return his generosity. I offered to bring him into my project. We pooled our resources and paired my tract with some land he owned and we made more money than either of us can spend in a lifetime. He lives in New England now. Retired after thirty years of teaching math at a level that would give Einstein a migraine."

"All because a little bully finally realized what was available to him if he would just shape up."

Jim smiled. "It's amazing how you can turn anger into a productive force," he said as he worked on his Cobb salad. Ted munched on a mixed green salad with lite Italian dressing. He had resolved to maintain his post-adventure weight and to work on the creaks and aches he noticed in his older self. No more donuts.

"I spent most of my childhood pissed at my old man. Then you showed me how to change it all."

You just needed a little push."

"It wasn't a *little* push, Ted. It was a well-deserved smack to my head. Your gang of heavy-hitters got me straightened out. Nobody cared before. The caring was as important to me as what came of it. I started getting good grades. I saw the benefits of getting my sh—my act together. There was a whole world waiting for me I didn't know about. I'm a better man because of what you and the Carbonville High School SWAT team did for me."

"You sure don't sound like the Jimmy I used to know."

"I'm nicely set up for retirement, thanks to some advice from a wise young fellow."

"I even took some of my own advice," Ted said. "Unfortunately, not all of it and not as soon as I should have. Still, I invested well. I'll be comfortable and my son will be assured of a college education with no student loan hanging over him."

"I've got two grown kids; a girl and a boy," Jim said. "And I never laid an angry hand on either of them . . . or my wife."

"You didn't become your father after all."

"Didn't miss it by much. I had some bad moments where I thought I might fly off the handle. A shrink helped me deal with it."

"Good man. Are your parents still living?"

"The old man died about twenty years ago. Liver disease from all the booze. We never did make up. I don't have any regrets. He was a brute. Mom divorced him in the nineteen-sixties, not long after you moved away. She cleaned up her own act and married a nice, boring guy who treats her like a princess."

"Spoken like a fully-vested adult."

"Teddy, let me ask you a question . . . something that has been on my mind all these years."

Ted knew what was coming. And he knew Jimmy was as reluctant to ask as Ted would be to answer.

"My dad never smacked me around again after he showed up one night with a messed up face. I thought you might have done something."

Ted poked at his salad.

"Why would you think I was involved?"

"The thing is, it stopped right after you saw him beat up on me. After the way you handled Wally Whatzizface who, by the way, is doing life in prison for murder, I put two and two together and came up with Teddy McBride."

"Your father and I had a discussion and came to an understanding with regard to your welfare and safety."

"Was it anything like the understanding where I agreed to stop jumping you on the way home from school and you agreed not to pound the piss outta me?"

"Well, I was a persuasive kid. I probably should have gotten into sales instead of computers."

"Details, man . . . I need details."

Even though Blaine Deavers had been abusive, the man was still Jimmy's father. Ted saw no point in getting specific.

"Jim," he said. "Why don't we let the dead rest."

"Maybe some day you'll tell me?"

"Maybe when you're older."

"Ted, I'm fifty-four years old."

When Ted remained quiet, Jimmy made a sound like air escaping from a balloon. Mercifully, he backed away from the subject.

Ted thought it was interesting that Jimmy Deavers, who had been his enemy, had become his friend. Charlie Freeman, who had been his friend, became a stranger.

In parting they agreed to stay in touch. Jim gave him John Wilson's phone number and the names of some people who might know where Grace Simpson lived. That was a high priority.

CHAPTER 47

CONSIDERING ALL THE CHANGES HE HAD WITNESSED, it occurred to Ted that he might still be married to Maggie. He dialed her number not knowing what to expect . . . or whether the phone number was still the same. She picked up on the second ring.

"Hi Maggie," he said. "It's Ted."

"*All right. Just a minute,*" she said without further greeting and put down the phone. He heard her call for Tim.

That answered that question.

Despite any changes that may have come about as the result of the new Ted, he realized his ex-wife would still have the same rigid set of requirements for a mate. Even if he had been more self-assured and assertive, Ted knew Maggie's quest for the perfect husband would have found reasons to be unhappy with him. That would also apply to anyone else who had the misfortune to marry her. He wondered whether the relationship he had with his son would be the same as before his trip back in time.

Tim finally came to the phone.

"*Dad! Dad! You're back!*"

Ted was startled at the boy's outburst. Previous calls were usually met with fidgeting, lots of 'ers' and 'ums' and a lack of enthusiasm. Ted had assumed Tim would be anxious to get off the phone. This was a welcome development.

"*I was starting to worry about you,*" Tim said. "*You okay?*"

"I just got here and I'm fine, son. What's up with you?"

"*I've been working at the airport on Saturdays, cleaning the rental planes and doing odd jobs around the flight office. The chief pilot takes me up when business is slow. He even lets me take the controls.*"

"Great. It's what you've always wanted to do."

"And, Dad, they actually pay me."

"Well don't let them know you'd do it for free or they might let you."

So, another unexpected positive change in Ted's life. After his experience as an adult among teens, Ted had apparently developed a better understanding of his son as he grew up, including Tim's desire to fly airplanes. The result was a happier son and a more solid father-son relationship.

Ted felt some regret that he could not recall any of his altered life after his family moved to the farm. He certainly must have become a better father. Memories of his life up to the time he rode the mud bed to his past remained the same as before. He had missed the new version of his son's growing up years. Well, he would just have to be certain that their future relationship continued to be an improvement.

"You know," Ted said. "There's an air show at the Wilkes-Barre/Scranton Airport a week from Sunday. I thought the two of us could go."

The Tim Ted knew before his trip would never have believed his dad would have considered going to an air show.

"I heard about the show, but didn't have any way to get up there. Mom doesn't much like the idea of me flying."

Ted had not been in favor of it either. But that was before he realized he could not dictate his son's passion. No more than his own father had a right to put restrictions on Ted's fascination with computers.

"How is your mother?" Ted said. It was a test question.

"She's fine. Her and Jeff got back from their honeymoon two weeks ago."

Ted was actually relieved to hear that he was no longer married to Maggie.

"You like her new husband?"

Tim hesitated for just a beat, which told Ted a lot.

"He's okay. He treats me good" Tim lowered his voice. *"But he's not you."*

"Life is full of twists and turns, Tim. I'm still your dad and I'll always be here for you."

Ted felt regret that he had not been near by when Maggie remarried. Tim probably had some emotional issues to deal with and Ted could have been supportive.

"I'm sorry I wasn't here when all that was going on. Are you sure you're okay with the new arrangement?"

"Like you say, life is full of twists and turns. Just another thing to deal with."

"That's my boy. Okay, we're set for the air show . . . maybe a check ride with an instructor if you're not tired of flying by this time?"

"That's never gonna happen. Won't I see you before then?"

Another surprise. Tim typically invented excuses to get out of spending time with him. It was as though Ted had a brand new son who was born at the age of fifteen.

"We'll get together anytime you're free."

"How about this weekend?"

"You're on, kid. Check with your mother about that and about the air show. If it's okay with her, get back to me and we'll plan something spectacular . . ."

" . . . and aeronautical."

Ted laughed. "And aeronautical."

Tim lowered his voice. *"Dad, can I ask you something?"*

"Anything, any time."

"Do you think I could come and stay with you?"

In Ted's wildest imaginings he would not have believed Tim would want to live with him. It had been just short of impossible even to hold a phone conversation of any length with the boy.

"Things bad there, son?"

"Not bad. Just kind of . . ."

"Strained?"

"Yeah, that's the word."

"I'd love it," Ted said. "But we don't want to hurt your mom's feelings or wreck any future relationship you might have with her new husband. I'll talk to her and see if we can ease into it."

"Soon, Dad."

"Soon, indeed."

There would be some logistical challenges: changing schools, two guys living in a small apartment. Nothing that couldn't be worked out. Maybe he'd buy a house. Ted was pretty sure Maggie would go for the idea. She was probably feeling the strain, too.

After they hung up, Ted thought back to his objections to Tim's passion for flying. That was a whole other Ted. Father and son disagreed on the career path the boy should take . . . more accurately, the path Tim should *not* take. Ted had considered Tim's use of his computer a waste and his desire for a flying career as dangerous and immature. Their relationship was stressed further by Tim's natural growing pains and his parents' divorce.

Even before Ted returned he had known his attitudes would have to change. Judging from Tim's enthusiasm on the phone, the relationship had already been patched up. Ted just needed to be set straight on the care and feeding of teenagers.

Just because you have a lot of years behind you does not necessarily mean you are a grownup.

Ted once envied people with no children because he believed they were lucky not to have anyone to worry about.

Those poor bastards.

CHAPTER 48

Ted's phone rang.

"Hiya, big brother."

It took Ted a moment to realize the voice at the other end was Emily. His sister, who barely tolerated him before he tinkered with time, had actually telephoned him. Thinking back to the sullen adult that Emily had become, he could not remember her ever having called him before.

That was a whole other Then. This was a brand new Now.

Ted was remembering the little girl he had gotten another chance to know and like. He was not absolutely certain which Emily was on the other end of the line.

"Hi, Em," Ted said. "Where are you?"

"Right here at the farm in deepest, darkest Pennsylvania. We stashed the kids with Rob's parents and we're on our way to a Mighty Chicken franchisee conference in New York City. Rob's the keynote speaker."

Rob? Husband? Ted had never met him. Not in this dimension, anyway. In that other life she was twice-divorced and pretty much a flop in the relationship department.

"Ah. You're the surprise Mom mentioned when she invited me to dinner."

"Darn. I spoiled it."

"No you didn't . . . I'm surprised. How long will you be staying?"

"A couple of days. I wanted to spend some time here. You're coming, I hope."

He pictured those times when he helped ten-year-old Emily with her homework and the fun they had.

"I'm looking forward to seeing my baby sister."

"Watch it buster."

" . . . my sweet, younger sister."

"Much better. Dinner at Mom and Dad's this evening then."

Mom *and* Dad.

For a few seconds Ted couldn't speak.

"If we can pull him away from the shop, that is."

Ted's knees grew weak. He had to sit down.

"Teddy?"

"Wh . . . yeah."

"Are you okay?"

"Uh . . . great," he was finally able to say. "I'll be there."

"See you then."

Ted was stunned. Before he could figure it all out, he was sobbing.

Ed McBride had apparently gotten the medical help Ted recommended. Ted had become so accustomed to the idea that his father was dead that it never occurred to him that Ed survived . . . or that he would care. The negative feelings toward the man had been deeply embedded. In the short time he revisited his youth he had grown to love his father. The seed was always there, but it didn't have a chance to grow until each did what they had to do to nourish it.

The ill feelings had been a rejection of his father's rejection. Ted assumed everyone wanted acceptance by their parents. When they didn't get it, they tried to convince themselves they didn't need it and they made other emotional arrangements. Having established a new connection, Ted was actually looking forward to seeing his father.

If you don't stay alert, life can really bite you in the ass.

CHAPTER 49

TED ALWAYS THOUGHT THE TRIP TO THE FARM was like driving through a picture postcard. He passed stretches of lush woods and glorious panoramas along streams and fields. He drove through terrain that rose and fell dramatically where prehistoric seismic and geothermal energy upheavals had created a meandering countryside, the rough edges worn smooth by wind and rain and time.

Curving roads wove among remnants of a fading agricultural past. Land use had changed considerably since Ted was a boy, when small family farms dominated the region. The population expanded farther from the city. Housing developments appeared on fields where Ted spent summers of his youth helping farmers bring in their hay and grains.

As he pulled into the lane at the farm he noticed there was an addition to the side of the barn that had not been there before.

Ted's heart rate increased noticeably in anticipation of what he would find here.

His sister saw him as he pulled up to the house. She looked somehow different from the last time he saw the adult Emily.

"Teddy," Emily called out from the porch. In that other dimension, if he had cared at all, he would have considered himself fortunate that Emily had even acknowledged his presence. This time she ran across the driveway, threw her arms around her brother and gave him a gooey kiss on the cheek.

Instead of the pinched face and permanently dour expression, Emily had the look of a happy and well-adjusted adult.

"Hiya, brat," he said.

She stuck out her lower lip. "I not a brat . . . I big girl."

"Yes you are," he said, turning her around and taking a look at her backside. "And getting bigger."

"Mom," she yelled to their mother, who was standing on the porch, "Teddy said

I'm fat."

"Did not either, Mom," he shouted back and put an arm around his sister as they walked to the porch where the others were waiting. "You look great, kid."

Ted looked out at the new addition to the barn and choked up again as he saw Ed McBride wave at him and start walking to the house.

It felt good to be home. The old farmhouse represented security, Ted's home base, a safe place to come when the world got too big to handle. The house was nestled among tall trees that provided cooling summertime shade and let warming sunshine in after the leaves dropped in the fall.

Ted hugged his mother, but she gave no indication she knew of his trip through time. He did notice that she had more brown hair on her head and fewer worry lines on her face since his last visit to the farm before the adventure. Apparently the years since had not been as troublesome as they were in that other dimension.

The initial shock of seeing that his father was still alive quickly subsided. He looked much older than he had just a day earlier. . . forty years ago. The time before that was when Ted saw Ed in his casket, dead at forty-three. Yet there he stood, alive and apparently healthy, in his late seventies.

Emily's husband, Rob, had the appearance of a galoot, fresh off the farm. He shook Ted's hand warmly. Rob had no way of knowing his brother-in-law had never laid eyes on him before.

Now, if I can just find out about this guy without looking like an idiot.

With careful questioning, Ted learned Rob and Emily had two pre-teenage boys. His sister and her husband were both Georgetown University educated—Rob with an MBA—and, with Emily's support, was an astute businessman in their fast food enterprise. They owned a half-dozen successful fried chicken franchise restaurants throughout the Midwest. So much for outer appearances.

In Ted's previous existence, multi-married, multi-divorced Emily had not gone on to college, thus she had not met Rob or made anything of herself. The Emily for whom Alma McBride had been unable to afford college had gotten an education and a future after all.

Alma seemed to be looking more intently at her son than usual. She had a disconcerting half smile.

Ted got his father away from the others and they stood on the porch. "You're looking happy and healthy, Dad. Mom must be feeding you good."

Judging from the aroma wafting out of the kitchen, she was getting ready to feed them all.

"I've slowed down a lot."

"You mean you're not twenty years old anymore?"

"I'd settle for being sixty again," he said with a cackle.

"You've created quite a business."

"Your mother takes care of the business part. I just build furniture."

"Emily says they practically have to drag you away from the shop," Ted said, gesturing toward the new building he assumed was his father's work space.

"I have six months of back orders and I like what I'm doing."

"Maybe you ought to take on some help."

"When someone buys McBride Creations furniture, they're getting something I made with my own hands."

Hard-headed, as always.

"Dad, did you know that Michelangelo and most of the great Renaissance sculptors had a lot of help with their work. Sometimes the artist merely created the idea and their helpers chiseled away the marble."

A whiplash moment.

"Get outta here."

"Yep. Michelangelo did some of his works in miniature and on paper . . . or was it papyrus? Anyway, his underlings did the chipping. Meanwhile, Mike was off painting chapel ceilings and such."

Ted may have given the creative genius of the Middle Ages less credit than he deserved, but it was a parable of a sort, accurate enough to make the point. Ed put his hands in his pockets in quiet deliberation.

Ed shook his head. "I wouldn't feel like I was giving the customer his money's worth."

"Here's the thing, Dad," Ted said. "As it is now, you *are* your business. When you're gone, the business is gone. It would put Mom in a pickle."

Ed McBride had evidently never given that much thought.

"Your mother will be okay," he said. "We've invested well. But it would be nice to keep the business going."

After a long pause he said, "I suppose you have a suggestion."

"Does a penguin have cold feet?" Ted said. "Find skilled people. After a reasonable probationary period, when they become worthy of being sidekick to the King of All Things Wooden, hire them on a permanent basis. Provide benefits they can't get anywhere else. Treat them respectfully and value their suggestions. Give them an additional bonus or a share of the profits for as long as they're with you. They would be much less likely to jump ship and go into business for themselves or go to work for someone else with those kind of incentives. With you doing the designing and looking over their shoulder, you could let them turn out as much of the work as you can part with.

Ted could see his father's reluctance. "I don't know . . . ," the old man said.

"Maybe you could do some of the finish work on each piece. That way it would still have been touched by the master. That would take care of the backlog, double your output and significantly increase your income. You could spend more time on the creative side and accumulate a stack of designs ready to be doled out over the coming years. The business could continue in the hands of your crabby old business manager. Even . . . heaven forbid . . . without you."

Ed looked at his son and smiled. "I took your advice once, long ago. I've never been sorry."

Although his father could not have known it, he had benefited twice from Ted's advice. The result of getting medical help was standing right there with him on the porch.

"I'll think about it," Ed said.

"Here's another suggestion," Ted said. "Let's eat."

He put his arm around his father's shoulder and led him to the dining room where the rest of the family waited.

Dinner was wonderful. The company was awesome, as never before. In that other past, family get-togethers were gatherings of adversaries. Emily had carried her jealousies through the years. Until the day he died, Ed McBride had never gotten past his resentment over the trap he was in. Only Ted and his mother had always had a peaceful connection.

All had changed for the better because Ted was able to make adjustments to his past.

When the dishes were done, Alma McBride was finally able to get Ted away from the others. She seemed to be working her way cautiously to the subject hanging in the air.

"Okay Mom, I guess I'll have to be the one to bring it up . . ."

"I can't imagine what you're talking about, Teddy."

"Stop it. . . you know what I mean."

She laughed. "Oh. . . you mean that trip you took."

"Do you know where I went?"

For a moment Ted was afraid she didn't remember what had happened.

Finally she smiled and said, "I do know where. And I know *when*."

Ted sighed deeply and was amused that his mother had played a trick on him.

"Whew. I thought maybe I'd been dreaming . . . except for the part where Dad is still alive and Emily actually doesn't seem to hate me."

"When did Emily ever hate you, Teddy?"

He realized that in this dimension he'd had an entirely different relationship with his sister than the first time around.

"Doesn't matter, Mom. You haven't said anything about this to anyone, have you?"

She shook her head. "No one would have believed me."

"They would have hauled you off to the booby hatch."

"You were right about your father's health problem, Teddy. The surgeon who performed the operation said the aneurysm was large enough for great concern. It saved his life. But he works so intensely that I sometimes want to murder him."

"Don't do it before he hires shop help. You had money problems in that other dimension."

"He'll never get help."

"Just watch," he said.

Ted explained how his memories after leaving Carbonville were the same as before he left. The rest of his life until he returned to the 21st century had changed in every way, but he could not remember any of his own past in this layer of the time onion.

"All those things you told me came true," she said. "I think when they started putting the holes in the hoods of Buicks again, that's really when I believed the time travel story. Oh. . . and the moon landing."

"It just goes to show you . . . you should listen to your son more often."

"You know, Teddy, that money you gave me helped get your father started in the custom furniture business. Those few hundred dollars amounted to a lot more then. He started selling his work right away. Then it got to where he was doing better with the sideline than with his railroad salary. Plus, the commute to his job, especially in the wintertime, was getting to be too much. So, one day he went to the company office and turned in his notice. He had put in enough years to get a small pension. That helped out, too."

Ted thought back to the pleasant, life-changing conversations he and his father had in the old man's basement workshop.

"I hope that can of coins I gave you did some good," he said.

Alma suddenly took in a breath.

"I forgot all about those." She put a hand to her cheek and looked around as though searching her mind as well as her house. "Now what did I do with—"

Ted had a moment of panic. "We're talking about a real treasure, Mom. I hope you didn't give them away or spend them like regular money."

"No, I wouldn't—wait—I know."

She led Ted to the closet where the family treasures sat idle, threatening to compost while waiting to be put back into service. She burrowed through the accumulation of shoes and boxes of pictures and old board games and came out with a securely taped box containing the long-forgotten can.

"Voila," she said and sat it on a table in front of him with a jingle and a thunk.

"There you go," she said.

"Don't give it to me, Mom. I got it for you and Dad."

"We don't need it anymore. The business is quite successful and we have money in the bank. You take it."

As he was about to protest, Ted had an idea. "I know exactly what I'll do with it," he said.

His mother raised that magical single eyebrow.

Ted wondered whether he might get the hang of that if he practiced.

CHAPTER 50

ABE KIRBY FOUND HIMSELF FLAT ON HIS BACK where Ted had knocked his kick-boxing instructor.

"Wow, Ted," Abe said. "That was unexpected."

The session at the YMCA was the first since Ted returned.

"Shouldn't be a surprise, Abe," Ted said. "It's what you taught me."

"Yeah," Abe said, getting back to his feet. "But you were never that aggressive before."

"I guess your advice stuck."

"That trip you took apparently did you some good."

"More than you could possibly imagine, Abe."

Ted had filled Arnie in on the changes he found, confirming that Ted's activities had actually produced some positive differences.

Ted also told Arnie about the coins he had sent to the future. His friend recommended a coin dealer he knew. He assured Ted that the aptly-named Joseph Silverman had an excellent reputation for honesty and fair dealing.

Ted found the little shop in an alley near the county courthouse. He sat the container down in front of Mr. Silverman, removed the tape and said, "This will be the first time the can has been opened since the mid-sixties." He removed the tape and pried the lid off.

"Amazing," the old man said, his eyes wide at the sight of the large pool of precious metal staring back at him. The old man put on a pair of white cotton gloves as he listened to the story behind the coins. Ted skipped past the time travel part. He could tell by the dealer's expression that he was doing a mental calculation, envisioning the truth of Ted's earlier prediction that there would be lots of genuine silver and valuable collectibles among them.

When Silverman called a few days later, the result of the tally was beyond Ted's expectations. Much of the bounty was only worth the denomination of the coins or the weight of the metal. But, among the dimes, nickels, quarters, and half-dollars were hundreds of in-demand early issues worth far more than their face value.

Apparently Benny the bookie had made change from the upper levels of the canister.

"The deeper I dug in the can," Silverman said, "the older and more valuable the coins. He offered just over two-thousand dollars for that lot.

"But, Mr. McBride," the coin dealer said, "the star of the show was an 1859 Liberty twenty-dollar gold coin in near mint condition."

It was anyone's guess as to how it had gotten into Benny Hubbard's common change container without being noticed. The coin was about the size of a quarter and may have been mistaken for one. One of his horserace bettors may have inadvertently paid Benny with it.

Ted accepted the dealer's two thousand dollar offer for that one alone. The more than four thousand dollars would go a long way toward helping Tim train for his private pilot's license. Ted would take care of the difference, if necessary. The boy could start ground school immediately to learn the Federal Aviation Administration's rules and the physics of flying. At sixteen he could begin flight training. It would probably take most of a year to get ready for the FAA flight test when he reached the legal licensing age of seventeen.

Maggie would have to give her okay, of course. If she approved, Ted knew what his son was getting for his sixteenth birthday, just a few months away. If she did not approve, Tim would resent her forever. Ted wondered if it was a character flaw in him for enjoying that thought.

The gift would come to his son from both his mother and his father.

CHAPTER 51

Ted was becoming more and more frustrated as he called former Carbonville High School students to try to find Mrs. Simpson. The men who stayed in the area were easy to locate because they still had the same last names and were listed in the telephone book. The married women would have their husband's names. But one female classmate took back her maiden name after she divorced. Carbonville High School no longer had its maiden name either. It was now part of a large joint district. The woman had been keeping track of alumni and teachers to contact them for reunions. The most recent information she could provide about Ted's former English teacher's location was at least five years old.

It was early evening when Ted drove to the address he had been given. On the way he noticed a billboard advertising Eddie Stolsfus and his "Mountainaires" dance orchestra. They were appearing at the Shrine temple.

So, my old band mate turned pro after all.

He had been directed to a plain, unattached single-family house along the eastern edge of the city. It was typical of those built in the early part of the previous century. Originally clapboard, the small house was covered with a light green metal siding. A recent model mid-size Chevy sedan sat in the driveway. Flowers bloomed along the foundation. An ancient milk box sat on the porch, a relic of earlier times when a milkman still delivered dairy products to the home.

As he walked up the sidewalk to the front door, Ted tried to imagine what Mrs. Simpson would look like today. He estimated she would be in her late seventies or early eighties and would probably only slightly resemble the person he remembered.

No phone number was listed in the city directory. The only option was to drop in unannounced and ring the doorbell.

When the door opened, the term 'taking one's breath away' never had a clearer meaning for Ted. The woman who answered was not much older than when he last saw her.

"Mrs. Simpson . . ." Ted managed to stammer. "It's not poss—"

"Oh . . . no," she said. I'm Alice Simpson-Curtis. You're thinking of my mother."

"Alice! The resemblance is amazing. How is she?" Ted asked.

As though a cloud had passed over the sun, Alice turned very serious and in that instant, Ted knew.

"Sadly," Alice said, "my mother passed away two years ago."

Ted was stunned. It was as though lightning had struck him, leaving him numb. He had a sudden need to sit down. He leaned against the wall of the porch.

Alice sensed the effect the news had on Ted.

"Are you all right?"

"Alice," he said, stinging from the tragic news, having trouble catching his breath. "You may remember me from when we went to school together at Carbonville High School. I'm Ted McBride."

"Teddy!" She cried and swung open the screen door. "Of course I remember you. Oh, I shouldn't have blurted it out like that. I know you and she were close."

Another regret to add to his list. All the years wasted when a diligent search could have located her. Of course, he did not know her as well in his original youth as he did the second time around.

"I've had some time to adjust to her being gone," Alice said, taking him by the arm and guiding him into the living room. "I know it's difficult for you, just finding out."

Ted stepped inside. The home reflected the same warmth as their original place, with inviting touches throughout.

"I'm so sorry to hear about your mother," he said, scarcely able to get the words out. "She had not only been my favorite teacher, she was the person I most admired in my life. I've never known anyone wiser or kinder."

"She spoke of you often. She said in all the years she taught, you were her favorite student."

"You are the living saintly image of her."

No," she said. "My mother was the Simpson saint. I think there is only one saint allowed per family."

"Well, there's St. Mary and St. Joseph," he said, "so there is precedent."

Alice had not lost her little girl giggle.

"There's so much I wanted to talk with her about."

"Me too," Alice said. "I think of things every day that I want to ask her or tell her."

Alice held onto his arm as familiarly as if no time stood between this moment and their previous meeting. "Sit and tell me about it."

"I see you don't wear braces on your teeth anymore," he said, accepting the invitation.

She squeezed her eyes shut and looked embarrassed. "Those were horrible."

"No they weren't horrible," he said. "Braces and glasses are just appliances."

He noted that Alice no longer wore glasses either. She apparently had discovered contact lenses or lasik surgery.

"You were one of the few boys who didn't treat me badly or ignore me altogether."

"They didn't know there was a smart, good person inside a somewhat awkward young girl. Their loss. I notice you outgrew the awkwardness, too."

"Oh, Teddy, you're still that nice boy I used to know."

"And you're still the prettiest girl in Carbonville."

Alice searched his face for some sign he might be teasing her.

"You told me that once," she said. "I never could believe it."

He thought it was interesting that some people still blushed, even after they reached their fifties.

Ted's emotional state wavered between grief at the loss of his old friend and elation at seeing Alice.

"Besides getting even prettier, what have you been doing since I last saw you?"

Alice's eyelashes fluttered in the way people do when sorting through memories. "Oh, I graduated from high school, went to business school, got a job with the state where I've been ever since, got married, had a daughter, got divorced, do some oil painting and here I am. Your turn."

Both laughed at the staccato delivery and Ted rattled off his own resume.

"Graduated from high school and college, got my doctorate, started teaching computer science at Penn State, got married, had a son . . . who may be coming to live with me soon. . . got divorced, still teaching, play the trombone in a old duffer Dixieland band . . . and here I am."

"I'm sure neither of our lives could have been that simple," Alice said, a little sadness at the edge of the smile.

Ted's eyes wandered to an array of remarkable artworks hanging on the living room walls. A closer look revealed the name, 'Alice Simpson'. "You're an artist."

"More like someone who smears paint around on canvas," she said. "Mom hung them there. I would have put them in storage."

Ted tsk-tsked the idea. "Inappropriately humble, as always."

"Well, I'm not good enough to turn professional, but it gives me pleasure."

They spoke of some of the people they knew back in their day.

"Remember Clark Erickson?" Ted said.

"Of course. Clark is Harrisburg's Andrew Wyeth. His picture is constantly in the newspaper for some good deed or charitable gift. I'm certainly not in his league. His work hangs in some of the country's top galleries. I couldn't even afford to buy one of his paintings."

Ted hesitated to tell her of his own purchase.

"I saw a dozen or so of his paintings," Ted said. "I had lunch at a downtown restaurant I understand he owns."

"Chez Paree. I've had lunch there quite a few times," she said. "It's owned by Clark and his partner, Kevin Bachman. I haven't seen Clark since high school. He's never been in when I've gone there."

By 'partner', Ted wondered if that meant 'in life', as well as in business.

"There's an oil of a red barn and a stone farmhouse," Alice said. "A fall scene with a stream in the foreground. The water looks so real you can almost feel the movement and smell the fresh country air. The food at the restaurant is wonderful, but I honestly think I go back to see the painting more than for the food. I've been afraid someone would buy it and I'd never see it again."

Ted was beginning to wonder whether his mother's ESP skills had rubbed off on him or if he and Alice were simply aligned in their artistic tastes.

"Wait here," he said. "I'll be right back." She looked puzzled, but waited patiently as Ted went outside.

When he returned with the nearly forgotten package he tore off the wrapping.

"Someone did buy your painting," he said, turning it around for her to see.

She put her hand to her mouth and Ted thought she might cry.

"Oh my . . ."

With no hesitation he said, "I want you to have it."

"Teddy, that is very nice, but I couldn't accept it."

"I bought it for you," he said. "I didn't know it at the time, but I did. I only admire this painting. You love it. That makes it more yours than mine. Besides, having it here will give me an excuse to visit you again."

"You don't need an excuse, Teddy, you're welcome anytime. You don't even have to call first."

An invitation was nice. However, Ted had already made up his mind in that regard. Looking at the woman who was no longer that gangly girl so much younger than he, Ted wished he had found the Simpsons all those years ago.

"I've often wondered what happened to some of the others from those days," he said. "Jimmy Deavers gave me our old science teacher's phone number. He's retired and lives in New England."

"Yes, John Wilson is a math genius with a worldwide reputation."

"I called him," Ted said. "We're going to meet somewhere in the middle this summer. I also want to find Marlene Sutton."

"And she will want to see you, too. After all, you saved her life."

Ted's surprise must have shown.

"Yes, Teddy," Alice said. "You did save her life. You saved all our lives."

"I helped her with a problem she was having. It was your mother who did the real work." The lump had returned to his throat. A sob was down there, as well, but it would have to wait.

"I know all about the 'problem', Alice said. Marlene told me what happened even before you beat up her molester. I often wondered how a fifteen-year-old boy could have bested a grown man like that . . . especially one as mean as he was."

Ted shrugged. "A tiger defending his cubs, I guess."

Alice smiled. "Marlene and I became best friends after she came to stay with us. When people weren't nice to me, Marlene would be all over them. She lost friends by coming to my rescue . . . if you could call those people 'friends'. Those were some of the happiest days of my life."

Ted was truly surprised. "Your mother said she would help Marlene. I had no idea. I thought she was only going to stay with you temporarily."

"'Temporarily' turned out to be seven years. After my parents divorced, mother adopted Marlene and made her my official sister. Marlene Simmons became Marlene Simpson. She had a few rough years, but got some professional help."

"The best thing that ever happened to her," Ted said, "was living in a place where people cared about her."

"She married a wonderful guy. They live in Delaware. They have a son, a daughter, a grandchild, and another on the way."

"She finally got the life she deserved."

Ted noticed Alice got a faraway look. "Her mother was beaten to death by a drunken boyfriend," she said. "Joel died in prison, apparently at the hands of inmates who didn't think much of child molesters."

Ted thought about the part he played in Joel's fate. "He was a monster. I have no regrets about putting him in that position."

"Marlene spoke so fondly of you that I used to get jealous," Alice said. "I'm going to call her. She'll want to see you. We'll organize a reunion party."

Neither said anything for awhile. The silence and her lovely hazel eyes were comforting.

She spoke at last. "You must know that I was in serious puppy love with you."

He smiled. He did know, but now was not the time to tell her how he knew.

"Three years was a big age difference then," he said.

"I'm still three years younger than you," she said. The information came with a musical laugh.

"Let's see . . ." Ted did a quick mental calculation. "The last time I saw you, you were twenty-percent younger than I am. Now you're only about five-and-a-half-percent younger."

"I'm catching up," she said with that girly giggle. "At this rate, pretty soon I'll be older than you."

Regretfully, it was time to leave.

"You must come back," she said. "To visit your painting."

Ted was certain there could be better reasons for future visits.

Meanwhile, there was some thinking . . . and some grieving . . . to do.

As he returned to his car, Ted could not recall ever having such intense, yet mixed, emotions. It was a tug-of-war between the high at seeing Alice again and the low at learning of the loss of the woman who had been so important in his life.

If the past had remained as it was before the adventure, Ted thought he would probably not have thought much about most of the people he had known in that part of his life.

If only Alice knew what he knew. Maybe one day it would be possible to tell her.

As best Ted could interpret what had happened, there must be another dimension where nothing had changed from before his voyage through time. But, in this layer of the 'time onion', lives had been saved that would otherwise have been wasted or lost.

Ted finally understood that allowing oneself to care for people risked the pain that would come when they were gone. His life had been quite different before he got to know Grace Simpson as he had the second time around.

Alice watched from her window as Ted got into his car and drove away.

Was it her imagination, she wondered, or were the colors of the flowers in her yard more vivid now than they had been before Ted's visit? And did the sky seem bluer?

In the years since she last saw him, Alice had thought of Ted often. She compared every man she had ever known to Ted McBride. None matched up very well. Least of all, as it turned out, the man she married. Silly, she thought, to have set up a fifteen-year-old boy as the male gold standard. But she remembered his kindness and his solid values. Now he was back. And he wasn't fifteen-years-old anymore.

She was impatient to see him again.

She would not have to wait for long.

CHAPTER 52

TED ASSUMED IT WAS MORE LIKELY THAT CLARK would be at his restaurant in the evening than at lunchtime. The place was bustling with dinnertime patrons. Music was playing over the sound system, a genre and volume perfectly aligned with the welcoming mood. Thoughtful touches included ceilings slightly lower than the standard height, for greater intimacy. Fresh-cut flowers sat on each table and an unhurried waitstaff treated those they served with respectful informality. The entire establishment embraced the diner.

The man greeting patrons alongside the hostess looked just enough like the boy Ted had known that he was able to recognize him.

"Clark?"

"Good evening, sir," he said, "did you have a reservation?"

"No, I came to see you. My name is Ted McBride and—"

"Ted McBride?" he said. Smiling, he grasped Ted's hand warmly. "Savior of lost souls."

"Savior—"

Clark seized Ted by the arm, still shaking his hand, whisked him away from the hostess station and rushed him into a small office at the back of the restaurant where another man sat at a desk.

"Kevin, I want you to meet an old friend from high school. Kevin Bachman, Ted McBride."

"Ted McBride," Kevin said, rising to vigorously shake his hand. "Now there is a name I am very familiar with. Clark has spoken of you many times."

Clark nodded. "I told Kevin how you took down one of our high school's worst bullies on my behalf and helped me through a rough spell."

Ted glowed at the knowledge that what he did had changed the direction of a young boy's life and resulted in the man who stood before him.

"I heard Baumgardner is a permanent guest of the state now," Ted said. "I recall enjoying that athletic field incident."

"Dear boy, it may have been recreation for you, but that and some things you said to me afterward changed my life."

His very presence and demeanor were proof of it.

"Surely you remember what you said, Teddy."

"Vaguely," he lied, thinking it better to let Clark remember it his way.

"You said there were others like me out there and I should find them and be happy."

"Did you . . . and are you?"

"I did," he said. Putting his hand on Kevin's arm, he added, "and I am."

Ted turned halfway, as though to leave, and said, "Well then, my work here is done."

The two men roared with laughter. "Until then," Clark said. "I thought I was the only one in the world like me."

"You are, Clark," Ted said. "There is no better Clark Erickson anywhere."

"You sound just like the Teddy I remember. Something wonderful happened after that. The kids treated me differently. Before you intervened, I was an untouchable; someone to be shunned, teased, laughed at and bullied. People who had never spoken to me before came forward. I'm friends with some of them to this day."

"I'll bet none of them caught '*it*'."

Kevin and Clark laughed so hard that Ted thought they might pass out from a lack of oxygen.

"Teddy, you are a wonder," Clark said, through laugh-inspired tears. "If there is ever anything I can ever do for you, just let me know."

"Actually, Clark, there is."

"It's yours . . . whatever it is."

"I won't hold you to that because I know it's an imposition."

"Doubtful. Name it."

"Do you remember Mrs. Simpson, our high school English teacher?"

"Of course . . . a wonderful woman. I heard she died several years ago."

The ache returned to Ted's throat and chest and it took a moment before he could continue. "I just found out today about her passing."

Clark was obviously affected, as well.

"She had a daughter," Ted said.

"Alice," Clark said. "A sweet girl a few years younger than you and I."

"I spoke with her this afternoon. She described you as the Andrew Wyeth of

Harrisburg."

"A great compliment. One of the benefits of engaging an aggressive PR firm."

Not a pretentious bone in this man's body.

"You are too modest, Clark. I've seen your work. It would not surprise me to hear the late Andrew Wyeth referred to as the Clark Erickson of Chadd's Ford. I bought one of your oils. A farm scene."

"You're the one. I wish I had known that was you . . . I'm refunding your money."

"No you are not. I won't let you deny me the snobby right to claim to be a patron of the arts. But you could do me the favor I mentioned."

"Speak of it."

"Alice is an artist of some skill, although she would be the last person to describe herself as such. I wondered if you would look at some of her paintings, possibly give her some encouragement—maybe some pointers."

"I thought you were going to ask me something difficult. I would adore seeing her again. It would be my great pleasure to look at her work. Soon, I hope."

CHAPTER 53

IT WAS EARLY EVENING WHEN ALICE ANSWERED THE DOORBELL. Clark stepped out from behind Ted.

She recognized him immediately.

"Teddy." she said, breathlessly. "What have you gone and done?"

"I've gone and done brung an old friend to visit."

"Alice," Clark said, shaking her hand. "It is wonderful to see you again. You are the image of your beautiful mother."

"See," Ted said. "I'm not the only one who noticed."

Alice recovered somewhat and said, "Clark, I am absolutely astonished—and impressed."

"Well don't be too impressed," he said. "I'm still the kid who took Home Ec in high school."

She held the door open wide. "Come in, both of you."

Ted could see that Clark was immediately absorbed into the warmth of the home. His eyes were drawn to the artworks hanging around the living room; including the one Ted had given Alice. It was already hung in a prime location.

Clark went to one particular landscape and there was a sudden intake of breath as he gazed at the work.

"Oh, Clark," Alice said. "I'm embarrassed for you to look at my paintings."

"Never apologize for artistic expression, Alice," Clark said. "Whatever finds its way onto canvas is personal and requires no explanation. If others also happen to like it, so much the better."

Clark stood back from the painting Alice had done of the Appalachian ridge as seen from their mutual hometown, a field of brilliant yellow daffodils in the foreground.

After taking in the scope of the work from across the room, Clark moved in for a closer look at the detail. "I love what you've done here, where the mountain meets the sky."

Alice beamed when he said, "Amateur artists usually leave a sharp line between contrasting objects, almost like a cartoon outline. You have made a skillful transition from light to dark. Your composition is outstanding and your colors are an extraordinarily creative blend. I have seen such hues in nature, but never so successfully transferred to canvas. Your cloudy sky is magnificent; the whites, the grays, the pinks . . . Alice, you have a real talent."

"I couldn't ask for a nicer compliment," she said. "But I just paint for my own enjoyment."

"As do I, Alice. I don't consider myself an artist who owns a restaurant. Rather, I'm a restaurateur who paints. It just so happens that enough people like what I do for fun that I've been able to make a nice sideline out of it."

"You're sweet to say that, Clark."

Clark smiled, amused at her humility.

"I should tell you, Clark," Ted said, "Alice has always underrated herself."

Clark was quick to reinforce the praise. "I hope you won't think that is an empty compliment Alice, just because Ted asked me to see your work. People constantly want me to look at their paintings. Frankly, most of it is pretty low-quality stuff, with raw colors straight out of the tube, barely a step up from paint-by-numbers. I say, in all sincerity, this is far, far . . . *far* beyond anything I have ever been called upon to give my opinion. The only difference between you and a professional artist is that you don't get paid for it."

"I usually just give them to friends."

"I predict that one day those friends will be very rich."

If Alice had been nervous about having a renowned artist look at what she regarded as modest works, much of the tenseness had evaporated in Clark's kindly presence.

"Teddy, you did this for me."

"Not just for you. For the art world at large."

"The art world was getting along fine without me."

What happened next no doubt registered a ten on Alice's personal Richter Scale.

Clark took her by the hand and said, "Alice, if you can find some time I'd consider it an honor if you would come to my studio and sit in with me occasionally."

The suggestion practically knocked the wind out of her. Her eyes went wide.

"I—"

"There's a fine artist inside you, Alice. Let me help you bring her all the way out.

I'm sure I could learn some things from you, as well."

Ted was also caught completely unaware. It was not something he had expected, nor would he have considered asking it of Clark. It had certainly scrambled Alice's vocabulary before she recovered enough to work out a schedule.

"Teddy, you could have given me a heart attack with this surprise."

"I can't tell you how delighted I am that you survived."

It was time to get Clark back to the restaurant. Hugs all around.

"I'll wait for you in the car, Ted," he said.

There is no end to this man's sensitivity.

Alice looked at Ted with those soft hazel eyes.

She moved closer, stood on her tiptoes and gave him a soft kiss on the lips. "I've wanted to do that almost since the first time I saw you when I was six years old."

Love of the lasting kind is a long-term process and not 'at first sight' as some believe. Alice and Ted may have gotten a head start; Alice for the gentle boy she knew when they were children; Ted for the delightful girl of his youth who shared so many of the qualities of her mother, who was a treasured friend.

Ted realized in that moment that he had been in a dark place because he'd had no one to share his life with.

He was looking forward to sorting it all out.

"It's hard to believe it has been forty years," Alice said.

"Really?" Ted said. "It seems like only yesterday."

Made in the USA
San Bernardino, CA
02 April 2016